THE COMPANY WE KEEP

Also by Mary Monroe

She Had It Coming
Deliver Me From Evil
God Don't Play
In Sheep's Clothing
Red Light Wives
God Still Don't Like Ugly
Gonna Lay Down My Burdens
The Upper Room
God Don't Like Ugly
Borrow Trouble (with Victor McGlothin)

THE COMPANY WE KEEP

MARY MONROE

Based on the original screenplay by
Roy Campanella II

KENSINGTON PUBLISHING CORP.

www.kensingtonbooks.com

DAFINA BOOKS are published by

Kensington Publishing Corp.
850 Third Avenue
New York, NY 10022

All Kensington titles, imprints, and distributed lines are available at special quantity discounts for bulk purchases for sales promotion, premiums, fund-raising, educational, or institutional use.

Special book excerpts or customized printings can also be created to fit specific needs. For details, write or phone the office of the Kensington Special Sales Manager: Kensington Publishing Corp., 850 Third Avenue, New York, NY 10022. Attn. Special Sales Department. Phone: 1-800-221-2647.

Dafina and the Dafina logo Reg. U.S. Pat. & TM Off.

ISBN-13: 978-0-7582-2551-1
ISBN-10: 0-7582-2551-2

First Printing: March 2009
10 9 8 7 6 5 4 3 2 1

Printed in the United States of America

CHAPTER 1

Teri Stewart had no idea that two of the secretaries she worked with were secretly trying to set up a date for her with a popular male escort. It was going to be expensive, but worth every penny. That didn't matter, though. The money was going to come from the company's petty cash fund that the two secretaries controlled.

"John, if that woman doesn't get some dick soon, we are all going to be in therapy," complained one of the secretaries with a weary look on her face.

"And if this escort thing doesn't work, I'll screw her myself! I've been gay to the bone for my entire thirty-seven years and have never even *seen* a woman's pussy, so you know this is serious," moaned the terrified male secretary. "Either that or you'll have to strap on one of those dildo dicks and do it. We can't take too much more of her foolishness."

Unfortunately, the scheme didn't work. The only agency that the two desperate secretaries could afford had only one black escort. And he had dates lined up for the next two months. When the agency suggested another one of their studs, a very dark-skinned Iraqi, the two secretaries considered him until they saw what he looked like. That poor man looked enough like bin

Laden to be his twin. Teri was very patriotic. She'd never sleep with a man who looked like the enemy.

"All we can do now is hope that the upcoming New Year will be better for Teri," the female secretary said hopefully. "And better for us . . ."

Teri had not been involved in an intimate relationship with a man in six months, and it was beginning to get on her last nerve. She had gradually become a tense, frustrated, abrupt Donna Karan–wearing bitch. She knew she was beginning to get on the last nerves of *everybody* she came in contact with. Just yesterday she actually saw the guy from the mailroom duck into the stairwell as soon as he spotted her thundering down the hall trying to track down a fax she'd misplaced. And the two nicest secretaries in the company had started looking at her in some of the strangest ways. She had no idea what was going through their heads, and she didn't want to know.

It wasn't that no man was interested in her. That had never been the case and probably never would be. If for no other reason, men came on to her because of her looks. Most didn't care about anything else she had to offer. Few could resist her big, shiny brown eyes; smooth mahogany complexion; and full lips. Not to mention her hourglass-shaped body on legs that would put Tina Turner's to shame and a mane of dark brown hair that didn't need a prop like a weave to cascade around her shoulders like a silk scarf.

It seemed like the older she got, the more men she attracted. She predicted that forty years from now she'd be beating off dirty old men with her walking stick. Just last week somebody had stopped her on the street and asked if she was Kerry Washington, one of the most attractive black actresses in Hollywood. So why did her pussy feel like a condemned piece of property on no-man's-land? Beauty was not the cure-all for loneliness that some people thought it was. She was probably one of the best-looking lonely women on the planet. But in her case, it was by choice. And it was all because the *right* man had not approached her in six months.

"At least you still got your health and a good job," somebody—she couldn't even remember who—had told her a few days ago.

That same person had advised her to contact an online dating service. An *online dating service!* If that wasn't the last refuge for the truly desperate and a paradise for predators of all kinds, she didn't know what was. She'd made it emphatically clear that she was not that desperate . . . yet.

"I'm doing just fine, thank you very much." That was how she always responded when some busybody's nose sniffed in her direction and asked about her love life.

No, she wasn't getting any and didn't know when she ever would again. What the hell. She could live with it. She still had more things to be thankful for than a lot of other people. Yes, she did still have her health and her job and had been thinking about getting a cat.

Right now her job was the main focus in her life. She enjoyed being the Executive Publicity Director for Eclectic Records. The prestige and all the perks that went along with her high-profile position meant as much to her as the fat paychecks she collected twice a month. This was one sister who didn't have to worry much about where she was going in the hectic business world and how she was going to get there; she had already arrived.

Unfortunately, a lot of Teri's peers hated their jobs, so they didn't share her vision or enthusiasm. She didn't know of a single person in L.A. who *wanted* to be at work on New Year's Eve. It was hard enough for most people to come to work on the rest of the days in the year. But work was where Teri Stewart was tonight (she'd also worked well into the night on Christmas Eve, too). Not because she wanted to be, but because she had to be.

Teri didn't give a damn what everybody else in L.A. was doing. If nothing else, she was disciplined and considerate. To her, every commitment she made was important. Last year on a much-needed vacation to Puerto Vallarta, she had offered to take her friendly hotel maid and her kids to dinner. She didn't think to ask the woman how many kids she had, but she expected at least two. When the maid showed up with all *nine* of her kids in tow, including the eldest boy's wife and their two kids, Teri didn't back out. Now here she was on New Year's Eve trying to finish a monthly media report that was late because one of her sources had dropped the ball.

The building that was home to Eclectic Records was almost empty. But that didn't bother Teri. There was a pit bull of a security guard at the front desk on the first floor at all times. The sixteen-story building was located on a busy street near downtown L.A. Even though there had been a few muggings in the area recently, it was still fairly safe compared to other parts of the city.

Holiday lights were still in place, inside and out. The soulful R. Kelly jam emanating from a CD player in the center of Teri's cluttered desk in a corner office on the sixth floor didn't do a whole lot to make her feel more at ease. Her mood was dark, and she was more frustrated than usual. The impatient frown on her face and her pouting bottom lip, which would have made a less fortunate woman look like a hag, made her look even younger than her twenty-nine years. She mumbled profanities as she searched for a document that contained information she needed to complete her report. "Shit!" she hissed as she thumped the button on the speakerphone next to the CD player, speed-dialing her secretary at home.

"Nicole, you didn't put a copy of Reverend Bullard's report on my desk," she insisted, glaring at the telephone as if it were the source of her frustration. There was no answer. "Nicole, are you there?"

"Uh-huh, I'm here," Nicole finally replied with a mighty hiccup. Somebody had popped open a bottle of champagne in the company break room to jump-start the New Year's Eve festivities. Like a fish with a long swallow, Nicole had guzzled two glasses before she left the office two hours ago.

By the time Teri had concluded a tense conference call with two long-winded clients on the East Coast and made it to the break room, all the champagne was gone. If she ever needed a liquid crutch, it was now. She appeased herself with the reminder that she would make up for it in a couple of hours.

"I thought I told you to put a copy of the Bullard report on my desk. You know we can't afford to not get our artists mentioned in the tabloids and the music rags whenever they do something good." Teri was convinced that a story about an ex-con preacher making gospel CDs for troubled teenagers would be good press for the preacher and for Eclectic Records. "I thought I told you twice."

"Well, I *thought* I did," Nicole said with a burp. "I meant to . . ."

"You thought you did and you meant to, but you didn't," Teri snapped.

"Will you please calm down? You're making me nervous."

"Calm down, my ass. I've got a job to do and I can't do mine if you don't do yours." Teri paused and let out a loud breath. "I'm sorry. You know I don't like to take out my frustrations on you. I just want to finish what I started and get the hell up out of this place." Teri let out another loud breath, inspected her silk-wrapped nails, and glanced around the spacious office that she spent as much time in as she did her condo near Hollywood.

"That's better," Nicole mouthed.

Nicole Mason sat on the edge of her bed in the apartment she shared with her son. With a heavy sigh, she rose and wiggled her plump but firm ass into a pair of black lace panties. "Try the file cabinet behind my desk. The report should be in the top drawer in a green folder," she said. The panties felt a little too tight, just like almost everything else she owned. Especially the black slip she had on now. She made a mental note to curtail her ongoing relationships with Roscoe's House of Chicken 'n Waffles, Popeye's, Marie Callender, and Sara Lee or else she'd have to introduce herself to Jenny Craig and Richard Simmons. "Teri, you know you are my girl, so I know you won't take this the wrong way . . ."

Teri responded with an exasperated snort.

"Girlfriend, you need to get a life," Nicole told her. "You know it and I know it. Everybody else knows it, too."

"I have a life, thank you. I am on my grind," Teri reported, as she continued her search. She entered Nicole's work area, which was right outside her office. She fought her way through an assortment of large, live green plants on the floor that decorated the area like a rain forest. She found the green folder right where Nicole said it would be. With another frown, she returned to her office with the folder and leaned over her desk, glaring at the phone. She sucked in her breath so hard her chest ached, but before she could speak again Nicole's voice cut into her muddled thoughts.

"Miss Girl, I thought we were supposed to be hanging out tonight. Come on, this is New Year's Eve and we happen to be in one of the most exciting cities on this planet. And, in case you forgot, Lincoln freed the slaves."

"I have a job to do, Nicole," Teri reminded her.

"We all do. But we all have lives outside of our jobs, too," Nicole said firmly.

"I know, I know. I just need to tweak a few more sentences on this damn report. It won't take that long. And why are you rushing me? You are not even dressed yet."

"How would you know that?" Nicole quipped, tugging on the waistband of her panties.

"Because I know you," Teri remarked. Flipping through the green folder, her eyes got big and a smile formed on her lips. "I found it!" she exclaimed, clutching the missing document to her bosom as if it contained the secrets of the universe. She breathed a sigh of relief and flopped down into her chair, which was so comfortable with its soft black leather and adjustable seat that she didn't want to move again. "Let the games begin!"

Nicole rose and stood by the side of her bed, which was just as cluttered as the rest of the bedroom. She ignored the clothing and music magazines that she had tossed to the foot of her bed. "Uh-huh. So, now you can—" She was cut off by the annoying buzz of a dial tone. "Hang up on me then, bitch." She laughed, shaking her head. "I'm too scared of you."

CHAPTER 2

As soon as Nicole hung up the telephone, she rolled her large, inky black eyes and let out a deep breath. Then she raked her fingers through her thick, shoulder-length, charcoal black hair—a weave that only her hairdresser knew about.

She would never admit that she wore a weave. Why should she when it was the same shade and texture as her real hair? All pure black women weren't as bald-headed or hair and scalp challenged as some people implied. Half of her female cousins had thick hair halfway down their backs and it wasn't because of an Indian ancestor or the result of a fling with an Irishman or whatnot.

Before her weave-wearing days, she'd possessed a beautiful head of hair. Now she had more bald spots on her head than a dried-out cornfield. She blamed the permanent hair loss on the stress of once being married to a violent asshole. The hair that the stress didn't destroy had been pulled out in clumps by the violent asshole during some of their many battles. But she'd survived somewhat intact. At least physically. But like a lot of abused women, she wore her scars on the inside. Now, thanks to the hair that had once belonged to some female in Ethiopia, she still looked good. She lifted a hand mirror and gazed at her reflection. "Call a fire truck because I am so hot," she said, mimicking Paris Hilton.

But she wasn't a Paris Hilton; she had to *work* for a living. She had to work in an office and deal with workaholics like Teri Stewart five days a week—then get calls from her after she got home.

"Yes, Miss Whip Cracking Thing, you can call my house after hours and you can hang up on me. I don't mind. Just keep signing my paychecks and giving me my bonuses on time," she said, now glaring at the telephone she had just hung up.

And she didn't mind. Nicole loved her job and she loved Teri, which was why she had canceled a date so she could accompany Teri to another party that Teri didn't want to go to on her own.

Nicole made a mental note to cancel her part in a scheme with another secretary to set Teri up with a paid male escort. She knew for a fact that that dude was a firecracker in the bedroom. Her cousin Lola had tricked her into going out with him during a dating slump she'd slid into last year. She laughed and shook her head. If the other secretary still wanted to pay somebody to fuck Teri, he'd do it without her assistance. She had decided that her relationship with Teri was too important to risk.

A loud, sour belch rose in Nicole's throat, then popped out of her mouth, almost making her gag. She was still feeling the effects of the champagne she had consumed. The cup of coffee she'd picked up from Starbucks on the way home, hoping it would help reduce her buzz, hadn't helped. She was as dizzy now as she'd been before she left work. But that didn't matter one way or the other. It was party time and she was going to party her big ass off tonight.

The panties she'd just slid into seemed even tighter now as she patted her stomach. The elastic in the waistband was stretched so tight she was afraid it might snap in two. It was a consolation to know that the bloating around her middle was mostly premenstrual water retention that would last only a few hours.

Standing in the middle of her bedroom floor with her hands on her hips, she looked around her cluttered bedroom. She didn't have much, but she was thankful for what she did have. Aside from her family and a few close friends, at the top of her list was a job she loved. It was demanding and it didn't pay as much as she would have liked, but it was a job, and she worked with people she admired and respected.

Living in L.A. and working in the music industry, she was surrounded by wealth and a fast-paced lifestyle that she admired from the sidelines and secretly envied. Who wouldn't? She dealt with people who paid more for one pair of shoes than she paid for rent. She'd met and socialized with some of the biggest recording stars in the business. Last year, she'd been treated to lunch at Mr. Chow in Beverly Hills with a Grammy-award-winning rapper. And even though it had been part of her reward for taking the rapper's dog to the vet, she had enjoyed it.

Despite the fact that the rapper in question was a first-class fool, she'd been attracted to him and they'd spent the night together in his Hollywood Hills mansion. He had admired her good looks and spunk. He had made a bunch of promises—ones she knew he wouldn't keep—while he was on top of her, his dick slapping the side of her thigh as if it were his favorite sport.

A week later, when he was supposed to call her again and didn't, she saw him on an entertainment TV show grinning into the camera as he exited a church with the supermodel he'd just married. The last time she saw him was six months after his wedding. He was strutting his newly divorced ass down a street in West Hollywood. He'd flirted with her again, not even realizing he'd already sampled her fruit. The last thing she wanted to be was the same fool twice. Karrine Steffans, the ultimate black groupie, had already cornered that market and then told the world about it in her two tell-all best-selling books.

Like all the other women connected to the music industry on some level, Nicole wanted to lead a more glamorous life on a regular basis. But for the time being, all she could afford was a one-bedroom apartment, which was always cluttered with items she was still paying for.

Nicole was just a few months younger than Teri Stewart, a boss that she not only admired but envied. But her envy did not include malice. She adored Teri, and the feeling was mutual. But Nicole didn't have to drop to her knees and kiss a bunch of funky butts to make people like her. She was "all that" anyway—sensitive, thoughtful, and charming. She had to do very little to win admirers. Especially with the men she came in contact with.

Despite the fact that she was not a beautiful woman by Hollywood's standards or if she went by what the black music videos depicted, a lot of men found her casual eroticism and icy aloofness appealing. She had a nice body but a face that she felt was too round. She also felt that her eyes were too big for her face and that her nose was slightly crooked. However, nobody but Nicole noticed her "flaws." She knew how to work with what she had and turned heads everywhere she went.

Nicole looked toward the bedroom door, then glanced at her watch and moaned like a woman in labor. The one person she knew who had her at the top of his shit list was on his way. And her trifling ex-husband was the last person she wanted to see tonight, or any other night for that matter. This man had broken not only her heart but her spirit as well.

"Mama, I can't find my Transformer." The small voice coming from the doorway leading to the living room belonged to Nicole's five-year-old son, Chris. The small living room, with cute little pieces of furniture and knickknacks that Nicole had picked up at places like Ikea and other discount stores, contained a pullout sofa where the boy slept. He was the only reason she still had a relationship with that sperm donor she'd once been married to.

Nicole whirled around, blinking hard. "Uh," she started with a sniff. "Honey, your daddy should be here soon to pick you up. Get all your stuff ready. You know how he doesn't like to wait."

Chris gave her a puzzled look, as if he were hearing this for the first time. The fact that he looked so much like his no-good daddy made his reaction that much more irritating to Nicole. "But what about my Transformer?" He pouted with his bottom lip sticking out.

"Can't you go just one night without that thing?" Nicole snapped.

"No way," Chris snapped back, shaking his head so hard his ears wiggled.

"Well, tell your daddy to buy you another one," Nicole suggested, rubbing her chest.

Nicole had chest pains almost every time she thought about that man. Seeing him in the flesh was enough to make her sick. Chris opened his mouth to speak again, but a loud knock on the living room door made him hold his breath. Nicole braced herself and held her breath, too.

CHAPTER 3

"Ask who it is before you open that door," she ordered, knowing damn well who it was. She slid into the tiny bathroom next to her bedroom and threw on a long, loose terry cloth robe. It was one of several she owned that had seen better days. The belt was missing and the one pocket below the waist had a hole large enough for her foot.

"It's Daddy," Chris announced from the living room, which smelled of fried food coming from the kitchen and floral scents coming from the bathroom.

Gregory Mason, dressed in dark brown corduroy from head to toe, reluctantly entered the living room with the grim look of a pallbearer on his handsome, dimple-cheeked face. He shook his head in disgust and smoothed back his thinning, wavy black hair. He and Nicole were the same age, but Greg looked at least five years older. That was because he had frowned so much the last few years that the frown lines on his forehead and the sides of his mouth had become permanent. Looking around the room, shaking his head, he rubbed the beaked nose that he had inherited from his Jewish grandfather on his mother's side. Then he sniffed and coughed as if he'd just stumbled into a room full of cow dung.

"Hey, Dad," Chris offered, more interested in his misplaced toy than his father's presence. Chris was used to seeing his daddy look and act like the giant booger he was. Greg had started exhibiting this rude behavior before he moved out.

But Chris loved his daddy as much as he loved his mama and wanted to spend time with him whenever he could. Unfortunately, they were not together that often because Greg had his own agenda and it did not include babysitting his own son when there were a lot more important things he could be doing.

Gregory Mason was an angry black man and had been for years. He blamed the source of his rage on the black woman. She had contributed to his downfall and had been an ongoing thorn in his side for years. An ass-kissing, female Uncle Tom of a black woman had beaten him out of a managerial position at Southwest Airlines where he worked as a personnel rep. His own mama had physically abused him and then dumped him off on his grandmother when he was thirteen for her to finish raising. And that old hag had beat the shit out of him more than his mother. When his mother came to visit, she and her mother took turns beating his ass for one thing or another—masturbating, torturing animals, and trying to look under girls' dresses. As far as he was concerned, his only crime was just being a boy and doing what all his male friends did. All three of his sisters were bitches on wheels, and the one six-year-old daughter he had, whom Nicole didn't know about, was already walking around with an attitude, rotating her little neck and rolling her eyes. Black women were more trouble than they were worth. No wonder they couldn't keep their men out of the white woman's bed. But he wasn't into white women, thank God. They'd gotten so big for their britches lately that, as far as he was concerned, Asian women were the only ones worth a man's time anymore. Shit.

Nicole let out a heavy sigh from the bathroom, leaning toward the slightly ajar door so she could hear and see what was going on in the living room.

"Hey, chief! How're you doing?" Greg yelled, coughing some more. He rolled his eyes at Nicole as she exited the bathroom and strutted into the living room, straightening magazines on the coffee table and rearranging chairs as she moved. "Don't you ever cook anything but cabbage, greens, and neck bones? This place smells like an outhouse, as usual," he said with a sneer.

"Hello, Greg," Nicole said, sounding as cordial as her temper would allow. She wanted to stomp his smug face into the ground for the way he had disrespected her residence and the way he was looking at her. From the look of contempt on his face and the way he treated her these days, you would have thought that it had been she, not he, who had ruined their marriage by sleeping with every Chinese, Vietnamese, Japanese, and Filipino woman in the area. He was now married to a Korean woman, and they had a two-year-old daughter who Greg treated like gold. "From the looks of things, seems like it's time for you to replace your toupee," Nicole remarked, talking out the side of her mouth. She knew damn well that all the hair on Greg's head was his. But he should have known better than to insult her because she was the one person who knew what button to push to piss him off. She knew that his hair was and had always been a sensitive issue with him. Just like hers was with her, thanks to him. He knew from his premature receding hairline, and the bald spots on the back of his head, that he'd be completely bald by the time he turned forty, just like his father and all the men on his father's side. He ignored her comment.

Greg smoothed back his hair with his hand again. He blinked hard and chewed on his bottom lip to keep from saying something else to Nicole that would set her off. He had come to believe that black women were like land mines, just waiting to explode and destroy or disfigure their men. Was it any wonder that there were so many black men walking around with no balls?

"You ready to go, chief?" Greg asked his son, shifting his weight from one foot to the other and sliding his hands in and out of his pockets. He wanted to leave. There was no doubt in Nicole's mind that this was the last place he wanted to be. And it was the last place she wanted him to be, too.

"Almost, Daddy. I have to find my Transformer first," Chris replied.

Nicole was glad she still had a slight buzz. Had she not been so mellow, there was no telling what else she might have said, or done, to Greg. To keep from saying or doing something crazy anyway, she went to the bedroom to look for Chris's toy. "You're two hours late," she told Greg, talking with her back to him.

"Kim Loo had a few errands for me," he responded, entering the bedroom like it was still his. He didn't even try to hide his exasperation. Neither did Nicole.

"As usual," Nicole replied. "The new wifey needs you to play houseboy, so your son comes last."

"I am surprised you can find anything in this mess," Greg remarked, looking around with disgust at the messy room. With the tips of two fingers, he lifted a week-old newspaper from the nightstand next to an empty pizza box. He shook his head and mumbled profanities.

"And while we are on the subject of being late, you are two months late with the support payments," Nicole reminded him, with her arms folded.

"I found it!" Chris yelled from the living room, grabbing his bulging Spider-Man backpack from the coat hook by the door.

"Good. Let's get up out of here!" Greg hollered, purposely ignoring Nicole's last comment. He shook his head some more, waved his hands in the air, and spun around so fast he almost fell trying to get back to the living room in a hurry. He wasted no time opening the front door. But before he could usher his son out, Chris held his arms out to his mother for a good-bye hug.

"Have fun, little man. I'll see you tomorrow night," Nicole told Chris, covering his cheek with hungry little kisses.

"Come on, Mom," Chris whined, embarrassed. "I don't want to keep Daddy waiting."

"I don't want him to wait either, son," Nicole said with a smirk. "And I hope he doesn't keep us waiting, either."

"The check is in the mail, woman," Greg snapped, slamming the door behind him as he scurried out.

CHAPTER 4

It had been an hour since Teri had spoken with Nicole. While Nicole was still in her apartment stewing over her latest face-off with her ex-husband and trying to decide what to wear, Teri was still at the office, stomping out fires with both feet.

"Look, Paul, I have to get back to the other line. I am trying to finalize some arrangements for one of our artists. One of our A-list stars," she said proudly. "I've been playing phone tag with his tour promoter for days, so I really need to take his call. I promise we'll talk later in the New Year." She didn't wait for a response from Paul Bailey, the high-strung realtor she'd met at a party a month ago. Since he couldn't get her to go out with him, he was determined to sell her a new condo. She clicked back to the other line. However, before she could announce that she was back, she heard the loudmouth tour promoter, Ronnie Thigpen, complaining about the fact that she was involved in the tour arrangements for one of his most important clients. The tour that she was so committed to. That punk!

Teri held her breath as she listened. "That uppity bitch is with the fucking record company, not the artist. Young Rahim is the artist. Compared to him, she ain't nobody! I don't know why, but he trusts that woman to make sure all the details are correct.

Why? There is no reason in the world we need her help! Hold the line a minute, man. Let me get my beer."

Ronnie had recently recovered from throat cancer, and it had taken three surgeries to save his voice. However, he would sound severely hoarse until the day he died. Under normal circumstances, Teri would have felt sorry for a person who had to live with such a condition. But in Ron's case, his voice was particularly irritating because of the harsh words coming out of his mouth about her. She bristled but managed to remain composed as he continued.

"We've got our own people that can get the job done." He paused again to take a long, loud drink from his beer can. Then he belched, coughed, and sneezed for almost a full minute. "Excuse me! That shit went down my windpipe. Anyway, how hard is it to hook up a goddamn tour, anyway? That bubble-butt heifer likes to meddle as much as she can just so she can get more money. If I didn't know any better, I'd swear she was kissing Rahim where the sun don't shine. Either that or he's heard how she can suck a mean dick and wants to get him a few blow jobs before he goes on his tour this summer. Ha! If it was up to me, I'd tell her to kiss my black ass and bark at my asshole!"

Teri exhaled quietly. She had to cover her mouth to keep from laughing; she wondered what Ronnie would say if he knew that she hadn't even seen a dick in six months, let alone sucked one.

If there was one thing she couldn't stand it was having somebody disrespect her, even when it wasn't to her face. But since it was the holiday season and she was planning to get loose before the night was over, she let Ronnie slide this time.

She cleared her throat to make sure she could be heard. Without hesitation, she directed the tour promoter's attention to a list of eccentric items that his artist had demanded to have on his tour.

"Ron, I'm back," she announced. "I apologize for leaving you on hold for so long . . ."

"Oh! Well, let's talk business, honey. I was just telling Jake about how much I enjoy working with you." Ron's voice was so

sweet and gentle now; it was hard for Teri to believe that it belonged to the same man who had just trashed her. "Now, where
were we, T?"

"As I was saying, Rahim wants several cases of Cristal, several
cases of Jack Daniels, and several cases of Jose Cuervo tequila."

"Now, when you say several cases, are you talking about three
or four or what? Several is a vague word," Ron told her.

"Last count was five cases each. Before that it was three. I don't
know what it'll be the next time I talk to him," Teri said.

"All right, consider it done. Is that all?"

"He wants *several* dozen lambskin condoms, several cases of
Evian water, his own manicurist and barber, somebody to take
care of his dogs, and the phone numbers to the most exclusive
brothels in each of the twenty-two cities on the schedule," Teri revealed with a grimace.

"Is that all?" Ron asked again, holding his breath.

"That's all that I'm aware of," she replied in a stiff voice.

"Well, if any of this is going to be a problem, you need to let me
know and you need to let me know now so I can deal with it. We
can always get our people to do what you can't do."

"I can do whatever he wants, as long as it doesn't involve standing on my head," Teri said, trying to make the conversation less
painful.

"But I bet you could do that, too, if you had to, Miss Teri," Ron
muttered.

"There won't be any problems. At least not on my end," she
promised.

"Uh, I hope you're right. I need to know that a job can get
done the way it's supposed to get done."

"That's why I'm here," Teri said dryly. She had been flattered
and annoyed at the same time when the artist in question had
insisted that she help organize his tour. She could have turned
him down but she liked adding feathers to the many caps she
wore.

"All right now. I'm counting on you. I've heard a few good
things about you. If anybody can take care of business, it's you."

"That's good to know," Teri said, her voice dripping with sarcasm. She was surprised that they were able to reach an agreement without a fight. "Well, uh, how can I get the contract to Rahim ASAP?"

"How ASAP?" Ron asked gruffly. His voice was beginning to sound like a frog croaking for his dinner. "After all, it is New Year's Eve."

"Like tonight? I know this is short notice and all. I'm sure you must have plans for later tonight, so I apologize in advance for the inconvenience."

"Uh, Teri, I do appreciate all your hard work. You make your company look good," he offered. "In more ways than one, if you don't mind me saying so."

"Thank you." That was all she said before a long pause.

Ron gasped and blinked. His eyes were burning almost as much as his throat. What the hell was with this woman? Couldn't she tell when a man was trying to show a little interest in her?

"Messenger a copy of the contract to me," she said, pausing to look at her watch. "Within the next hour. I'll see Rahim later tonight."

"Oh? I wasn't aware of that. Will you be visiting him at his office on Melrose?"

"No. I received an invitation to attend his New Year's Eve party at his place. I will give it to him there."

There was an excruciating moment of silence before Ron responded. "Oh. I . . . I see," he stammered.

"Will you be there?" She knew he wouldn't because he would have mentioned it by now.

"Uh-uh. My brother's home on leave from the air force so there's a family thing I have to attend . . ." Poor Ron. He didn't want to admit that he didn't even know about a damn party until she brought it up. That was bad enough, but not receiving a party invitation from one of his most important clients made it even worse. And he was too embarrassed to admit it.

"Well, that's a damn shame," Teri said. "You'll be missed," she added, trying to think of other ways to rub it in. But he refused to give her that satisfaction. Without another word, he hung up.

Teri shrugged her shoulders and looked at the telephone, talking to it as if it had a brain. "He could have at least wished me a Happy New Year." She chuckled.

With a loud sigh, Teri whirled around in the soft leather chair that had begun to feel like it was glued to her butt. She wasted no time getting up, turning out the lights in her office, and calling it a day.

CHAPTER 5

Teri didn't know that it had started to rain until she drove out of the enclosed garage beneath the building she lived in. But minutes after she'd pulled out onto the street, it stopped. She was glad she didn't have to haul an umbrella around with her, too. She felt like she was dragging enough already. But it had been a productive year for her, and she had to admit that ending it at one of the most anticipated parties of the year, an invitation-only party at that, suited her just fine. She had already begun to perk up.

It had been a while since she had attended a party. And even longer since she'd attended one on her own. Well, she was not exactly going to the party alone. The engraved invitation that she had received by messenger a week ago had indicated that she could bring a guest. Other than her secretary, Nicole—or executive assistant as Nicole liked to be called (as the metal nameplate on her desk said)—she couldn't think of anybody else whom she could tolerate socially to invite to another one of these music people parties.

Teri picked up Nicole about twenty minutes past eleven o'clock. When Teri saw Nicole exit her apartment building dressed in black from head to toe, she did a double take. The black turban wasn't so bad. But the black woolen poncho, the black leather pants, and black boots were a little too much. Teri had on a simple green silk dress, matching green earrings shaped like four-leaf clovers, and a pair of low-heeled black pumps. A pale beige shawl lay across her shoulders.

"You spent hours on end trying to decide what to wear and that's the best you could come up with?" Teri teased as Nicole climbed into the front passenger seat of her BMW. Nobody would have guessed that Teri was Nicole's boss. The truth of the matter was, they'd been best friends for more than twenty years.

"What's wrong with what I have on? A lot of people wear black all the time," Nicole protested.

"Yeah, and that's fine if your name is Johnny Cash. But we are going to a party, not a wake. Black is too depressing for a party."

"But it goes with everything," Nicole whined as she brushed lint off the front of her poncho.

"So does white."

"Well, all my bedsheets were dirty." Nicole gave Teri a playful tap alongside her head and laughed. "Let's roll. I hope you didn't forget to bring that contract to give to Rahim," Nicole said, looking at Teri's small black suede purse on the armrest.

"I didn't. If I didn't want to get this damn thing signed so badly, I'd be on my sofa with a glass of wine and a bowl of popcorn."

"Well, I'm glad you decided to come out tonight, Grandma. I know I sure needed to get out tonight. Even if it is just with you . . ."

"Well, you don't need to pout about it," Teri said, glancing at Nicole. "You didn't have to break your date with what's his name. I didn't beg you to come with me tonight."

"It's not that," Nicole admitted.

"Oh. I forgot Greg was coming by to pick up Chris. Was he in a good mood?"

"Yes, if you can call acting like a rabid rottweiler being in a good mood. I tell you, Teri, men are such chameleons. Don't you wish we had other options?"

"We do. But licking another woman's pussy doesn't quite appeal to me," Teri said with a shiver.

It was a smooth twenty-five minute ride. The streets were wet and slick so Teri had to drive carefully and more slowly than she normally did when tooling around L.A.

She kept her eyes on the road and bobbed her head along with the music on a jazz radio station she had discovered by mistake one night.

Nicole was tired. It was hard for her to keep her eyes open. Dealing with her ex-husband had worn her out. But she was not about to let that stop her from enjoying herself tonight. She leaned back, glad that she had a turban on her head. It hid her hair, which was in desperate need of a touch-up and some tightening up assistance.

Teri's silver BMW, a year old but still exuding that new car smell, moved through an intersection in the direction of an exclusive neighborhood near the Hollywood Hills. One that also happened to be predominantly white. Nicole could always tell a white neighborhood from a black or Hispanic neighborhood. White neighborhoods had yogurt shops and delicatessens and quaint little churches all over the place. The black and Hispanic neighborhoods had their share of churches, too, for all the good it did them. But the liquor stores, the overextended funeral parlors, and the pawn shops ruled the minority neighborhoods. Nicole glanced from one side of the street to the other, admiring the expensive homes.

"Now this is what I call my kind of neighborhood," Nicole said in an eager tone of voice and a look of envy and awe on her face as she scanned the neighborhood.

"I am definitely hearing that, girl," Teri agreed with a vigorous nod. "I wouldn't mind living in this zip code myself."

"Well, you're a lot closer to it than I am," Nicole reminded with a loud, exaggerated sigh. There was a bail bondsman's office on the ground floor of her building with a steady stream of losers in and out every day. There was a garishly decorated Korean nail shop, the same one that Kim Loo was working in when she stole Greg from her, on one side of her building. There was an open-all-night, dollar-a-load Laundromat on the other. It also served as a makeshift motel for some of the homeless people who patrolled the block. A deserted school bus with no wheels squatted near the corner of a vacant lot across the street. Homeless people avoided the bus because it wasn't as clean and warm as the Laundromat.

"Being close to it and being in it are two different things. But socially, these folks have their own 'hood problems. Did you see that derelict stretched out on the ground a couple of blocks back? Or those well-dressed white kids huddled in a corner in front of that office building sharing a joint?" Teri asked.

"No, I didn't. I was too busy admiring all these gorgeous homes," Nicole replied, still looking out the window with the wide-eyed awe of a child. "So what's your point?"

"My point is, this is still a small world. No matter where we live, or who we are, we've all got some of the same problems on some level."

The party was in full swing by the time Teri and Nicole arrived at the rapper's house. Handsome young black and Hispanic valets were parking cars and greeting guests. They all wore stiff red jackets and sharply creased black pants. Fake smiles were plastered on their faces. They knew that the friendlier they were, or appeared to be, the bigger the tip. The scene outside was a media frenzy with ambitious reporters hopping around like rabbits and rude paparazzi waving cameras like weapons.

The only things missing from this frantic scene were a red carpet and Joan Rivers. Nicole took all this in with a stunned expression on her face. From her body language, you would have thought that she didn't know which way to turn.

"Smile for the cameras and stop drooling. You've been to these things before," Teri reminded Nicole, something she'd done on dozens of similar occasions.

"Yeah, but each time seems like the first time. I just saw two of the world's biggest stars going inside!" Nicole stopped talking long enough to whip out her compact to check her makeup. "I don't know if I will ever get used to all this," she admitted.

"Well, you'd better. It is part of your job," Teri warned Nicole in a low voice as they walked up onto the front porch of Young Rahim's eighteen-room white mansion. It was as outlandish as it could be. A large Greek-looking statue of a naked woman holding a bowl of fruit stood on one side of the double doors. On the other side was a life-size ceramic lion with his mouth opened in a menacing yawn. The white draperies covering the front windows displayed large, green dollar signs. "People who can afford to live like this are no better than you or me," Teri added.

A scowling, portly man dressed like a penguin opened the door and waved them in without a word. He ignored the invitation Teri held out to him. Shaking her head, she slid it back into her purse, wondering why Young Rahim's assistant had advised to bring it in the first place.

"No better than you or me? That's easy for you to say. But if I were you, I wouldn't let them hear that," Nicole replied, looking around the spacious living room, trying to price the expensive furnishings. On one wall there was a large cheesy painting of a man who looked like James Brown but was supposed to be an illustration of a black Jesus in dreadlocks and silver earrings. Nicole had a cheaper and much smaller version of the same picture on her living room wall that she had picked up at a flea market in San Jose when she visited her aunt Bertha last year. Who needed three couches in the same room? And they were the loudest colors in the spectrum: one red, one orange with green leaves jumping out, and one yellow. Each had clawlike feet and arms wide enough to hold a large baby. Had she not already known that this all belonged to a black man, she would have guessed it anyway. She had learned a long time ago that when black folks got their hands on some money, they made sure everybody in the world knew about it. Then they spent it as if it grew on vines in a backyard garden, buying ten or twelve of everything they didn't need or appreciate. She gasped at an antique vase sitting in the middle of a brass leg glass-top coffee table. What did an ignoramus like Young Rahim know about antique vases? Other than his music, what did he know about anything else?

Young Rahim moved about the party room, strutting and looking more like a peacock than a rapper in his red suit jacket, yellow silk pants, and white Panama hat. He was not a bad-looking brother by anybody's standards. As a matter of fact, except for the shoulder-length dreadlocks, he looked like a younger version of Denzel Washington. He had nice white teeth, capped no doubt.

But at least there wasn't a gold one among them. That pleased Teri and Nicole. In their business, they saw enough gold teeth to replenish Fort Knox. If nothing else, Teri found these glorified dog-and-pony shows entertaining, to say the least. She was glad she had come.

CHAPTER 6

Armed security guards with walkie-talkies patrolled the area inside and outside of the rapper's house. Dressed in somber dark suits, dark hats, and dark glasses, they looked like an advertisement for that old John Belushi and Dan Aykroyd movie, *The Blues Brothers.*

Marcus Boggs was Rahim's head of security and looked the part. He was built like an ox, had a face like an angry gargoyle, and a neck that looked like the trunk of a large oak tree. He towered over Young Rahim and most of the other guests.

The guests were a smorgasbord of ethnic diversity. White people were gadding about with their hair in dreadlocks, braids, and even afros. Some even had the nerve to wear African attire. Black folks, male and female, were prancing around with platinum blond hair. There were others present whose ethnicity, and gender in several cases, could not be determined.

Other guests included popular DJ Harrison Starr. He looked out of place in his dapper three-piece suit, but he was as cool and smooth as he looked. He was tall and solidly built, and he had the look of a man who liked to be pampered. His handsome coconut brown face was as smooth as the faces of some of the women present. He owed that to good genes, a balanced diet, and plain old luck. His slanted black eyes scanned the room and had been

doing so from the minute he'd arrived—a few minutes before
Teri and Nicole.

He was surprised but glad to see Teri in the mix. That's when
he stopped looking around the room, because he'd found what
he'd been looking for. As far as he was concerned, they had some
unfinished business to address. From the way he was smiling at
her, and trying to steer her by the arm to a more private spot, it
was obvious to some of the guests close by that he had a "thing"
for her.

"I'd like to talk to you before you leave tonight," Teri told him.
They did have some unfinished business, and she had a thing for
him, too. He was the last man she'd been with. Their relationship
had ended before it even got off the ground. It had started with a
chance meeting at a charity function, a few dinner dates followed
by nights of passion she had not experienced before (or since),
and then it was over. Sometimes it seemed like it had never happened.

Their hectic lives were complicated by work and many other interests. And even though they were both still fairly young, they
were settled in their ways and unwilling to bend too far in another person's direction. Harrison had wanted her to spend more
time with him, stroke his ego, be his trophy, and be the woman
behind him.

She had scoffed at the notion of being *behind* him, or any other
man. "If I can't be beside you, I won't be with you," she had told
him, laughing as she said it. But he had taken it the wrong way.
Harrison had sulked for days and ignored her repeated telephone messages. And by the time he'd come to his senses, it was
too late. His telephone messages to her went unanswered, and
twice when he was bold enough to ring the buzzer at her residence, she'd ignored him. He finally gave up when he attempted
to visit her at her workplace and was brusquely turned away by
the pit bull security guard, per Ms. Teri Stewart's instructions.

"We can talk now," Harrison told her with a nod, still holding
on to her arm. They hadn't encountered each other since their
breakup.

Teri nodded. "I heard about you going around speaking to the kids at some of the inner-city schools. I admire you for doing that," she told him, meaning every word.

"Did you also hear that I got robbed and beaten at the last school I spoke at?"

Teri gasped and shook her head. "I'm sorry to hear that. I hope that doesn't discourage you from going back. Those kids need people like us, now more than ever. I visited the girls in juvenile hall last month. I didn't think they'd want to hear anything I had to say about my work."

"Did they?"

"They were more interested in who did my hair and what famous people I hung out with." Teri laughed. "But I'm going back in a couple of months anyway."

"So am I. And to one of the most violent schools in Crenshaw. As a matter of fact, the boys that jumped me turned themselves in and apologized. I got all of my shit back, too. They said it was my talk that had made them think about what they'd done once the excitement of robbing my ass wore off."

"See? That just goes to show you that anybody can change," Teri said hopefully.

"This is not what I want to talk about, Teri," Harrison said, grinding his teeth. "What I meant was, I wanted to talk to you about me. It's now or never." His lips tightened and he gave her a defiant look, staring at her with his eyes narrowed into slits.

She didn't like his brusque attitude and she let him know by giving him one of the harshest looks she could manage. It didn't take her long to decide that since he had just acted so uppity, she would make him work his ass off to get more of her attention tonight. He would have to compete with all the other men at the party. "Excuse me," she said bluntly, attempting to leave. He grabbed her wrist and held her in place. "Please don't do that," she ordered, removing his hand. Her attitude didn't even faze him, though. He was glad to see that she was still a challenge. But he wanted what he wanted and he wanted it now.

Unlike Teri, Harrison had not been spending his days and nights alone. His bed and his arms were rarely empty. He and Teri had the same biological needs, but for different reasons.

Knowing what a firecracker she was in the bedroom, he had assumed that she'd kept herself busy in that location, too. He would have been horrified and amused to hear that Teri had been on a self-imposed "pleasure strike" since their breakup.

Harrison Starr had never denied himself the pleasures of nature. As long as he could get it, he would. But he had high standards when it came to women. He wouldn't fuck just anybody. Beauty was one of the main requirements that he looked for in a woman. That shit about looks not being important was hogwash and had to be something that an ugly person had come up with. In his position he couldn't afford to be seen in public with a woman who looked like a frog princess. But even having all the physical requirements was not enough. He had to like the woman, not enough to take home to Mother or to give her his name, but just enough to keep the flame going until it burned itself out.

"Do you want to talk to me tonight or not?" he demanded, his impatience showing.

"Maybe later," Teri replied, pulling away with a smug smile on her lips. A disappointed look slid across Harrison's face. Teri Stewart had been and still was his biggest challenge. He offered her a smile and another nod. Even though he had not been with a woman in two days, he could wait another two days, or two weeks, for Teri.

One of the many things that Teri didn't like to do was rush. And the unfinished business that she had with Harrison Starr was something that she wanted to resume in her own time. After all, it had been six months since she'd been with the man. Another six months wouldn't kill her.

CHAPTER 7

Teri latched onto Nicole's arm and guided her to a long table in the center of the living room. There was something on that table for everybody, from crispy, golden fried chicken wings and fried okra to bite-size quiche and caviar. Teri and Nicole ignored the feast on the table. But they each snatched a flute of champagne off a passing waiter's tray.

"What was up with that?" Nicole wanted to know, an amused look on her face.

"What do you mean?" Teri took a long swallow of her champagne, then wiped her lips with the back of her hand.

"You know damn well what I mean, girl. That was Harrison Starr. He was looking and acting like he wanted to lick you up one side and down the other," Nicole said with a leer and a hand on her hip. She wanted to do that "neck rolling" thing that black women had made so famous. But she didn't because judging from all the gum chewing, blond-weave-wearing, loud-talking, scantily dressed sistahs already on the scene, the ghetto was being represented enough tonight.

Teri didn't respond for a few moments. But a mysterious smile crossed her face. Her mind was on the thought of Harrison's tongue on her body.

"Well?" Nicole yelled, jabbing the side of Teri's arm.

"Well what?" The smile was still on Teri's face as she adjusted the shawl on her shoulders and drank some more champagne.

"What's up with you and Harrison? Tell me all the details," Nicole demanded.

"It's a long story," Teri said with a mysterious look on her face. She glanced over her shoulder to see that Harrison's eyes were still on her. She smiled at him but quickly returned her attention to Nicole.

"I like long stories. I've seen *Roots* eight times," Nicole told her. "Start talking."

"Well, like I said, it is a long story. But I will give you the short version. It's, uh, all history now, but Harrison and I were very close once upon a time. It lasted only a few weeks. That was about six months ago."

Nicole stared at Teri for a few seconds. "Hmm. With those powerful-looking thighs, I bet he had your ass flipping and flopping all over the damn bed," she said with lust on her face.

Teri gave Nicole an exasperated look. "We enjoyed a lot of other things, too."

"I bet you did," Nicole added with a wink and an obscene gesture with her tongue. "If I remember correctly, you were walking mighty bowlegged around that time."

"Girl, you are hopeless," Teri insisted with a sharp wave of her hand. "There was more to our relationship than my body."

"Tell me about it. Your body was just one of the props. Now I know why I stumbled across all those sex toys in your condo in the cabinet beneath the sink in your bathroom . . . about six months ago."

Teri glared at Nicole. "Why you nosy heifer," she snarled. "Now I know why you looked at me with such a bug's eye and a shark's grin." She was used to Nicole's loose attitude when it came to talking about sex. And it pleased her to know that she was one of the few people that Nicole felt comfortable enough with to talk the way she did. "Anyway, Harrison and I enjoyed each other's company. We parted on fairly good terms and I'd like to keep it that way. It was a good business move."

"A good move in what way? Other than the obvious, what else can he do for you now? Even I can tell that he's happy to see you up in here tonight. Either that or that big bulge on the side of his thigh is one big-ass gun." Nicole fanned her face with a napkin and sipped her drink. "And while we are on the subject, I'm beginning to feel a little horny myself around all this testosterone."

Teri gave her friend an exasperated look. "Now don't you even go *there*. Like I said, remaining somewhat friendly with him was a good business move. And not just for me, but for everybody at Eclectic Records."

"Well, that everybody includes me and unless you tell me, I don't have a damn clue what a good business move it was for you to stay on good terms with Harrison Starr." Nicole was talking trash, but she was also serious. The solemn expression on her face told Teri that.

"For your information, he is the lead DJ at one of the few radio stations that will play our music cuts frequently. As a matter of fact, every hour on the hour. They are one of our strongest support systems. That's a relationship I can't afford to lose."

"Uh-huh. Well, I guess that is as good a reason as any for you to keep him happy."

Nicole and Teri blended into the crowd, smiling and air kissing a few people they knew. Another one of the more interesting guests was a wildly popular basketball player named Dwight Davis. Teri had not expected to see him at the party, and when she did, she stumbled. She was glad that Nicole didn't notice her reaction. She was not in the mood to tell her that she and Dwight also had a "history" and that he was also in her slush pile.

The fact was that she and Dwight had had a brief but very hot affair before Harrison entered the picture. But unlike her situation with Harrison, a relationship that was only on an extended pause (she'd realized that as soon as she saw him tonight), the intimate part of her association with Dwight was over as far as she was concerned.

There he stood, just a few feet away from her, gnawing on a chicken wing with his eyes closed. If he didn't look countrified and ghetto, she didn't know what did. A large gold hoop earring dangled from his left earlobe. He was the only person present who had on a jean outfit. With his long sexy legs and high firm ass, he couldn't have looked sexier if he'd been naked.

Nicole noticed Teri fanning her face with some folded papers she'd removed from her purse. "Are you ok? Don't you think you should eat something before you finish that drink?" Nicole asked. "I don't care how expensive that shit is, you shouldn't drink too much of it on an empty stomach."

"I guess I could use some of that quiche," Teri decided, moving back toward the table. She looked at the document in her hand. "Let me find Rahim so I can give him this damn contract before I forget." It took Teri several minutes to track Rahim down. And it took her another ten minutes to convince him to take the contract and put it in a safe place for the time being.

"Girl, stop thinking about work and get loose," Rahim told her. "Get out there and have some fun." He handed the contract to a nearby assistant and dismissed Teri with a slap on her ass. She started to walk back to the buffet table, but she stopped when she saw that that was where Dwight was. She pretended to be admiring the artwork on the walls and the other décor until Dwight had moved away.

Harrison's presence, and that little chat she'd just had with him, had been enough for her. Despite her "I'm going to make you work to get me back" attitude with Harrison, the longer she remained in the same house with that luscious man, the more she realized she wanted him back sooner rather than later.

Teri could feel herself beginning to weaken, especially in the knees. There was some hot, tingling, throbbing, moist activity going on between her thighs. The champagne had contributed a lot to her meltdown, but it also helped her feel less inhibited. She didn't know if that was a good thing or a bad thing. Because now that Dwight had been added to the brew, she knew that if something happened between her and Harrison tonight, or between her and Dwight, she wouldn't be responsible.

CHAPTER 8

It was Nicole's idea to leave the party early, but not with Teri. A drummer from an up-and-coming reggae group, and Nicole's recent past, had arrived late. As soon as he had spotted Nicole, he was ready to grab her and run. Nicole was feeling hornier than ever. She was ready, and as anxious to run with that drummer as those daredevils who ran with the bulls through the streets in Spain every year. She plowed through the crowd like a backhoe trying to get to the bathroom quickly, with Teri nipping at her heels.

"Did you know your maintenance man was going to be here? Did you know he'd be coming here solo tonight?" Teri asked, speaking to Nicole in a low, controlled tone of voice, even though they were off by themselves in a corner outside one of the three upstairs bathrooms. Nicole had just emptied her bladder and touched up her makeup.

Teri had to admit that she couldn't remember the last time she'd had more fun than tonight. She'd danced off and on for the past hour. She had consumed so much more champagne she didn't give a damn who saw her hovering over the table snatching fried chicken wings with both hands. Before that, she had devoted her attention to the caviar and quiche. Her lips were so greasy, at one point, a snotty black woman who had avoided the black entrees because she didn't want the non-black guests to think of her as just another Negro rolled her eyes at Teri in disgust. To show that despite her status she was still a "sistah" with obvious ties to the 'hood, and proud of it, Teri gave that blond-weave-wearing bitch the finger. Then she grabbed several more chicken wings and slapped them onto a saucer. She chewed like a squirrel as she spoke to Nicole.

"You mean Carl?" Nicole asked with a blink and a twitch of her bottom lip. Despite the fact that she had just checked her makeup, there was still some lipstick on her teeth and some grease on the side of her cheek.

"Whatever the hell his name is," Teri snapped. She used the same napkin she had just employed to wipe grease from her bottom lip to wipe Nicole's cheek.

"No, I didn't know Carl was going to be here tonight, *Mama*," Nicole quipped. "And of course he's here alone. What do you think I am? Some hoochie who would leave a party with some other woman's date?"

"You're going home with some other woman's *husband*. Is there a difference?"

"Carl and Debbie are separated. They've been separated for two years. The only reason they are still married is because wifey is such a bitter bitch that she wants him to suffer, so she refuses to give him a divorce. They lead separate lives."

"They still live together, girl. You told me that yourself. And you and I both know how people in our business talk."

"I also told you that he was still there because of his son. The boy is fifteen, so in three years, Carl can leave."

"And be with you full time? Three years is a long time to wait for somebody's leftovers."

"Unless we are talking about virgins, everybody is somebody's leftovers," Nicole snarled.

"Greg hurt you when he left you for that other woman. I don't want to see you get hurt again."

"Greg was my husband. He had certain commitments to me that he didn't fulfill. Being with Carl and the other men I see these days is all about me having a good time. Nothing more. If I don't get much more than that, it's still all good because I don't expect it."

"So you let Carl use you?"

"Use me! Ha! If anything, I'm using him. The last time I hooked up with him, he couldn't even bust a nut. But I *always* get mine. With him and every other man. Shit." Nicole laughed and folded her arms. But then she looked more serious than she had at any other time that night. "What's your point?"

"Sex isn't everything, Nicole," Teri said in a weak voice. "Don't you want more?"

Nicole nodded so hard her turban slid to the side. "Right now I want more sex," she admitted, rearranging her headgear. "T, you know I love you to death. We both say a lot of shit to each other when it comes to our love lives. I know that what I say to you goes in one ear and out the other. You should know by now that it's the same way with me. I'm a big girl and I can do whatever the hell I want and with whomever the hell I want. Life is too short and I want to enjoy it while I still can. And you should, too! Shit. If I were in your Jimmy Choos, I'd have thrown Harrison over my back like a sack of flour and hauled his black ass to the nearest motel room as soon as I saw him tonight. But you didn't!"

"That's not what I came here for," Teri insisted, leaning against the wall. They stopped talking and waited for two other female guests to pass by and enter the bathroom, both so drunk they didn't even notice Nicole and Teri, anyway. Teri maneuvered a thick slab of meat off the chicken wing bone with her tongue. "At least I'm enjoying the food," she said with her mouth full.

"That's not all you're enjoying. I saw the way you looked at Harrison. You looked like you wanted to fuck that man out the door. Then you had a second chance to do the same thing with Dwight! Girl, just about every other woman in this place tonight would have done just that. What you do is your business, honey. And what I do is mine. Let's not forget that, okay? Now help me get this damn poncho back on straight." Teri helped Nicole adjust her black poncho and then she watched her stumble down the steps like a wino. Teri shrugged and started to attack another one of the chicken wings on the saucer in her hand, even though she already felt like a sow gone wild.

Before Teri could leave the spot she occupied, Nicole returned with a sheepish look on her face. "Uh, I just wanted to let you know that Harrison is still here."

"So?" Teri managed, still chewing.

"He's been keeping to himself most of the night and I'll bet it's because he'd rather spend his conversation on you . . ."

Teri stopped chewing. "Where is this conversation going?"

"Teri, I don't know what you are waiting for. And maybe you will get exactly what you want one of these days. Knowing you, you will. But in the meantime, have yourself some fun, girl. There is nothing wrong with that. You could probably wrap Harrison or Dwight, or any other man, around your little finger if you wanted to. Do it while you still can."

Nicole's words gave Teri something to think about, but not for long. However, it did make her lose her appetite. She set the saucer on a table outside the bathroom, even though a couple of chicken wings remained. "Are you through? Is there anything else you need to say to me?" Teri asked, licking grease off her lips. She couldn't remember the last time she had behaved so "ghetto." It was a liberating experience.

"I had a dry spell—by choice like you—for a year after Greg did his disappearing act. It didn't bother anybody but me." Nicole paused and shrugged, then gave Teri one of her sharpest looks. "I decided that if I couldn't beat 'em, I'd join 'em. I hooked up with a couple of . . . uh . . . on-call maintenance men, as you like to call them, and I've been happy ever since. I want you to be happy, too," Nicole concluded with a pleading look on her face.

"I am happy," Teri insisted, dismissing Nicole with a wave as they both moved toward the steps.

Teri decided to locate Harrison and wish him luck in the New Year. She decided that that was the least she could do. But by the time she and Nicole got back downstairs, where she had summoned enough nerve to locate and approach Harrison, it was too late. Teri spotted him walking out the door with the same bitch who had rolled her eyes at Teri when she saw her gobbling up those chicken wings a little while ago.

Teri looked at Nicole and blinked. Nicole saw what Teri had just seen. She looked at Teri, shook her head, then gently rubbed her arm. Teri felt as stiff as a board and was hot to Nicole's touch.

"We'll talk tomorrow," Nicole offered. "Right now, I've got a man waiting for me outside. But if you need me, I can send him on his way." Teri gave Nicole a sorrowful look and shook her head. "All right then. Listen, you drive carefully," Nicole told her before she left.

CHAPTER 9

The afternoon after the rapper's party, still slightly hung over, Teri attended service at the same church with her beloved grandparents. The predominantly black congregation spilled out of the old white building with its tall steeple.

It was warm for January, even for L.A. The rays from the sun stung Teri's eyes. She was sorry that she didn't have her sunglasses with her. Some of the two hundred members looked and behaved like they couldn't get off the premises fast enough.

"Baby, we know you probably want to spend the rest of the day with the other young folks," Teri's grandfather said, knowing the reaction he would get from Teri. He said the same thing every time they left church together. He knew her response was always going to be the same, but he liked hearing her say it anyway.

"Don't you start that," Teri scolded, brushing lint, ravels, and fuzz off the lapels and arms of the blue serge suit he wore, which he should have disposed of thirty years ago. "I am with the folks I want to be with today," she said, shaking her head in mock exasperation. "Now let's get to the house and do some serious kicking back and some serious eating. We want to start the New Year off right."

The elder Stewarts had raised Teri after her parents died in an automobile accident when she was eight. And as far as they were concerned, they were still "raising" her. Despite their advanced years, their minds were still fairly sharp and they still applied a lot of good old-fashion common sense when it came to most things. But Grandma Stewart would have still been spoon-feeding Teri if she had her way.

The light green adobe house with the neat lawn and cobblestone walkway that the Stewarts owned was nowhere near as opulent as the mansion that Teri had partied in the night before. But given a choice, she would have chosen the modest single-family home in a middle-class black neighborhood over anybody's mansion any day. It was one of the few places where she felt totally at peace. It was also the one place she could go where she didn't have to do a damn thing to gain anybody's approval. She could eat greasy chicken wings here all day and all night and not worry about some uppity so-and-so looking at her as if she had brought down the whole black race.

"What are you thinking about, girl?" Grandma Stewart asked Teri as soon as they parked in the driveway and got out of the Lincoln that Teri had cosigned for them the year before. Teri had also made an ample down payment and paid the first six notes. Financially, the Stewarts could afford to manage on their own. With their combined pensions after forty years' service, each working for the post office, and the fact that they had made some good investments over the years, they were more than comfortable. But Teri had a six-figure income, a first in her family. She had everything she wanted or needed. With no children or siblings to shower with affection and gifts, she did more than she needed to do for her grandparents, whether they wanted it or not. Last year, she almost had to hog-tie them and have them carried onto the cruise ship where she'd booked them a seven-day cruise to the Mexican Riviera as a surprise for their fiftieth wedding anniversary. They'd come home wearing sombreros, smelling like tequila, and grinning like teenagers.

"Oh? Who me? What am I smiling about? Oh, I was just thinking about what Reverend Upshaw said about Lot's wife . . ." Teri told her grandmother.

"Wasn't that a wonderful holiday sermon? I swear to God,

whenever Reverend Upshaw gets loose in that pulpit, I feel Jesus go through me to the bone. Don't you?"

"I sure enough do. Uh, let's get in the house and get comfortable," Teri insisted, escorting her grandmother into the house with her arm around her shoulder.

The Stewarts' furniture was old but sturdy and well-cared for. A maroon couch, a matching love seat, and a La-Z-Boy dominated the cozy living room. Doilies that Grandma Stewart had made and shaped with starch and beer bottles covered the dark oak coffee table and the end tables and lined the windowsills. High-back chairs faced the big-screen TV in the room that was also a dining room where meals were served on a long, low wooden table covered with a crocheted white tablecloth. Brocade draperies covered the windows in every room except the kitchen and bathroom. Everything in the house could easily last another twenty years before it fell apart. Grandpa Stewart had built this house that Teri loved so much many years ago with the help of some of his church members. And just like it was with Teri, this house also felt like home to a lot of the church members, too.

This was a typical late-afternoon dinner gathering, served buffet style so it was every man, woman, and child for himself. It didn't take long for every single person to have a plate in hand. Old, stout Maybelle Hawthorne, wearing a white floor-length frock that looked like a bathrobe, had a plate in each hand. Both contained generous mounds of food threatening to spill onto the freshly waxed linoleum floors. Some folks stood in groups of three or four, talking as they ate. Others sat or meandered throughout the house.

The destination for most of the males was the room with the big-screen TV where a previously recorded Lakers game was on, featuring Dwight Davis. There was almost as much emotion displayed in the living room as there had been during Reverend Upshaw's fiery sermon. This was the "down-home" atmosphere that kept Teri focused and balanced. This was where her character had been formed. This lifestyle had made her the caring, hardworking, no-nonsense person she was today. No matter what happened in her future personal life, this was what she would always measure her sense of values against.

Grandma Stewart had spent most of the day and half of the night before "cooking up a storm," as she had declared. In addition to a deep-fried turkey, five Crock-Pots full of collard greens, four platters of corn bread muffins, six mac and cheese casseroles, and enough yams to feed a small army, there were six huge pots of black-eyed peas—more than enough for every person present to have several helpings. Grandma Stewart didn't care how much everybody ate. And she made it clear that she didn't want anybody to leave without eating some black-eyed peas.

"Everybody knows that if you want a New Year to start off right, you got to start it off with some black-eyed peas," Grandma Stewart announced, spooning peas onto a huge plate for herself. Black-eyed peas on New Year's Day had been a family and cultural tradition for generations. For a woman who liked to cook and eat rich food, Teri's grandmother was a petite woman with an attractive but chubby face that resembled a chipmunk. Black moles dotted her warm brown face. Her husband was only slightly larger with a mole-like face, a head that resembled a coconut, and sparse, wiry white whiskers on the sides of his face that looked like they belonged on a cat. Teri had her grandmother's eyes and her grandfather's full lips, but she had inherited her five foot seven inch height from her mother's side. One of her biggest sorrows was that her maternal grandparents had both died before she was born so she'd never know what else they'd passed on to her.

Teri enjoyed good southern cooking as much as everybody else in the room. And even though she didn't think of herself as a superstitious woman, she ladled more peas onto her plate than anybody else. There was nothing else on her plate, not even one of the golden corn bread muffins that her grandmother had just removed from the oven with steam still floating above them like miniature clouds.

"Girl, I know you are not going to bypass that turkey and those greens," Grandma Stewart commented, frowning at the contents on Teri's plate.

"The peas are enough for me right now," Teri declared, stirring a few drops of hot sauce onto her meal.

"Well, if all you are going to eat are the peas, you're going to wind up with enough gas to light up Florida. Are you all right? You look a little peaked. I hope you didn't stay out too late last night. I woke up and called your house around eleven-thirty last night and you hadn't come home yet. I hope you are not running around with the wrong crowd, drinking and doing whatnot. You know how we worry about you, with you still out there by yourself as manless as a nun . . ."

CHAPTER 10

By herself? As manless as a nun? Teri was so sick and tired of everybody constantly reminding her that she was still by herself. What in the hell was wrong with a woman being by herself? What did she have to do to convince people that she was doing just fine by herself? The fact that she never complained about being alone should have told them something.

"Grandma, you don't need to worry about me. I can take care of myself." Teri occupied a seat next to her grandmother at the table in the TV/dining room. She recalled how she had badgered Nicole the night before and now she knew why Nicole had been so irritated. She felt the same way now.

"Your mama used to say the same thing and look what happened to her. I don't want you to end up dead. I want you to settle down and get married so me and Grandpa Isaac won't spend eternity worrying about you, too."

"Getting married won't save me. It didn't save my mother," Teri reminded. "Let's change the subject." Teri leaned to the side and kissed her grandmother's puffy cheek.

A few minutes later, Grandpa Stewart left his seat in front of the television set. He shuffled over to the table where Teri had just finished eating her black-eyed peas.

"Girl, you need to eat like you got some sense," he complained.

"Let me dip you out some of these peas. Black-eyed peas on New Year's Day mean money."

Teri didn't protest as her grandfather piled more peas onto her plate. "And don't you worry none about gas. Sop up some turkey gravy with a piece of that corn bread before you go home. It works better than charcoal pills when it comes to dealing with gas," he told her, burping like a baby, excusing himself between burps.

"Uh-uh. I take back what I just said about peas meaning money," Grandpa Stewart said, shaking his head as he reached for his own plate, which he promptly filled with peas. "Corn means money. Peas mean good luck," he said with a grin. "That and a little gas if you overdo it," he added with a chuckle. He sniffed and dropped another spoonful of peas onto Teri's plate. She thought she would scream if she heard another reference to gas.

"I'm not *that* hungry," Teri said again, rolling her eyes at her grandfather.

"You always did eat like a little bird," Grandma Stewart gently complained, then chewed on a deep-fried turkey leg.

"It's her nerves if you ask me," Grandpa Stewart suggested, both of his cheeks full. He was a good match for his wife. She looked like a chipmunk. He looked like he had the mumps. Juice from the peas glazed his bottom lip like lip gloss. He sat down hard in the chair on the other side of Teri, groaning like a man in pain.

Teri rolled her eyes up to heaven. A few minutes later she followed her grandmother into the living room with Grandpa Stewart close behind, holding onto his plate and grumbling all the way.

"Isaac, Teri's just trying to hold on to her girlish figure like all the rest of these youngsters," Grandma Stewart said, giving Teri an affectionate pat on the butt. "Baby, I need to show you something." Teri gave her grandmother a puzzled look as she followed her out of the room.

"Trying to keep a girlish figure my foot. Her nerves are what keep her from eating right. And prayer is the only thing that can help that," Grandpa Stewart said in a gentle voice. He had stopped in the middle of the living room floor. As soon as Teri and her grandmother disappeared, he plopped down into a chair and that was where he planned to stay until his bedtime.

"Amen to that," said Old Man Carson, who occupied the seat directly across from Grandpa Stewart.

"Well, I'm praying that there's some corn bread left." Grandpa Stewart turned to see Teri's young cousin Rudy running into the living room with an empty plate. Normally, eating in the living room was off limits. And that was a rule that Grandma Stewart enforced with vigor. But today was an exception. There were more than two dozen guests in the house and it was a holiday.

"Girl, did you find a job yet?" Grandpa Stewart asked Cynthia, Teri's nineteen-year-old cousin, as she eased down onto a hassock near the doorway, crossing her long, freshly waxed legs. She was hoping that somebody would notice how good her legs looked and pay her a compliment. Nobody did.

"I'm still looking," Cynthia said, rolling her heavily made-up eyes. A job was the furthest thing away from this girl's mind. She wasn't a man, and as far as she was concerned, work was for men. A woman's "job" was to keep her man happy. She was one of the few relatives that Teri had little or no use for. Especially after Teri refused to hook her up with some of the musicians she worked with or to make arrangements for her to shake her shapely ass in somebody's music video. Instead, Teri—with her jealous old-maid self—had offered her a *receptionist* position as a backup to Nicole. Cynthia had looked at Teri as if she were crazy.

"Well, you better look harder. Don't you want to be like your cousin Teri?" Grandpa Stewart asked, frowning at the way his granddaughter displayed her naked legs. Had young people become so loose that they had no shame left whatsoever? That had to be the case.

"Not if I can help it," Cynthia said with a snort, shaking her head.

"In the meantime, pull your skirt down and cover your shame, girl," the old man ordered.

Teri and her grandmother talked about trivial things as Grandma Stewart searched for some documents in the dresser drawers in her bedroom, spilling contents to the floor like a burglar.

Every few minutes, Grandma Stewart brought up the fact that Teri was "still single" and that that wasn't normal for a woman her age. But each time Teri's marital status came up, she steered the conversation in another direction.

"Sister Hawthorne is looking mighty healthy these days," Teri commented.

"Healthy? Baw! She'd better look healthy with her pig-ear-eating, three hundred pound self. Brother Hamilton asked her to marry him last month and she jumped at the chance. Can you imagine that? I don't know what this world is coming to. But with her being a widow going on two years and him just losing his wife, and them living next door to each other, it was bound to happen sooner or later. Now if she can get a man, even one that looks like a baboon and smells like a nanny goat like Brother Hamilton, a girl like you ought to be able to get somebody like Obama or Denzel."

Teri looked around the room and sighed. She wondered what her grandparents and Nicole were going to complain about once she did get a man.

"There's a sale at Kelsye's furniture store." Teri pitched her words like a baseball.

"That reminds me. I saw the Kelsye's older boy the other day. The one that spent twenty years in the military. He's going to make somebody a good husband. You want his phone number? I'll ring up his mama before you go home today."

"Nanny, listen to me. I am happy being alone. How many times do I have to say it? What do I have to do or say to make you and Grandpa stop worrying about me being by myself?"

Grandma Stewart gave Teri a stern look and let out wind from both ends before she spoke, excusing herself first, though. "Get married, I guess," she said, fanning the fumes she'd just released. The old woman gave Teri a hopeful nod. "Grab the Kelsye's son before somebody else snatches him up."

Teri was too exasperated for words, but she knew that if she didn't continue to defend herself, her grandmother would wear her out.

"I don't need you or anyone else to help me find a man. I can do that on my own," she insisted.

"Then why don't you?"

"Why don't I what?"

"You work with men every day. What's wrong with one of them?"

Teri gave her grandmother a thoughtful look. "There is nothing wrong with the men I work with. I used to date one of the guys in our personnel office," Teri confessed. "But things didn't work out."

"And why didn't things work out? It don't take much to keep a man happy, if you know how. And I am not talking about all that bedroom foolishness. The first time I was with Isaac in the flesh, you would have thought he was tearing down a house the way he rode me. The whole time I was laying there under him, all I could think about was how I was going to wash all his sweat and jism off my sheets."

Teri stared at her grandmother in slack-jawed agony. "Do I really need to hear this?" She had to look away to keep from laughing at the thought of her stuffy grandparents having sex.

"Once you put that physical part in the proper perspective, the rest is easy. You feed your man what he wants to eat, make him think he's some kind of king—and all that means is telling his dumb ass a lot of barefaced lies, and keep his house and kids clean. That's all it takes. That's why divorce is a stranger to most of my generation."

"The guy I dated from work wanted a mama . . ." Teri admitted with a pensive look on her face. She recalled how heartbroken she had been when Derrick Hardy told her that the only reason he'd asked her out was because she reminded him of his mother. That same day, she had stopped at the mall and purchased a more youthful wardrobe on her way home from work. Derrick no longer worked for Eclectic, and she made sure that every piece of clothing she purchased came from the most youth-oriented boutiques—for women in her age group, of course—that she could find.

CHAPTER 11

Teri ignored the look of disapproval on her grandmother's face as she smoothed the sides of her short black skirt.

Like everything else in the Stewart home, the bedroom furniture was old, but well cared for, too. There was the bed that looked more like a wagon that Teri was not looking forward to inheriting.

Watching her grandmother rooting around in her dresser drawers reminded Teri of how she had searched for the document that she needed to complete her media report before the party last night.

"Here they go," the old woman said with a sigh of relief. She beckoned for Teri to join her on the bed. The old bed's springs squeaked like a herd of mice when they sat on it. "We haven't signed these yet."

"What is all this?" Teri asked, reaching for the beige folder in her grandmother's gnarled hand.

"Just some paperwork." Grandma Stewart held the papers out of Teri's reach. But Teri took them anyway. She frowned as she read. "This is just to renovate the front of the house and replace the front porch," Grandma Stewart said, stroking the side of Teri's head. "And look at all that good hair. A man would love to run his fingers through it."

"You can't sign these papers. We could lose this house!" Teri exclaimed, rising. "We need to get Grandpa in here."

"We can talk about all this later. After everybody's gone. I don't want the whole world to know my business," Grandma Stewart told Teri. She motioned for Teri to return to her seat, but Teri refused, shaking her head like a defiant child.

"Let's go," Teri ordered. With the papers still in her hand, she ushered her grandmother out of the room.

They found Grandpa Stewart back in the dining room standing at the table. Nicole stood next to him with a plate in her hand. Teri was glad to see her. Nicole was always a reliable defensive tool for her to use when she had to deal with her meddlesome grandparents. No matter what her grandparents said, Nicole always took Teri's side, unless it involved Teri not having a man.

"Hey, girl," Nicole said in the light and cheerful voice that made her such a joy to be around in situations like this. Sometimes all Teri needed was Nicole's presence to get her spark back. "How come you didn't wake me up for church this morning?"

"I thought you were busy," Teri replied with a smirk then a wink. Teri's grandparents gave each other a puzzled look.

"Where's that young'un of yours, Nicole?" Grandpa Stewart asked, clearing his throat as if he were trying to remove a frog.

"He's with his daddy," Nicole answered with a sigh of mild disgust that only Teri detected. She already knew that she was going to have to give Nicole a pep talk after Greg came by to drop Chris off later that evening. Teri had never liked Greg and he despised her. However, whenever she ran into him in public, or if he happened to drop by Nicole's apartment when she was there, she went out of her way to be cordial. But he treated her no better than he did a dog he didn't like.

"Nicole, did you and your husband get back together yet?" Grandma Stewart asked with a hopeful expression on her face. Teri and Nicole looked at each other and cringed.

"Greg has remarried," Nicole reminded in a stiff voice. It was obvious to Teri that Greg was the last thing that her girl wanted to discuss with the Stewarts or anybody else. Nicole cleared her throat, then grabbed a napkin and started to nibble on a turkey wing.

"Now there you go, eating like a bird, too, girl," Grandpa Stewart complained. "You and Teri are two peas in a pod. No wonder you're both still single . . ."

"Can I talk to you two in private?" Teri queried, looking from one grandparent to the other. Then she looked at Nicole. "You can stay if you want. You're family, I guess."

Nicole gave Teri a confused look. She didn't like the serious look on Teri's face. She decided that whatever Teri wanted to discuss with her grandparents, she didn't need or want to know. She dealt with the ups and downs of the aged enough in her own family. "I think I'll join the crowd in the living room, if you don't mind," Nicole said. "You and I can chat later."

"Later," Teri said, giving her friend a defeated glance. Then she turned to her puzzled grandfather, waving the documents she had taken from her grandmother in his face. "Whose idea was this?"

"What is all that?" Grandpa Stewart wanted to know. He looked at the documents as if he were seeing them for the first time. Then he looked at his wife. They both shrugged. "I thought we settled this."

"As long as you didn't sign them, nothing has been settled. Whoever this man is, he's a straight-up crook. And don't you dare sign any papers he brings to you," Teri ordered.

"Isaac, Teri said we could lose the house," Grandma Stewart said with increasing alarm. "I told you that man didn't look honest to me. He had enough grease on his hair to fry a chicken gizzard."

"How do you know so much about this?" Grandpa Stewart asked Teri, giving her a suspicious look. "Do you know this man?"

"I know that people like you are getting scammed out of everything left and right these days. Our accountant's parents got swindled out of thousands of dollars last month in a similar scheme," Teri revealed.

"Was it the same outfit? The King Associates?"

"I don't know if it was the same outfit, but it was the same scam.

Look, I know a lot about these things. Please trust me. It's been all over the news lately."

"Why would anybody want to cheat us out of anything, Teri?" Grandpa Stewart asked with the wounded innocence of a child. And this was why it was so important to Teri for her to keep an eye on them.

"Because they can, that's why. But they won't if I can help it. You're the two most important people in my life now. I am not going to let anybody take advantage of you." Teri ripped the documents in two.

"What do we tell that Mr. Brinkley when he calls next time?" Grandpa Stewart asked.

"You give him my telephone number and have him call me. In the meantime, don't even let anybody into this house trying to sell you anything unless I know about it. I don't care if they are trying to sell you a fly swatter, you call me before you let them into this house," Teri said in a stern voice, shaking her finger in the air.

"Well, I guess that's that. I didn't think we needed all that mess anyway," Grandma Stewart said, leaving the room with her husband behind her mumbling under his breath.

Teri didn't enjoy being in the position she occupied in her grandparents' lives. But in a way she was glad she was. The fact that she always had to be highly alert to keep them out of trouble kept her on her toes in other areas. She knew that as long as she had her wits about her and could hold her own, growing old alone didn't seem nearly as ominous as everybody tried to make her think it was.

"Is the coast clear?" Nicole asked, peeping around the doorway, then easing back into the room. Teri stood by a window, looking out at the backyard. Her old swing set and sandbox were still in place next to the brick barbeque grill that she and Nicole had helped Grandpa Stewart build fifteen years ago.

"It's fine. Come on in. How was your date last night?" Teri asked, frowning at the half-dollar-size purple sucker bite on the side of Nicole's neck. She promptly replaced her frown with a smile.

"Oooooh, it was nice." Nicole swooned with a grin and a wink, rubbing her neck. "I can barely walk."

"Oh, shut the fuck up, you nasty buzzard!" Teri snapped, pinching Nicole's arm as she joined her by the window. "Happy New Year, girl," Teri said, giving Nicole a big hug. "But if you don't show up for work tomorrow, you're fired. You look like you've been mauled."

"Oh, you mean this?" Nicole said, rubbing her neck.

Teri inspected Nicole's neck for a full minute, shaking her head the whole time.

"Say what you've got to say about it so we can get it over with," Nicole suggested.

Teri let out a loud breath before she spoke again. "I hope I get one soon," she said earnestly. Nicole gasped and looked at Teri as if she'd just sprouted another head. Then they both burst out laughing. "Let's go to my room," Teri invited. Nicole followed her to one of the two bedrooms upstairs.

Just like the backyard, Teri's old room looked like she had never left it. And it was the only room in the house that had a youthful touch. There was a brass bed in the center with a blond nightstand on either side. A bright chenille bedspread covered the bed. A few stuffed animals still occupied a high-back chair in front of a vanity table.

"The dreams I used to have in this room." Teri sighed. "Would you look at us?" She pointed to a framed photo of herself and Nicole on top of the vanity table. "This is the only picture that the folks wouldn't let me take. We both look like a pair of crazy women trying to imitate Tina Turner with our flyaway wigs and short skirts."

"We were the original crazy women." Nicole laughed, looking at the picture as if she were looking at a picture of two sideshow freaks.

"Tell me about it," Teri responded with a nod. The nostalgia brought tears to her eyes, causing her to blink hard and sniff a couple of times.

"And now look at us." Nicole paused. "Speaking of crazy, do they know?"

"Know what?"

"That your crazy ass is seeing a shrink?"

"Are you kidding? I'd rather run naked down Sunset Boulevard before I let them know that. You know what their generation thinks about shrinks. Besides, I don't think of Carla as a shrink in the traditional sense."

Before Nicole could respond, Elliot, one of Teri's other young cousins, came tearing into the bedroom.

"The Lakers won! Dwight Davis hit a three pointer at the buzzer!" the boy reported.

"Boy, get your knotty-headed self out of here," Teri ordered. Elliot did a jig, crossed his eyes, and stuck out his tongue before he ran back out of the room. "That's what you have to look forward to in a few years with Chris," she told Nicole.

By five o'clock, most of the Stewarts' guests had left. Teri and Nicole volunteered to stay and help clean up. They ended up doing all the cleaning. Grandpa Stewart had returned to his favorite chair in the living room and was now snoozing like a baby. Grandma Stewart kept trying to help, but all she did was get in Teri's way.

"I appreciate your coming over," Teri told Nicole just as they were about to finish their chores. "I know you'd rather have spent the day with your son."

"You're right about that. But you know how inconsistent Greg is. And Chris absolutely adores that fool. I have to let him see his daddy whenever I can get him to come over. I don't want my son to grow up resenting me someday because he didn't get to spend enough time with Greg."

"Well, you're raising the boy right and that's all that really matters. Let's just hope he turns out to be a better specimen of a man than his daddy," Teri said. "We could use a few more good men in our race."

"Oh, we already have a lot more good ones than we know. We just have to find them," Nicole offered with a laugh. "It might take a lot of searching, though. And I know you don't want to hear this from me *again*, but if you don't get busy, you never will get one . . ."

CHAPTER 12

It was the first day back to work in the New Year for some people. Teri and Nicole both knew a lot of their friends and associates were still celebrating or recovering from the arrival of the New Year and had called in "sick." Bobby Ming, the young Chinese man who delivered the mail twice a day, had called to say that he was "so sick he couldn't even get out of bed." But two of his coworkers saw him on their way to work that morning cruising down Olympic Street with his fiancée, grinning like a man who didn't have a care in the world. The bookkeeper who occupied the cubicle next to the break room had called to report that her flight from Cancun had been cancelled so she had no choice but to take another day off.

Nicole, loyal and dependable to a fault, had arrived an hour earlier than her usual time. She wanted to jump-start her first workday in the New Year, make a pot of coffee, and have Teri's schedule printed and on her desk when she arrived.

Just as Nicole was about to open the door to Teri's office, she heard somebody coughing. It was coming from behind the double doors that led to Teri's office. Nicole sucked in her breath and glanced at the telephone on her desk, wondering if she should call security. Then she sniffed and smelled the aroma of coffee coming from the break room down the hall. Before she could decide what to do, she heard Teri's voice. "Nicole, is that you?"

Nicole eased open the door and entered Teri's office. "Teri, what are you doing here at this hour?" She was pleased to see how well rested Teri looked. Before they'd left the Stewarts' house the evening before, she had noticed how tired Teri looked. Now she looked like she'd slept for three days and was ready to take on the world. She wore a navy blue suit with a light blue blouse underneath. This was the ensemble that Nicole jokingly referred to as Teri's kick ass armor.

"I'm working," Teri replied with a laugh. "I just made a fresh pot of coffee." She was bent over her desk with a thick pile of papers and folders in front of her. There was a pencil perched behind her ear. Her thick hair was piled on top of her head and held in place by one of those light blue squeegee-looking things.

"Thanks for making the coffee. I sure need a cup, and I am too lazy to go down to Starbucks and stand in that long-ass line for twenty minutes," Nicole said, rubbing the back of her head. She had on a pair of black slacks and a purple turtleneck sweater to hide the love bite that was still visible enough for people to notice. She wore her hair in one long braid, wrapped around her head like a crown.

"And I made it nice and strong because we're going to need it in the meeting," Teri said, moaning under her breath. "The first staff meeting in the New Year is always the hardest. It sets the tone for what we can expect for the next twelve months. Last year you would have thought that Victor was practicing to be the next Terminator. He fired three people . . ."

"Three lazy, incompetent motherfuckers who should have been fired a long time ago. Humph! Getting fired is the least of our worries," Nicole remarked. "The best-kept secret around here is that you and I are keeping this place from going to the dogs. If Victor fires us, or even one of us, they can rename this business Titanic."

"I don't know if we are that important around here. These folks were doing just fine before we came on board. I do know that it sure would do us a lot of good to take a break for a few days. Maybe we should go on that Caribbean cruise we've been putting off since last year," Teri said hopefully.

"I could be packed in five minutes." Nicole swooned. "All that black Caribbean gold running up and down those white beaches, dicks big as baseball bats, I hear . . ."

"Can you get your mind out of the bedroom for a few minutes?" Teri barked as she plopped down into her chair. She knew that she could not stop Nicole from talking about sex so much. But all that talk about sex didn't help Teri at all. If anything it only made her more frustrated. "Shit, get serious."

"Sorry. Whatever you say." Nicole bowed her head in submission. She removed the dreamy-eyed look from her face and tried to contain herself. "What were you saying now?"

Teri reared back into her seat and bit the side of her bottom lip. There was a serious look on her face. Her face was as beautifully made up as usual, but Nicole was surprised to see that Teri was not wearing any jewelry, not even earrings. "Work has become the most dominant thing in my life and . . . and it's still not enough. There's got to be more out there—and I'm not talking about a big dick. So please do me a favor and do not bring up Harrison Starr's name. Or the fact that he left Rahim's party with another woman." Teri shot Nicole a look that was so hot, it made her flinch.

"Okay, I won't." Nicole dipped her head and gave Teri a contrite look. "Happy?"

Teri nodded. "Like I was saying, there's got to be more to life than work."

"That's what I keep trying to tell you. But if you want more out of life, nobody can do anything about that but you, Teri. You *choose* to work your fingers to the bone, so don't complain to me about it."

"I'm not complaining. I'm just making conversation," Teri whined, which was something she rarely did. "Despite all the bullshit, I still love my job. And I want to give it everything I've got." Teri tilted her head and sniffed.

"And God knows you're doing that. Please tell me you didn't come here after I left you last night and slept here," Nicole pleaded, glancing at her watch.

"I didn't sleep here last night," Teri replied, looking at her watch, too. "I've only been here for a few hours. I couldn't sleep . . ."

Nicole shook her head and looked at Teri with pity.

"Did you have company again last night?" Teri asked, looking at Nicole out of the corner of her eye. She removed the pencil from behind her ear and started tapping it on the top of her desk.

"No. Why do you ask?"

"Because you look a little tired to me, Nicole."

"I could have had some company again last night, but I chose not to. I did take a rain check, though." There was a mischievous twinkle in her eyes. "Did *you* have company last night?"

"Now, don't you even go there," Teri hissed, shaking her finger in Nicole's face. She drank from a large green coffee mug with a bullfighter taunting a snorting bull on one side and I ♥ PUERTO VALLARTA on the other. It was a gift from the maid she'd treated to dinner during her last south of the border visit. "Now get your butt to work before I . . . before I write you up, or fire you, or something."

Nine o'clock crept up on Teri and Nicole like a mugger. But Teri would not have even noticed the time if Nicole had not buzzed her.

"I'm on my way," Teri said in a hurried voice. She suddenly wished that she had eaten more of her grandmother's black-eyed peas yesterday.

The conference room that often served as a battleground was a little too warm, but it was going to get even warmer. Victor Oliansky was the only person in the room who looked like he was there because he wanted to be. Everybody else looked like they were constipated and had been dragged to the meeting kicking and screaming. The attendees were shuffling papers, clearing throats, clinking coffee cups, checking BlackBerrys, and snapping cell phones shut. In addition to a few noticeable sighs and yawns, there were a few muffled comments about who had done what to ring in the New Year.

Had Victor attempted to play the part of a recording studio executive in a movie, every casting director in Hollywood would have said that he was too much of a stereotype. He was at least sixty, probably older. But it was obvious that he was doing everything his money could buy to look younger. Some of his employees knew that to be a fact, especially his secretary. John, a busybody of a secretary if there ever was one, snooped through Victor's BlackBerry and e-mail on a regular basis. He always knew when Victor had an appointment for a Botox treatment, and John made regular trips to a nearby pharmacy to pick up Victor's Grecian Formula hair dye and refills for his Viagra prescriptions. Every time Victor pissed off John, he blabbed Victor's most intimate business to Nicole, his unofficial confidante. They'd been thick as thieves ever since they'd attempted to set Teri up with a male prostitute.

Despite Victor's sixty-something years, he was in fairly good shape for a man his age. But his long, flat, black ponytail didn't do much to improve his appearance. In spite of his position and wealth, he looked more like the type you'd expect to see stretched out on a lumpy, three-legged couch in a trailer in a plaid flannel shirt and bibbed overalls drinking generic beer. The Armani suit he wore today was the same shade of pale blue as his eyes. He was slightly married to his fourth wife. According to the office gossip, he was trawling for wife number five.

Right after Nicole passed out the meeting agenda, Victor mumbled something to her and she slunk back out of the room. A few minutes later she returned with a spiral notepad and a large mug of coffee and handed it to Victor. He cleared his throat and looked at Nicole as if he were seeing her for the first time. She responded with a smile, but that didn't soften him. His lips were already thin, almost to the point of being nonexistent. They were now pressed together so tightly, had it not been for the line that divided his lips it would have looked as if he had no mouth. But that anatomical feature didn't fool anybody. Victor's lips hid a tongue that could be as sharp as a serpent's tooth.

Nicole gave Teri a conspiratorial look before she took a seat across from her.

"I can tell from the happy faces before me that you are all just delighted to be here with me. Right?" Victor began, looking at Teri as if she were the only other person in the room.

"*Hell* no. I can think of at least a dozen other places I'd rather be," she said sharply. Victor pretended that he didn't hear all the snickers going around the table. Teri didn't even look up from her notes.

"Now that we are all back on earth, let's get down to business," Victor continued, looking around the room. Within seconds there was a forced smile on every face.

Safety was always the first item on the agenda. It consisted of five minutes of dos and don'ts and a report on work-related injuries, if any. After a few more remarks, most of them unnecessary, Teri took the floor. Other than Victor, she was the only one who stood up when giving a presentation. All eyes were on her again as she flipped through her notes and cleared her throat.

"Teri, please proceed and be *brief*," Victor instructed. He slid the arm of his suit jacket up so he could see his watch. "I'd like to be out of this room by Easter."

"Let's get down to business now. Trevor Powell's first single from his new CD has just been released," Teri began, with her voice full of confidence and authority. There were several sheets of paper stapled together and clutched in her hand. She glanced at the first page, shook her head, and then casually flipped to another page, perusing it slowly and thoroughly. "Yes . . . hmm . . . oh! Here we go. I'm going to cut to the chase. If anyone is interested in reading my full report, let Nicole know and she will make you a copy." She paused, then cleared her throat some more. "The reviews have all been good, so far. And, even more important, the numbers are good. Very good. I'll be getting the team to focus on the up-and-coming release of his next CD." Teri gave a triumphant smile. But that smile faded as soon as Victor opened his mealy mouth.

"Thank you, Teri. That's a start, I guess," he muttered.

A *start?* What the hell was wrong with this damn man?

"I think it's a very good start, sir," Teri insisted, looking around the room for support. Nicole was the only one to respond.

"I agree," Nicole offered. "Thanks to Teri, Trevor was recently featured on the covers of two music magazines. And mentioned in *Jet* and *Ebony*."

"I don't read *Jet* or *Ebony*, and other than you, I don't know anyone else who does, either," Victor snapped, glaring at Nicole.

"Trevor's fans read those publications. They are the most prominent publications in the African American community and have been for decades," Teri said, her hand on her hip. "And for your information, I have a lot of non–African American associates who read those publications as well. I think it'll do us all a lot of good if we stay focused. Right now that focus is getting Trevor as much exposure as possible. And that's what I am doing, thank you very much." Teri concluded with a firm nod in Victor's direction. All he did was flinch and blink. There were seven other men present besides Victor. Not a one of them had ever had the nerve to stand up to him like Teri. But the men, as well as the four women present, silently agreed with every word that had just rolled out of Teri's mouth.

"You go, girl," Nicole said under her breath.

Teri eased back down in her seat, folded her arms, and looked around the table again. Her gaze stopped on Victor's beet-red face. "Any questions?" she asked, still looking at him, glad to see him squirming in his seat.

"Thank you, Teri," Victor managed. Then he coughed, sat up straighter, and glared at Miguel Reyes, directly across from him.

Thirty-year-old Miguel handled all the media-related work that Teri couldn't get to. He was almost as sharp and thorough as she was.

It was Miguel's job to procure and set up additional interviews and to get the artists' names mentioned in as many publications as possible, especially the weekly tabloids because millions of people read them on a regular basis. And it didn't matter if all the news printed about the artists was good or bad. Bad publicity was better than no publicity. R. Kelly had been accused of having sex with an underage girl, but even though that disgusted a lot of people, his name stayed in the news. And his sales were still fantastic. Every person in the room was well aware of what bad publicity had done for Paris Hilton, Britney Spears, and Lindsay Lohan.

They were more popular than ever because of all the bad publicity they received.

"Miguel?"

"Um, I'm still working on my report, sir. I will make a full report at our next meeting. I've been a little behind lately," Miguel explained, blinking his piercing black eyes and looking nervous. He also wore his black hair in a ponytail like Victor, and he was probably the most handsome man on the payroll. He was just a shade lighter than Teri and almost a foot shorter. But his height didn't hinder his popularity. Even though he was happily married, he still had to practically beat the women off with a stick. And he was so humble and charming it was hard for the men he interacted with not to like him. However, Victor was not one of Miguel's admirers at the moment.

"You've been more than 'a little behind' lately. As a matter of fact, you've been behind for weeks." Victor paused and made a sweeping gesture with his arm toward Teri. "See how easy it was for Teri. I suspect that she's doing her job and yours. Hmm? How is it she was able to pull together such a succinct report and be so prepared to deliver it at such short notice? What is your excuse, if you don't mind my asking. Hmm?" Victor folded his arms and glared at Miguel.

"I apologize, sir. I've had houseguests for the past three weeks and I guess I got caught up in the holidays," Miguel explained.

Victor dismissed Miguel with a snap of his fingers. Then he looked at the next person, who gave a report as brief and glowing as Teri's. Every other person who had a report to present did so with flying colors. But that was not enough for Victor. He grunted, made a few closing remarks, and then dismissed everyone except Miguel.

CHAPTER 13

Ten minutes after Teri had returned to her office, Nicole burst in with her jacket and purse. There was a wild-eyed look on her face, like a woman who had just escaped from a chamber of horrors. "Starbucks" was all she said, looking at her watch.

"Sure. Why not? But if Tiny's bar at the corner were open, I'd go there instead," Teri said flatly. "Victor's meetings usually make my temperature rise."

"Well, when the bar opens at eleven"—Nicole paused and looked at her watch again—"we can hit it, too. That meeting was pure torture."

"I'm buying. Let's get the hell up out of here," Teri told her. She rose from her seat and grabbed her purse. She was so hot she didn't need to bring her jacket.

When they got to the elevator, Miguel Reyes was standing in front of it holding a moving box under his arm that contained some personal items. The fake green papier-mâché plant that his son had made in school was under his other arm. He had on his jacket.

"Miguel? What the hell is all this?" Nicole asked. Nicole and Miguel's wife, Louisa, had been close for years. They'd once lived in the same apartment building in Encino. Miguel's son was in Nicole's son's class and the boys were very close. Miguel, Jr., had spent a lot of nights in Nicole's apartment sharing the pullout sofa bed in her living room with her son, Chris.

"I've just been fired," Miguel announced, his husky voice cracking as if he had suddenly developed a serious throat condition.

"For what?" Teri and Nicole asked at the same time, their voices sounding like an echo.

"Well, according to Victor, I am not doing what he's paying me to do." Miguel let out a deep breath and glanced at Teri with a hopeless look and shrugged. "He feels that I am more of a fuckup to you than a backup. Maybe it's time for a change anyway. My wife even said so. There are a lot of jobs out there, so I'm not worried." Miguel forced a smile. "I'll be okay."

"This is insane!" Teri said, her voice rising hysterically. "Has Victor lost his mind? I depend on you now more than ever." Before she could continue, her cell phone rang. She removed it from her purse and frowned at the caller ID. "Speak of the devil. Now he wants to see me ASAP," Teri said with a snort. "If he fires me, I want you both to know that I won't be responsible for my actions. Don't move!" she ordered, holding her hand in front of Miguel's face, then Nicole's. "I want both of you to wait right here until I get back. This won't take but a few minutes." She whirled around and rushed down the hall to the stairwell.

Eclectic Records was still considered a novice company by some folks, occupying only two floors in the building that had once been occupied by a law firm. The other floors were occupied by a real estate company, a plastic surgeon, a temporary employment agency, and an insurance company. Victor's massive office was one floor up, directly above Teri's. Even after she had closed the stairwell door, Miguel and Nicole could still hear her Jimmy Choos clip clopping on the stair steps like an angry Clydesdale horse.

"Miguel, I am so sorry about this. If you want to use me as a reference, please feel free to do so," Nicole said, gently rubbing Miguel's back. "Call me soon. We'll talk about you, me, the kids, and Louisa getting together for pizza or something."

"That'd be nice. Let's just make sure that wherever we go, they serve some pretty strong tequila." Miguel managed to grin, but there was still a sad look in his eyes. He set his box on the floor. "You know, I'd never worked for a gringo before I came to this company. After this, I don't think I ever will again." Miguel rubbed his temples with the ball of his thumb.

"If I didn't need this job, I would have left this place a long time ago," Nicole revealed with a heavy sigh. She looked toward the elevator as it stopped. The two young secretaries from the personnel department exited, and she greeted them with a smile. One was white, one was black. Nicole thought of them as Salt and Pepper. Both were plain, pudgy, and bitter. Neither could stand Nicole or Teri and talked about them like dogs every chance they got. They had even started rumors about Teri, everything from her sleeping her way up the ladder of success to her being a lesbian. If Victor was as smart as he thought he was, he would have fired Salt and Pepper a long time ago, Nicole thought, not someone as valuable and dedicated as Miguel.

"But it's the same all over. There are a lot of Victors out there," Miguel assured her. "We just do the best we can do, and when that's not good enough . . ." He stopped and shook his head. He gave Nicole a pensive look before he released a loud moan.

Five minutes after Teri had left the area, almost to the second, they heard her footsteps on the stairs again. She emerged from the stairwell, looking as if she had just won the lottery. "Miguel, you can return to your office. Victor had a sudden change of heart," she announced, intensifying the look of triumph on her face.

"Well, I'm scared of you," Nicole said, arching both brows. "We just might have to start calling you the fix-it lady."

A calm look appeared on Teri's face. "I can't fix everything," she admitted, in as humble a voice as she could manage at the time.

"Your nose is no browner than it was before you went to see Victor, so we know you didn't do any ass kissing on my behalf," Miguel told Teri, looking relieved. "So what *did* you do or say?"

"Not much. He did most of the talking. He said the place wouldn't be the same without you, I nodded, then he told me to call you back," Teri claimed.

She didn't feel that it was necessary to confess to Nicole and

Miguel that she had cussed Victor out for firing Miguel for such a flimsy reason and had dared him to fire *her.* By the time she got through with him, he was sweating like a stevedore and was as humble as the pope. It saddened her to know that she had so much control and power when it came to dealing with men she didn't have an intimate relationship with.

"I know there was more to it than that, but you don't have to say anything else. The important thing is, you got over on Victor," Nicole said proudly. "I'd like to walk in your shoes just once," she added, tongue in cheek.

"No, you wouldn't," Teri assured her, shaking her head. Miguel and Nicole both noticed the profoundly sad look that suddenly appeared on Teri's face.

CHAPTER 14

The house that Carla and Reuben Andrews regarded as their dream home was the most attractive residence on their block. It was a two-story, light beige stucco house with a garage large enough to accommodate their twin Jaguars and a silver Range Rover that was so new it still displayed dealer tags. Transplanted citrus trees surrounded the property like a fort.

Teri parked her BMW on the street in front of the house behind several other high-end vehicles. About a dozen of the Andrewses' guests, who had been invited to help celebrate Carla and Reuben's thirteenth Valentine's Day wedding anniversary, congregated outside on the spacious wraparound front porch.

The invitation had suggested casual attire but everybody, including Teri and Nicole, was dressed to the nines. Teri wore a blue suede pantsuit with a dangerously low-cut white silk blouse underneath.

Nicole, slumped in the front passenger seat of Teri's car like a wet noodle, had on a yellow leather skirt with a modest split up the side and a matching jacket with black buttons. It was one of the few outfits she owned that had been purchased from one of the super upscale boutiques on Rodeo Drive in Beverly Hills. And she had Teri to thank for that. Since Nicole's birthday was two days before Christmas, it had been a combination birthday/

Christmas present. Teri had removed the eleven-hundred-dollar price tag, and she didn't see any reason to tell Nicole that she'd bought it off the clearance rack, marked down by 40 percent. Hell, almost every designer outfit that Teri owned had come from the clearance community. But she was not a cheap woman by any means. She was a smart woman. She didn't get to where she was by being frivolous and stupid. It was one of the many reasons Grandma Stewart assured her she would make somebody a good wife.

This reminded Nicole of the night of the New Year's Eve party at the rapper's house last month.

"I bet there aren't too many of us in this neighborhood, either," Nicole pointed out, shading her eyes with her hand to see more clearly. Then she checked the knee-high black leather boots she had on.

"There you go again," Teri snapped, shooting Nicole a hot look.

"Well, it's true. There are not that many black folks in this neighborhood."

"There is tonight," Teri chirped. "And by the way, you sure are working that skirt. A little short for a woman your age, with a son . . ." she teased. "You'd better be glad I didn't wear my latest DKNY or you'd be outgunned."

"This was the only thing I had that fit the occasion. And the only nice thing I had in my closet that *fit* my fine brown frame. I'm still trying to work off all of those Thanksgiving, Christmas, and New Year's Eve calories." Nicole frowned, moaned, and groaned as if she were in pain.

"I feel you there," Teri admitted, sucking in her stomach. "And to tell you the truth, if you hadn't agreed to come to this shindig with me, I'd be at home on the sofa reading Carl Weber's latest book and nibbling on some barbequed ribs."

"I thought you loved spending time with Carla," Nicole said, sounding and looking confused.

"I do. Carla's a good friend. And as my shrink, she's done a lot for me. In some ways she's more like a spiritual advisor."

"Then what's the problem? Why did you even think about not coming?"

Teri shrugged. "No offense, but I'm getting sick of showing up at parties and other events with you as my escort."

"Well, you don't have to, you know. I thought you enjoyed my company. And I don't have a problem escorting you to these functions that you always seem to get invited to. The last thing I got invited to was my family reunion."

"You know what I mean," Teri said, her voice rising dramatically. "The same people seem to show up at every event I get invited to. I don't want them to start thinking I can't, uh, get a date with a man."

"Well, I hate to be the one to tell you, but I think you crossed that bridge a long time ago. You know how people talk at the office. You know about those two miserable secretaries in personnel with diarrhea of the mouth? Salt and Pepper? I've overheard them more than once wondering out loud why they never see you or hear about you being with a man. John's cubicle is in front of theirs and he hears practically everything that comes out of their mouths. But I know you don't care what gossips say. People are going to make assumptions no matter what. I know you're not a lesbian . . ."

Teri gave Nicole a sharp look. "Is that what people are saying about me?"

"It's been mentioned a time or two. But like I said, I know you don't give a damn what gossips say. And you shouldn't. I know the real deal. So do John and Miguel. But Victor couldn't care less if you are a lesbian or an aardvark as long as you continue to make the company look good."

Teri turned so Nicole could not see the hurt look on her face. But what Nicole had just said about her was true. She didn't care what people said about her most of the time. But what bothered her was the fact that she was losing her perspective in some areas. She had asked herself more than once lately if she had lost interest in men completely. She knew that that wasn't true just a few moments later when a silver Jaguar drove up and parked across the street. Nicole was absolutely dazzled. She wasted no time giving it an appreciative glance. Harrison Starr, looking better than ever, was in the driver's seat. Teri had not seen him since the rapper's party on New Year's Eve. But he'd been on her mind quite a bit since that night. Her heart started to beat so vigorously, she could hear it.

"Daaamn!" Nicole howled, fanning her face with both hands. She'd just experienced a severe hot flash. "Is it hot in here or what? I like *that*." She nodded toward the Jaguar.

"The car or the driver?" Teri asked, trying not to sound too interested. Despite her close relationship with Nicole, there were some things that Teri preferred to keep to herself. One was the fact that she wanted to be with Harrison again in the worst way. She just didn't know how to go about making that happen on her own. Her hope was that he would. "He's just another brother."

"Oh? Give me the goods on him. What's his story?"

Teri sucked in her breath, which tasted especially sour all of a sudden. "That's Harrison Starr . . . as in the FM station 98.6." Teri watched Harrison climb out of his car rocking the hell out of the black suit he had on. He looked more dapper than ever with his wavy black hair cut short. He didn't even notice Teri and Nicole sitting there staring at him like two magpies. "Don't you remember him from the rapper's party?"

Nicole squinted her eyes and stared at Harrison for a moment before responding. "Oh shit! I listen to his show every morning. Is it my imagination or is he twice as fine as he was on New Year's Eve?"

"The man does look good," Teri allowed, gripping her steering wheel.

"And he looks as good in person as he sounds on the radio. First time I heard that deep sexy voice, I thought I was listening to a younger version of James Earl Jones. I wonder why *he's* rolling up here alone. Didn't he come to Young Rahim's party alone, too?"

"He did. But he didn't leave alone," Teri said with a grimace.

"Well, I have no room to talk. I didn't leave that party alone either, remember?"

"I remember." Teri's mouth tightened and her eyes began to itch. For some reason it annoyed her to see Harrison looking as if he didn't have a care in the world. Men didn't know how good they had it when it came to affairs of the heart. She wondered why couldn't things have worked out between her and Harrison the first time so she wouldn't have to put herself through so much uncertainty now as far as he was concerned.

"I know you had a secret little ditty with him last year, but what's the rest of his story? How is it that a luscious brother like that can be running around loose? What's wrong with you, girl?"

"There is nothing wrong with me," Teri insisted, tired of defending herself. But she knew that if she didn't, people would never stop drawing their own conclusions about her. "Why does something have to be wrong with me because I am not chasing a man?"

"Well, I don't blame you for not chasing a man. But Harrison Starr is not just a man." Nicole looked straight ahead because she didn't want to see Teri's reaction to what she said next. "If I knew it wouldn't bother you, I'd go after him myself . . ."

"You can do whatever you want with Harrison. It's none of my business," Teri said, grinding her teeth.

"Teri, please! You know I'm just pulling your chain," Nicole declared. "For one thing, you know I don't go there." Nicole touched Teri's shoulder. "And if it really bothers you, I won't bring him into the conversation again."

Teri looked at Nicole with a mysterious smile on her lips.

"No . . . bring him up as often as you want to. I can't think of another man I'd rather discuss more."

CHAPTER 15

"If you couldn't hold on to him, I wonder just what he's looking for in a woman."

There were times when Nicole said something so stupid that it made Teri want to slap her. This was one of those times. But Teri was able to control herself. She gave Nicole's words some consideration before she responded.

"Why don't you ask him?"

"I don't think so. I just wonder how a man like that can still be single. It's beyond me, Teri."

Teri removed her compact from her clutch purse, checked her makeup, then patted her hair, which she had in a French roll. "He was married not too long ago. His divorce became final the last week that I, uh, was with him."

"Hurry up and slap me so we can get out of this car," Nicole said.

Teri whirled around to face her. "Slap you for what?"

"For messing with you like this. You know damn well I would never go after Harrison and it was stupid of me to joke about it. I want you to know right now, if he ever comes after me, all I'll do is send him back to you."

"Please don't do me any favors," Teri said firmly, her jaw twitching. "And please do me a favor and stop talking crazy. I've en-dured enough pain in the romance department."

"I'm not talking crazy, girl. One thing for sure is I know pain. I know what it feels like to be hurt." Nicole gritted her teeth and blinked hard. "That bitch Kim Loo was sitting on her dumpy, rice-eating yellow ass doing my nails every week and fucking my husband behind my back."

Teri gave Nicole an affectionate hug and waited patiently in si-lence until she cooled down a few degrees.

They remained in Teri's car until Harrison had gone inside the house.

"Well, the party's inside, and if we want to enjoy it, we'd better get our black asses in there, too," Teri said. Nicole gracefully un-buttoned the two top buttons on her jacket, making sure to ex-pose her perky breasts. Teri sucked in a deep breath and checked her makeup again.

The Andrewses' living room was jammed with people. Teri plowed through the crowd like a bulldozer with Nicole close be-hind, jerking her head from side to side as she stared in awe. She knew that the Andrews were well off, but not nearly as well off as the rapper. But their house had ten times more taste and class than his. African artwork, a stylish powder blue couch and match-ing love seat, and exotic plants dominated the living room. There was a wall-to-wall red oak bookcase filled with leather-bound books facing the couch. And Carla and Reuben had both read every single one of them. Red and white heart-shaped balloons dangled from the ceiling encircling a crystal chandelier. In the dining room, which was just as exquisitely furnished as the living room, sat on a table a huge heart-shaped white cake with a red heart in the center that contained Carla and Reuben's names. Other than her grandparents, Teri didn't know of any other cou-ple—black, white, or anything else—that seemed to be as much in love as Carla and Reuben.

Carla entered the dining room, looking like the wife of an African diplomat. Her salt-and-pepper-colored braids made her look ten years younger than her forty years, a fact that she never concealed or denied. Despite her owlish eyes, thin lips, and slightly crooked nose, she was considered attractive. Her voluminous, floor-length gown with a floral print hid a firm and youthful body that she worked hard to maintain. Her sensitivity and wisdom had earned her the respect and friendship of many people.

In spite of the fact that Carla was a prominent psychiatrist whose patient list included several of her friends and relatives, Teri considered Carla to be one of her most treasured friends. They'd known each other only for a couple of years, but in some ways, Teri felt like she'd known her a lot longer.

Carla read Teri like a book, in more ways than one. As if Carla didn't have enough going for her, she had been born with a special gift, a sixth sense that allowed her to glimpse into the future. It was not something that too many people knew, and it was one horn she didn't like to toot too loudly. Many years earlier, she'd learned the hard way that it was smart not to.

One dull night during her senior year at Spellman when she had nothing better to do, she'd surprised her roommate and sorority sister, Janette Spencer, by volunteering to do a psychic reading for her. Janette was skeptical and amused, but she agreed to it, anyway. She had nothing better to do that night herself. Carla told Janette that she was pregnant and that the baby's father was going to propose to another girl. Janette's period was already a week late at the time, but she'd been late before. And as far as her man even looking at another girl, she absolutely refused to believe that. She called Carla a damn fool and advised her to go read her Bible. The incident was forgotten until two months later when Janette suffered a miscarriage when she heard that the boy who had relieved her of her virginity was going to marry one of her rivals.

By the time graduation rolled around, Carla had been called a witch doctor so many times she lost count. She'd laughed it off for the most part, but it had hurt her feelings to be made fun of. She didn't even tell Reuben about her special ability until they'd been securely married for three years. She had never done a reading for him, and he'd made it clear early in their relationship that he didn't want her to. And it was not because he was a skeptic. He had been raised in New Orleans by a mother whose so-called healing hands had cured more afflictions than he could count. Anything that had to do with the paranormal, even slightly, frightened him so he left it alone. But he knew that Carla was not a dingbat. She took her gift very seriously. He didn't even know which of her friends and patients she read for, and he didn't want to know.

He knew that she wouldn't risk her credibility and reputation by broadcasting her business. She had too much to lose. And as a corporate attorney, he did, too.

"There are twice as many people here as we'd originally planned to invite. The list kept getting longer and longer," Carla said, addressing one of the caterers who looked worried. "And if that wasn't bad enough, my husband invited some that he forgot to tell me about."

"Not to worry. We'll manage," the caterer assured her.

Carla noticed Teri standing a few feet away sipping champagne. She rushed up to her, gave her a mighty embrace, and rubbed the side of Teri's cheek with hers. "Reuben must have invited everybody in Southern California," she mentioned. She turned to Nicole. "You must be Nicole. I've heard a lot about you." She gave Nicole a quick hug.

"Believe only the good stuff," Nicole quipped. She snatched a flute of champagne from the tray of a passing waiter and took a long swallow.

As much as Nicole respected Teri, she wasn't sure how to take the fact that Teri was seeing Carla on a professional basis and, well, she didn't know how to categorize that psychic thing. Seeing a shrink was one thing—a lot of people on Teri's level were in some kind of therapy. But this psychic thing in the year 2008? Nicole wondered what some of the uptight people she and Teri worked with would think if they knew she was being "advised" by a psychic shrink. She almost laughed out loud when she recalled how the media had exposed the phony television psychic Miss Cleo a few years ago. And before that, there was that story about Nancy Reagan getting caught up in some psychic astrology mess. The late-night talk show hosts had a field day with that.

Well, if anybody found out about Teri and Carla, it wouldn't be from Nicole. As a matter of fact, if Teri said the woman was good at what she did, that had to count for something. Nicole considered all the facts. Teri Stewart was not a gullible woman or a fool. If she endorsed something, it had to be worthwhile. Now that Teri had let her in on one of her "secrets" she would milk it for all it was worth. Why the hell not? She had nothing to lose but maybe something to gain.

"It was all good," Carla assured Nicole, giving her hand an affectionate pat. "But I already knew that." Carla added a wink to her declaration. She noticed Nicole and Teri exchanging glances. There was a dark cloud of confusion on Nicole's face. "It's all right. I know that you know what I do," Carla said in a low voice.

"Uh, yes, I do. And Teri tells me that you're pretty accurate," Nicole replied, almost in a whisper.

Carla nodded and beamed proudly. "Did you sign up for a reading?"

"I'd love to sign up," Nicole squealed.

"I'm glad to hear that, Nicole. I can already tell that you will be a good subject." Carla paused and looked around. "We can set up a time for later tonight."

Carla's husband, Reuben, feeling and looking his forty-two years, entered the room. From the dazed look on his reddish brown face, he was feeling no pain. There was a shot glass filled with Jack Daniels in his hand. He still had most of his hair, even though half of it was gray. And he was proud of the fact that it was naturally soft and curly. He liked to part it on the side and plaster it down with expensive pomade. But every time he had more than a couple of drinks, the alcohol had an odd effect on his hair. The strands of his curls separated and stood up and out, as if he had sprouted a head full of wire. With him was Mia Miller, the dream girl of almost every man at the party. But she was about as unnecessary, unwanted, and inconvenient as she could be as far as the women were concerned. She was the kind of woman no woman in her right mind would invite to her party. Especially a woman Carla's age. Had Mia not piggybacked her way into the party with another guest, she would not have been present. Carla would have made sure of that.

Mia was the daughter of a Vietnamese mother and a black father. She had just turned twenty-six. She did some modeling on the side, had no trouble latching on to a sugar daddy when she needed one, and had already appeared in half a dozen music videos. Carla trusted her husband, but she was not naive enough to think that he would never cheat on her. Especially the way the young bitches threw their asses at men these days.

CHAPTER 16

"How are you, Mia?" Carla asked, attempting to rub Mia's cheek with hers. Mia's reaction stunned Carla to say the least. Not only did she abruptly turn her cheek, but she moved back a few steps and glared at Carla as if she had tried to bite her.

"I'm fine," Mia replied, with her face and lips so stiff it looked as if her mouth didn't even move.

Teri and Nicole were even more stunned by Mia's blatant display of arrogance than Carla. But Carla handled the slight with dignity and class. "You're looking so lovely today, Mia. Welcome to our home. I hope you will enjoy yourself. And don't let this man of mine talk your ear off," Carla said with a laugh. Just to show that she was three times the woman Mia was, she gave Mia a friendly pat on the shoulder.

Mia flinched, but that didn't faze Carla, either. She continued to be graceful and dignified. "Reuben, honey, where are your manners? Get Mia a glass of champagne. This party was your idea, babe." Carla deliberately refused to look at Mia again. Teri and Nicole were so disgusted with Mia's behavior they discreetly nudged each other with their elbows and gave each other horrified looks. You didn't have to be a mind reader to know what they were thinking. Teri wanted Carla to take the bitch aside and order her to leave. Had this been Teri's house, that's exactly what she would have done. Nicole would have done the same thing, but she would have kicked Mia's ass first.

"I'd like some Evian, if you have it. I don't drink or smoke anymore. I gave it up years ago," Mia announced. "Nothing ages a woman quicker than alcohol and cigarettes," she added with a smug look on her face. She looked at the flute of champagne in Teri's hand and then at Nicole's.

"You stopped drinking and smoking? I never would have guessed that," Nicole quipped. Teri nudged Nicole's side again with her elbow. Carla snickered. "Looks like you stopped in the nick of *time . . .*" Carla covered her mouth with her hand, but Teri could still hear her snickering under her breath. Teri wanted to do the same thing, but she could see from the look on Mia's face that Nicole had made her point.

Mia gave Nicole a blank look and shook her head as if she were shaking rocks out of it. "What did you say?" she asked, glaring at Nicole even though she'd clearly heard Nicole's remarks.

"Nothing," Nicole mumbled. Now the smug look was on Nicole's face.

"Where is that photographer? Where in the world is that Eric Graves? I'm paying him by the hour," Reuben said to no one in particular, looking around the room with his neck swiveling like a barber's chair. His words were forced, but it was the only way he could think to change the subject at such short notice. He wanted to diffuse the situation going on with the women. He recognized a bitch's brew when he saw one. And a smackdown between two of his guests was the last thing he wanted to deal with on his wedding anniversary. He knew that he would never hear the end of it. Carla would make his life a living hell. "I want a shot of me, Harrison, and Dwight Davis for my office."

"Dwight is here, too?" Teri asked, obviously annoyed. It was one thing to know that Harrison was on the premises, *with his fine self*; she could deal with him. But Dwight's name was at the top of her shit list. She beckoned a waiter and had him refill her glass.

"Oh yes, Dwight is here. Lakers all-star forward." Reuben smiled. "And it wasn't easy to get him to come out here. A brother like him gets more invites than he can handle. Living over there in

Brentwood, everybody in his neighborhood wants him on their guest list."

Teri rolled her eyes and looked around the room, glad she didn't see Dwight. A passing male guest stopped and leered at Mia. It took him a few moments to notice Teri, Nicole, and Carla. Then he leered at them, too. "Why are all you foxy ladies hanging out in the dining room when all the eligible brothers are in the living room?" The women heard him but they all ignored him.

"Is Dwight here alone?" Carla asked her husband.

"He came with me," Mia volunteered before Reuben could even open his mouth. There was a satisfied look on her face.

"I figured that," Teri said, making sure Mia heard her.

"It was nice chatting with you ladies," Mia said, finally smiling. But a blind man could see how insincere her words were. Carla excused herself and led her husband away. Mia whirled around and pranced out of the room, strutting like a gay rooster.

"I hope I don't have to take off my earrings up in here tonight," Nicole said, watching Mia until she was out of sight.

"I hope you don't, either. I thought we left all that shit behind us in grade school. I haven't been involved in any violence since sixth grade."

"Well I have, and I can thank that *thang* I married." Even though there was no telling where Greg was tonight, Nicole still felt his presence. The last time he had come to pick up Chris, three hours late, he had lunged at her and grabbed her by the throat when she demanded her back child support payments. And she'd bounced her Crock-Pot off his head, leaving a knot the size of a lemon. "You used to be the one that handled more business than Mike Tyson. I'm surprised you didn't snatch that bitch bald," Nicole said.

"And don't you forget that every time you got caught up in a smack-down, you got your ass kicked. I'd hate to see that happen in here. Don't embarrass yourself or me. You should know by now that the world is full of skanks like Mia," Teri said.

"I bet I could whup that bitch with one hand tied behind my back," Nicole declared.

"Well, I don't want to find out. Now, you behave yourself. She is a guest here just like we are. Let's at least respect that, and the fact that this is Carla's house," Teri insisted. "I wonder what she did to Dwight for him to bring her here. He usually attends these kinds of things alone."

"Dwight's taste must all be in his mouth." Nicole huffed. "Mia's bubble butt must have more fingerprints on file than the FBI. He seems like the kind of brother who could do a whole lot better than a Mia."

"He used to. He used to make me so weak in the knees it makes me sick to think about it now," Teri confessed, her face burning with shame.

"Uh-huh. I can understand why. He's working the hell out of that bad-boy image. He's got that 'come and get it' scowl on his face, and the promise of a mean hump from the looks of that swagger in his hips. And hands that look as if they want to do the James Brown up and down your body. What more could a woman ask for? If you don't mind me saying so, Dwight is a few degrees hotter than Harrison."

"I wouldn't say that." Teri chuckled, shaking her head. "Harrison is on a Sidney Poitier level. Dwight is crawling around down there with the Snoop Dogs of the world." Teri guffawed at her own comment.

"The next time I see Snoop, I'll tell him what you said," Nicole jokingly threatened. Then she got serious. "I know that Dwight is here with Miss Saigon, but Harrison showed up here alone."

"So? What's your point?"

"I've seen him looking at you. And . . . I've seen you looking at him. This is a replay of Rahim's New Year's Eve party. Are you going to behave yourself up in here?"

"Now, you know you don't have to worry about me. Why do you ask?" Teri looked at the floor to keep Nicole from seeing the smile on her lips and the mischievous look in her eyes.

Nicole screwed up her mouth and gave Teri an exasperated roll of her eyes. She threw in a neck roll for good measure that was so profound it looked, and it was, painful. "I'm asking be-cause I need to know if I have to find myself another way to get home after this is over," Nicole replied, rubbing the side of her throbbing neck.

"What's that supposed to mean?" Teri wanted to know, staring at Nicole with her mouth hanging open.

"I don't remember the last time you admitted that a man made you weak in the knees. As a matter of fact, I've never heard you say something like that in all the years I've known you. And it has been a while for you. You must be climbing your bedroom walls by now."

"I'm just fine, thank you. And what I just said was, he *used* to make me weak in the knees," Teri stated.

CHAPTER 17

About ten minutes after Reuben had left the room with Mia, Reuben and Carla returned to the dining room, where Teri and Nicole were still holding court, chatting with two young brothers.

"Excuse me, young bloods," Reuben said, smiling from one of the young men to the other, then at Teri who looked bored beyond belief. "You won't get out of this house until you dance with me," he told Teri. He grabbed a relieved-looking Teri by her arm. He pulled her into the living room where music, mostly old-school golden oldies that he had recorded the day before, oozed from an entertainment center facing the fireplace.

Most of the guests were still in the living room. Before Reuben could get halfway through a dance with Teri, Harrison tried to cut in. As soon as he tapped Reuben on the shoulder, Reuben shook his head. Teri was so weak in the knees by now she felt like she was going to hit the floor.

After the song ended, Teri attempted to leave the floor, hoping that Harrison still wanted to dance with her. But another man grabbed her by the arm as soon as Reuben released her. Three slow dances later with the man's erection pressing against her pelvis like a Gatling gun, she left the floor, shaking her head and smiling. She was feeling better than she'd felt in a long time. Slow dancing was a long way from fucking, but just being in a man's arms had felt good. The thought gave her a warm feeling all over. She smiled at Nicole, who was now dancing with two men at the same time. Teri laughed to herself, wondering if she'd be going home without Nicole again.

She didn't have to look long to spot Harrison again. He stood a few feet in front of her clutching a bottle of champagne that had a red ribbon tied around the neck. She was impressed to see that it was Dom Perignon, Carla's favorite. But she was not surprised. Harrison was one of the most dapper and sophisticated men she'd ever met. She watched as he handed the bottle to Carla. After Carla kissed him on the cheek and walked away, Teri started to move in Harrison's direction. But she was not fast enough. Mia popped up out of nowhere and had Harrison on the dance floor within seconds. Her bold move didn't bother Teri half as much as Harrison's reaction. He wrapped Mia in his arms for a slow dance. And from the look on his face, you would have thought that he had just died and gone to heaven.

Disappointed, Teri turned her back to Harrison so she would not have to see what she didn't want to see. But she saw something else that she didn't want to see anyway. Dwight Davis stood in front of the fireplace surrounded by half a dozen women. The way they were drooling over him you would have thought that he was the Messiah. And he was enjoying every second of it.

Teri was disappointed to see that Nicole was one of the women drooling over Dwight. She let out a deep sigh and went out to the front porch because she knew that if she watched that spectacle any longer, it would make her sick. As soon as Nicole moved away from Dwight, Carla whispered in her ear, "Look but don't touch."

"Excuse me?" Nicole said, slurring her words.

"I could be wrong, which is rare, but I think our girl Teri still has a thing for Dwight."

"That's not what she told me," Nicole said, shaking her head. "You know, I've known Teri most of my life. I can't believe she told you about her little fling with Dwight and didn't tell me until recently."

"She didn't tell me," Carla said with a mysterious look on her face. She didn't wait for Nicole to speak again. "I know things before they happen and then some," Carla reminded.

Nicole gave Carla a pensive look. "I hope you'll have as much insight about me as you do Teri. I could use all the help I can get."

After a few minutes on the front porch chatting with people she had not seen in a while, Teri returned to the living room. Harrison was nowhere in sight. But Mia was dancing with Dwight this time, twisting her ass and dipping forward like she was having a spasm, swinging her coal black, waist-length hair from side to side.

Reuben was still looking for Eric. Eric had been present for more than an hour, and he'd been busy doing what Reuben had paid him to do: take as many photos of his guests as possible. Eric Graves was twenty-eight but because of his cute, round baby face and dimpled left cheek, a lot of people thought he was at least five years younger. His girlfriend, Yvette Staples, was with him, in a short, tight white dress that belonged on a stripper.

Yvette was a more ghettolike version of Mia, but she was more attractive than Mia. Her large green eyes and a pert nose in the middle of a heart-shaped face had opened a lot of doors for her. Usually to some leering man's bedroom, though. She used her good looks for all the wrong reasons, which usually meant short-term affairs for profit.

She had had a few that had lasted only a few days. Yvette was tall and slim enough to model and had tried it for a few weeks last year. She got bummed out after only three weeks. There was way too much hard work involved for her. All that running around from one job to another just about wore her out. And having to compete with a slew of other heifers for jobs was not her thing. She was the kind of woman who wanted everything handed to her, and on a silver platter if possible. But her biggest obstacle was her ignorance. She honestly thought that because she was pretty and only twenty-three, all she had to do was sit back and let things happen. Instead of being more proactive in securing a better life for herself, she had the nerve to think that somebody was going to discover her and give her the life she felt she deserved. Eric was all right for the time being. But she wanted more than a man with a Mickey Mouse photographer's job and the dead-end ass life he offered her. However, she'd decided that she'd get as much mileage out of him as possible. She firmly believed that if she hung out with him long enough and the people that he interacted with, her dreams would eventually come true.

But until that happened, she would have to drag along as a cashier in a punk-ass discount store in one of the most dangerous neighborhoods in L.A. And it wasn't even a dollar store, but a *ninety cent or less* store! After six years and no raises in two years because of her tardiness and frequent absences, she was getting desperate. That's where she'd met Eric three years ago. He had come in to purchase some Advil on his way home from his wife's funeral. A severe headache brought on by grief had sent him to her. Standing in her checkout line on a slow day he had told her how his wife, Lynn, had been diagnosed with breast cancer a year ago and died. Two days after his wife's funeral, he returned to the store to buy more Advil. That was when Yvette went in for the kill. She asked him for a ride home, and they ended up in a motel. Yvette knew the "power of the pussy" so once she got him into bed, he was dog meat. Poor Eric didn't know what hit him that night. But things had changed over the years. Yvette no longer went out of her way to please him. Now it was all about her.

She'd been living with Eric for more than two years now, helping him raise that nappy-headed brat of his. Other than a damn good fuck, he didn't do a whole lot for her. She would have moved out of his place a long time ago if she could have. But other than a cramped shit house in South Central with her alcoholic parents and six siblings, she had no place else to go. In the meantime, he had to do. She'd continue to eat a Happy Meal until somebody placed a filet mignon on her plate.

"Are we going to dance or what? All this time we've been here, all we've done is roam around from one side of this room to another," Yvette whined to Eric. From the sour look on her face, she was not happy. Her nose twitched when she was happy, sad, angry, or lying. It was twitching so hard now that she looked like a rabbit.

CHAPTER 18

"Yvette, please check yourself. I told you before we left the house that I'd be working. I didn't come here to dance. If you want to dance, you can dance with anybody you want," Eric told her. "And I wish you would stop all that whining. Go get yourself another drink."

"Drink? This shit they serving up in here ain't nothing but some glorified Kool-Aid," Yvette complained. She waved a flute with just a few drops of champagne left in it in Eric's face. "I want me some beer."

"There's a liquor store down the street," Eric retorted, a cloud of anger crossing his face.

Yvette's jaw dropped. "Fuck a liquor store. I ain't spending a dime of my money on no liquor store with all this free shit they got up in here." She looked like she wanted to laugh, and would have if Eric had not given her such a harsh look.

"Baby, there are some pretty important folks here. Lots of contacts," he told her.

Despite the fact that Yvette was actively looking for a bigger meal ticket than Eric, she still expected him to show her a good time.

"Contacts, my ass," she said with a sniff and a wave of dismissal.

She paused long enough to finish the drink she claimed she didn't like. "That's all you ever think about these days. What about me and you having some *contact?*" She giggled and rubbed her body against him. Eric got an instant hard-on and he gently pushed her away. "What about us having some damn fun?" He shook his head in mild disgust when she let out a loud belch, even though she immediately excused herself.

"Baby, I am having fun. Do you hear me?" he told her, looking around to make sure none of the other guests were listening and looking.

"And I want you to have even more fun," Yvette whispered in his ear. Despite the fact that Yvette was so tacky in other areas, she knew that the best way to get inside a man's head was through his dick. She gave Eric a quick massage between his thighs, making him even harder. She didn't bother to look around to see if anybody was looking, because she didn't care. Even though she had literally fucked Eric out of his bed and onto the floor before they left for the party, her little gesture was about to make him explode in his pants where he stood.

Reuben and Teri rescued Eric from embarrassing himself. "Man, I have been looking for you all evening," Reuben told him.

Eric cleared his throat and gently pushed Yvette to the side. "Well"—he shrugged—"I've been here all evening." Eric leaned forward and kissed Teri gently on the lips. "You are looking as beautiful as ever." He paused, released a mild moan, and kissed Teri again. Even though it was obvious that his show of affection was nothing but a platonic gesture, it made Yvette seethe.

"I want you to get a few shots of me by the fireplace. And if I can track down that woman of mine, I'd like to get quite a few shots of us together. And then a few of me with my man Dwight Davis. First, get one of me and my girl Teri," Reuben ordered.

You would have thought that Yvette had suddenly become invisible. The only woman that Eric and Reuben were interested in now was Teri.

"That bitch," Yvette muttered to herself, following behind them as they plowed through the crowd and strolled over to the fireplace.

After posing for half a dozen shots, two by himself, two with Carla, and two with Teri, Reuben decided to set out to find Dwight.

"In the meantime, Teri, do me a favor. Track down Harrison for me," Reuben said with a puzzled look on his face. "I had wanted a few shots of me, Harrison, and Dwight together. But Dwight is playing the player role. He will pose only if he's the only 'star' in the picture. He can't stand the thought of Harrison stealing his thunder."

"So why do you want me to find Harrison then?" Teri wanted to know.

"Because I want him to be ready when Eric finishes up the shots with Dwight and me. I don't want to spend the rest of the night looking for him, Eric, or anybody else. Shit," Reuben snarled. He had become so impatient, his jaw was itching.

The party was really blasting now. A few more guests had arrived. Even though Teri was enjoying herself, she kept glancing at her watch. She had no idea where the hell Nicole was. The last time she saw her, she was huddled in a corner with Carla and they appeared to be having a very serious conversation.

Before Teri could move from her spot a large familiar hand appeared in front of her face. For a moment, it seemed like it was disembodied. Her eyes traveled up the arm to see who it was connected to. Dwight had become like a boomerang. He just kept coming back. He held an hors d'oeuvres in front of him with his other hand. "Try this, baby. Prawns dipped in wine and wrapped in bacon."

Teri didn't even bother to give Dwight another brush-off. They seemed to have little effect on him, anyway. Besides, she was too tired. And since she knew in her heart that it was over between the two of them, she saw no reason not to give Dwight a little leeway from time to time. He had taken all he could take from her— which included a small chunk of her love and time—so she felt she had nothing else to lose. She took the snack from between his fingers and slid it into her mouth. "It is good," she said as soon as she swallowed.

"There's plenty more where that came from," Dwight told her, looking in her eyes in a way that made her wish she had brushed him off now.

"Thanks, but that's all right," she said, moving away. Out of the corner of her eye she saw Harrison a few feet away, still with that damn Mia. Dwight took Teri's hands in his and pulled her closer to him. So close that her titties were smashed against his chest.

He gently lifted her head. He was at least a foot taller than she was, but the way he had her positioned their eyes were just inches apart. "Can we go somewhere and talk?"

"What about?" Teri glanced to the side again. Mia had left Harrison and was now in another man's face. She was glad to see that Harrison was looking at her and Dwight.

"We can talk about whatever you want to talk about. I'd like to discuss a thing or three with you."

Teri shrugged and gave Dwight a dry look that he didn't appreciate. "I can't imagine what that could be," she replied, moving back. "Don't you have enough to discuss with Mia?"

"Who?" Dwight actually looked like he didn't know who Mia was. He gave Teri a thoughtful look. "Oh, her! Shit," he yelled, waving his hand and snapping his fingers. Then he said slowly and seriously, "Baby, you are worth about five of her."

"Is that right?" Teri questioned, with both eyebrows raised. "Well, let me circulate a little bit and if I can think of anything I want to discuss with you, I'll let you know." She didn't even give Dwight the chance to respond before she disappeared into the crowd. But the look on his face said it all. He had the long face and sad eyes of a puppy that nobody wanted.

Reuben and Carla had overheard the conversation between Teri and Dwight. They looked at each other and shook their heads, amused and confused. They had never seen a man as high and mighty as Dwight slide so low, so fast. Had his face drooped any lower, it would have been on the ground.

"Ow! I'm scared of Miss Teri. That sister could bring down

Telestar," Reuben muttered, his hand on his wife's waist. He gave her a quick peck on the neck.

"And without even trying that hard," Carla added with a nod.

As much as Teri wanted to find Harrison and be close to him, she didn't try that hard. And she didn't have to. Harrison found her.

CHAPTER 19

"I heard you were looking for me," Harrison said to Teri. Just the way he looked at her was enough to make her body stiffen. She felt like a mannequin. His eyes looked right into hers. She licked her bottom lip when she saw how moist his lips were. He cleared his throat and smiled. There were some people whose smiles seemed to brighten a room like a lightbulb, Teri thought. Harrison was one of those people. He beamed and it made her feel warm all over.

Eric and Yvette were nearby. By now Yvette was so disgusted with Teri she wanted to scream. She wanted to get back at her in the worst way and she promised herself that if the opportunity ever arose, she'd jump in feet first.

"Well, yes, I was. Reuben is determined to get his picture taken with you," Teri said, struggling to remain composed. She gave Yvette a quick glance. The tension between the two women was as thick as a horse blanket.

"Harrison, don't you move!" Reuben ordered, holding his hand in front of Harrison's face. Reuben laughed as he and Carla approached Teri and Harrison. "Eric, do your thing." Reuben clumsily wrapped his arm around Harrison's shoulder, pulling him close. "Baby, come on," Reuben invited, beckoning Carla. "Where are the kids? Let's get a few nice family shots," Reuben let out a mild belch and looked around the room. The two Andrews children, Reuben Jr. age ten and Carlena age twelve, had been escorted to their rooms by both parents and were told that that was where they'd be until morning. Carla had walked into the kitchen an hour before the party and caught the two of them guzzling wine coolers.

"The kids are in their rooms where they are supposed to be," Carla reminded her husband. "And if I catch you with another drink in your hand, that's where you'll be, too," she threatened.

Reuben looked at her as if he didn't know what she was talking about. Then he turned to Eric. "Brother, can you stay around for a while? As soon as the crowd thins out enough, I want to bring the kids down. If I don't let them get a few pictures with Dwight I will never hear the end of it."

"Since you are paying me by the hour, I'll stay all night if you want me to," Eric said with a chuckle. He didn't even have to look at Yvette to know the expression on her face. She looked as if she wanted to skin him alive.

"Tell you what," Eric said to Reuben, looking at his watch. "Why don't you bring the kids down in about twenty minutes. I will personally hold Dwight in place until we get as many shots as you want." Eric looked at Teri. "In the meantime, I could get a few shots of some of the other guests." He looked past Teri at Harrison. "My man, how about a few shots of you and Teri? Two of my most favorite people."

Before Teri could protest, Harrison had his arm around her and was grinning like Chuck E. Cheese. "It would be my pleasure," he said, meaning it in more ways than one.

"Get a little closer," Eric directed. Harrison pulled Teri so close to him she could feel his breath on her face. He smelled like cinnamon and some exotic spice that she could not identify. And coming from him, the aroma was erotic. She rubbed the back of her neck. It felt as if her neck hair had risen like the quills on a porcupine. Being in his arms again, even though it was for something as casual as taking a picture, brought back some excruciating memories of ecstasy. She felt like a criminal. What was going through her mind had to be against the law. Had she been made of wax, she would have been flowing to the floor like lava by now. She could only stand still long enough for three quick shots.

"That was nice, Teri. Thanks," Harrison said, kissing her lightly on her cheek. "You know, one thing I always regretted was the fact that I never got a single picture of you," he admitted. Why did he have to look at her like that? She felt as though he were looking clean through her.

Teri blinked and nodded. She cleared her throat to speak again. But before she could open her mouth, Mia slid back onto the scene. Teri could not have felt colder if somebody had flung a bucket of iced water in her face. Her lust had been reduced to a nagging pain in the ass and its name was Mia.

"Eric, how about a few shots with me and Harrison Starr," Mia purred, sucking on her capped teeth as she looked up at Harrison. "Your show is the only one I listen to," she said, lying. She would have said anything to make an impression on him, or any other man at the party for that matter. That cheesy-ass motherfucker Dwight didn't know how lucky he was to be her date, she said to herself. From the time they had arrived, he had spent most of his time skinning and grinning in every woman's face except hers—telling more of his lies, no doubt. *Well, fuck him,* she thought. Did that damn fool think his shit didn't stink? As far as she was concerned, there were much bigger fish to fry at the party than Dwight. All she had to do was reel one in.

There was a helpless look on Harrison's face as Mia wrapped her arm around his waist. He twisted his neck around and looked at Teri. She had no idea why he looked at her the way he did. He looked like he wanted to cry like a baby. What confused her was the fact that he made no attempt to escape from Mia's presence, or her embrace. If anything, the way he suddenly started to grin and blink, he was enjoying her attention.

When Teri started to walk away, Harrison grabbed her arm. "Is your phone number still the same?" he asked, his goofy grin gone. He looked more serious than she had ever seen him look.

"Yes, it is. Why?" Her eyes were on Mia, who still had her arm around Harrison's waist.

"Do you mind if I call you?"

Teri didn't know what to think. Here was the only man in the vicinity that she was truly interested in, being hugged by another woman, asking if he could call her. Did men have no shame? She gasped and looked him straight in the eye. "Honey, you can do whatever you want to do. Excuse me," she mouthed, strutting away like an ostrich.

Teri stumbled and stepped on the foot of a man she had danced with earlier. He was glad to see her, and even though he had a face like a baboon and the breath of a moose, she was glad to see him, too.

She danced three songs straight with the same man and was pleased that another one was waiting to dance with her afterward. She saw Harrison watching from across the room, even though Mia was still in his face. Teri forced herself to pay more attention to everything else around her except Harrison.

Reuben and Carla were dancing cheek to cheek and grinding against each other—even though "Billie Jean" was playing. Other guests were egging them on and yelling, "Get a room, y'all!"

Nicole was dancing next to Teri. Her partner was a man with so many gold teeth and so many gold chains around his neck he was glowing. His conversation was about as lame and tacky as he was.

"I'd like to cover your body with whipped cream, baby. Then I'd like to lick it off," he said in a hoarse voice. He was the only person present wearing dark glasses.

"If you step on my foot again the only thing you'll be licking is your wounds after I coldcock you." Nicole didn't like to chastise grown men but when she needed to do it, she didn't hesitate.

"Sister, that sure is cold," her partner told her with a contrite look on his face. "But I like you anyway. I love a spunky woman. If I wasn't already spoken for, I wouldn't stop 'til I got you . . ."

Nicole looked at Teri and shook her head. More than a dozen men, most of them with dates, had attempted to make a date with Nicole and she had declined them all. Other than Eric, she didn't see anybody else she'd like to get closer to. She hadn't seen Eric in a while, but he was on her mind.

Eric was busy. Somehow, Yvette had lured him to the downstairs bathroom near Carla's study, locked the door, and was slamming her body against his so hard against the wall that the mirror above the sink rattled.

"Yvette, didn't I tell you . . . I . . . I told you we should wait 'til we get home," Eric stammered, enjoying every thrust.

"I know you did," she replied, huffing and puffing. Her hands held his hips in place as she slammed against him. Eric's pants were down around his ankles, but she was completely naked. "I bet you don't care about trying to keep Teri happy *now*, huh?"

Eric's mouth was open but he couldn't respond. All he could do was grunt and moan, but a little louder than he meant to. When somebody suddenly knocked on the door his breath caught in his throat. He froze and gripped Yvette by her shoulders and held her in place.

"Shit!" Yvette hissed.

"Everything all right in there?" a woman's voice on the other side of the door asked. It was Carla's voice, but Eric didn't recognize it at the moment. "It sounded like somebody was hurt."

"Uh . . . uh, everything's cool," Eric managed. He waited, and held onto Yvette until he heard Carla leave. "Where was I?" he asked, breathing hard through his mouth.

"Right where you're supposed to be," Yvette told him, pulling him deeper inside her.

CHAPTER 20

"The company we keep . . ." Carla muttered, speaking in a low voice as if she was speaking to herself. "I don't even want to know what's going on back there in my bathroom," she said to Nicole as they entered her study. She shook her head, waved her hands in the air and chuckled.

"All I can say is, you and Rueben sure know how to throw a party," Nicole told her.

Carla was the first psychiatrist Nicole had ever met. And she was nothing like Nicole had expected. Instead of being one of those stiff, highfalutin bourgie sisters with an attitude, Carla wasn't that much different from the rest of the females she knew. Despite the fact that Carla was well educated and had class to spare, underneath it all she still had a down-home attitude that only black people could see in each other.

"Have a seat and we'll get started," Carla told Nicole, glancing at a large round clock on the wood-paneled wall. Carla plopped down into a high-back leather chair at a small oak desk and focused her attention on Nicole. Her gaze was so intense it made Nicole squirm. "Let's see what the future holds for you."

"Something good, I hope," Nicole said, easing down into the chair facing Carla, crossing her legs to keep them from trembling. She didn't want Carla to know, but she was just a little bit frightened. "Is this where you work all the time?"

"I had an office on Wilshire when I first got started. But that was a high-rent area that got to be a little too high rent for me over the years. My patients seem more comfortable here and I certainly do. There is nothing like working from home."

Carla nodded as she slid a stack of documents to the side of the desk.

The room was small compared to the other rooms in Carla's spacious house. Family pictures dominated one wall. An assortment of impressive-looking certificates almost covered another wall. Nicole wondered why professional people displayed their degrees, licenses, and all kinds of other documentation so prominently. And all that paperwork didn't really mean shit anyway. Anybody could get a phony diploma or award printed up at Kinko's. Just like a bogus plastic surgeon she'd seen profiled on the Discovery Channel.

Nicole's eyes quickly scanned the room. Venetian blinds covered each window. She could not see the backyard pool, the Jacuzzi, the lawn furniture, more citrus fruit trees, and the barbeque grill that Teri had told her about.

"You look frightened," Carla noticed, studying Nicole's face. "You don't need to be."

"I'm all right," Nicole told her. She uncrossed her legs and shuffled in her seat.

"Are you sure you're ready for this? Have you ever done this before?"

Nicole gave Carla a thoughtful look. "I've made a few calls to a few psychic hotlines. Why? Is it important if I have or have not?"

"Not really." Carla reared back in her chair and glanced at the door, which she had locked behind her. "I know that you and Teri are very close and I don't care what you share with her. But if you want some good advice, don't tell too many people about this. I take this part of my practice very seriously and I always have."

For about half a second Nicole almost changed her mind. The last thing she wanted people to know about her was that she'd got caught up in some hocus-pocus parlor game with a woman she hardly knew. But she trusted Teri's judgment more than anyone's. And Carla Andrews was one of the most prominent people in L.A.'s African American community. However, Nicole had to wonder how many of them knew about Carla's special gift.

Teri had met Carla at a Jesse Jackson function and they'd hit it off immediately. She had told Nicole that a lot of other people she knew were either Carla's friends or patients. One thing Teri didn't know was that Carla had more men as patients than women. And Harrison Starr was one of them.

"We haven't discussed money," Nicole said, squeezing her legs together to keep them from shaking.

"What about it?" Carla scratched her chin. "Who said anything about money?"

"How much is this reading going to cost me?"

"I don't do *this* for profit, Nicole." Carla was proud that she could make such a claim. "I don't need the money, and even if I did, I'd have a difficult time taking money for something I've been blessed with." She sniffed and smiled. "Will you please relax?" Carla looked toward the door again and glanced at the large clock on the wall behind Nicole. "I don't want to be missed, so let's do this now."

Nicole closed her eyes, massaged her temples, and held her breath for a moment. When she opened her eyes, Carla was staring directly into them.

"What's the matter?" Nicole wanted to know, ready to leave before the reading even got started. "I don't like the look on your face. If you don't see something good in my future, either tell me a lie or don't tell me shit," Nicole told her, holding up her hand. "Because if I've got some deadly disease, or if a bus is going to smash my ass into the ground, I don't want to know." She paused and sniffed. "Not unless I can do something about it."

"I don't see *all* of life's events, Nicole." Then Carla started speaking with her eyes closed. "I see a young boy. Watch over him, tell him everything is all right. He worries about you." Carla opened her eyes.

"That's my son, Chris. He's five," Nicole got misty eyed just thinking about her only child. "I'm not that close to my family so Chris means a lot to me."

"There is a man in your life." Carla paused and gave Nicole a guarded look. "In some ways, he's still a little boy, too. A lot of unnecessary drama seems to follow him everywhere he goes."

"That would be my ex. Gregory." Nicole said her ex-husband's name as if it were something obscene.

"It's not him," Carla said firmly, shaking her head. "You don't know this man that well . . . yet."

"Oh?" This piece of information peaked Nicole's interest.

"He's in your future," Carla said, confirming it with a hearty nod. She paused and looked into Nicole's eyes some more, making Nicole's eyes water.

Nicole blinked and gave Carla an inquisitive look. "I haven't been in a steady relationship for a while now. Do I already know this man?"

"That's something I choose not to answer. I don't think it would do you much good if I gave you too much information. That would limit your choices and possibly have a negative impact on your judgment."

"I see. Then what about my job?"

"You're in a very secure position right now. And as long as Teri is in the position she's in, you'll be fine." Carla rose.

"Is the reading over? Is that all you can see about me?" Nicole asked, disappointed.

"Readings are never over, per se. One thing I don't do is reveal more information to a subject than he or she needs to know at the time." Carla gave Nicole a warm smile. "Now if I told you everything I knew, you wouldn't have much to look forward to."

Carla remained in her office to make a few phone calls. Nicole shut the door on her way out and was so deep in thought as she made her way down the hall, she almost collided with Eric as he was coming out of the bathroom. Yvette was still inside, washing love juice off her throbbing body and touching up her makeup.

"Excuse me, Eric," Nicole mumbled, feeling and looking as flustered as he did. "I didn't know you were still here. I hadn't seen you in a while." She glanced toward the bathroom door. Before Eric could respond, Yvette pranced out, patting her hair and adjusting the straps on her dress. Nicole ignored Yvette. "I hope you will be working with Teri and me a lot, Eric," Nicole said with an infectious smile. It made him smile, too. He hadn't noticed how pretty she was until now.

"I hope I will, too," Eric told her.

CHAPTER 21

"*Oh no he didn't!*" Yvette said under her breath. No, Eric didn't flirt with that bitch right in front of her! But that was exactly what he'd done.

As far as Yvette was concerned, Nicole was one of the plainest bitches she'd ever seen in her life. She had a face like a pie pan! But the way Eric was looking at her, it was obvious that he didn't think so. "By the way, I noticed how you tore up that dance floor a few times. I hope you saved a few moves for me," Eric told Nicole, offering a playful wink.

"Anytime," Nicole assured him in a suggestive tone. She was preoccupied with a lot of other thoughts dancing around inside her head. But she could not ignore Eric and the way he was looking at her. She couldn't remember the last time a man looked at her with such adoration. She barely noticed Yvette standing next to him clinging to his arm like poison ivy.

Teri was more than ready to call it a night. It had been more than four hours since she'd arrived at Carla's party. She hadn't chatted with Nicole in a while. She was anxious to hear what Carla had revealed to her in her reading. But she promised herself that she wouldn't bring it up unless Nicole did. There were some things that a sister had to keep to herself. She could recall a thing or two that she'd shared with some of her friends in the past that had come back to haunt her. The worst being an abortion during her senior year in high school, which even the baby's father didn't know about. She'd told one person and within a week almost everybody in her senior class was discussing it. She had kept her relationship with Harrison a secret from Nicole until that night at Young Rahim's New Year's Eve party. She regretted that she had shared that information with Nicole. Now Nicole had something else to meddle her about. And the way she bristled so easily these days, she didn't know if her ego could take too much more.

Even slightly tipsy, she still couldn't think of a man she'd rather be with more than Harrison. For a while, she had thought that there was a chance that they would rekindle their relationship tonight. Unfortunately, from the looks of things, it wasn't going to happen. She had Mia to thank for that.

From the way Mia was hanging on to Harrison, and the way he was sopping it up, you would have thought that Harrison had brought her to the party, not Dwight. But she had to admit that Dwight didn't seem to mind what Mia was doing. He had more than enough attention to keep him busy. However, he still found time to pester her again.

"I let you get away from me earlier," he began.

Her jaw dropped and she shot him a hot look. "*You* let *me* get away? You make me sound like a runaway bride," she quipped, turning her back to him. He liked the way she looked when she displayed her emotions.

Dwight chuckled. "That was a good one. One of the things I really miss about you is your dry sense of humor. You know, Carla told me I'd see you tonight," he told her, speaking to Teri from behind. "That's the main reason I decided to come here," he admitted.

Teri let out an exasperated sigh before she whirled back around to face Dwight. When she did, she looked him straight in the eye and she wasn't smiling. "And did she also tell you that I'd tell you to go to hell? You had your chance and you blew it,

Dwight. When are you going to get that through your head?" She gently mauled his head with her fist.

"Aw, baby, don't be like that. I had a lot of things going on in my life back then. It was nothing against you. I just was not ready to settle down," he told her, blinking hard. He was trying not to show how much he really wanted her. "And to be honest with you, you never did tell me what I did to make you stop seeing me," he whined.

Teri's jaw dropped again. "You men amaze me. You didn't give me much choice. You stopped returning my calls, you stopped coming by. What else could I do? You wanted to see me on your terms. Which meant you'd see me only when it was convenient for *you*. Well, that wasn't good enough for me. I'm not a faucet that you can turn on and off."

"You never tried to talk to me about the way you were feeling—"

"I couldn't do that if you weren't around or didn't have time to return any of my phone calls. And when you finally decided you had some time for me, I told you I might be pregnant. You didn't waste any time putting the blame on me. You accused me of trying to trap you. I don't need to trap you or any other man. You got that?" Teri saw a few people staring at her but she didn't care.

"Look, baby. Nobody blamed you," he said, defensively, speaking in a low, controlled voice. He was seething with anger. But he didn't want any of the other guests to know that or hear him getting dressed down in such a brutal manner. So he forced himself to smile. In case anybody was interested, he made it look as if he and Teri were having a pleasant conversation. With his hand stroking her shoulder he said, "I want things to be right between us. Even if that just means we can only be friends. I can live with that. I would still like for us to have a drink or two sometime or, whatever . . ."

"You need to get right with yourself before you can get right with me. The way you are looking right now, I could swear you prayed to Jesus to be born again."

"Maybe I did. And maybe I am." Dwight looked like he didn't even believe his own words, and from the look on Teri's face, he knew she didn't either.

"Oh, please give me a break. Then, after the pregnancy scare, you didn't call me for two weeks."

"I was on a much needed vacation. You knew that!"

"Vacation?" Teri gave Dwight an incredulous look and shrugged her shoulders. "So what? You never leave home without your cell phone, and I am sure that wherever you went, you had access to a telephone."

Dwight didn't know what to say next. He just stared at Teri. Then he shrugged and threw up his hands.

"Forget you, Dwight."

"Forget me? Bah! You know you can't *forget* me, woman." He liked the sound of his words. He thought it was a good comeback. "I know you better than you know yourself, and I know what you want . . ."

"Oh really? Me and how many others? Well, let me give you some advice I am sure you can use. Keep on playing musical beds with all the groupies and hoochies and whatnot out there, and you won't be around for anybody to want you. This sister does not have to be part of your insanity."

Before Dwight could respond, a pretty young woman butted in, looking at him as if he were the only man on the premises. "Can I get your autograph?" she cooed, holding up a pen and napkin with nails so long they curled. "You are fantastic. Do you mind?"

"Sure," Dwight said with a recycled grin.

"You are so much cuter in person." The woman giggled.

"I wouldn't stand too close to him, honey. You don't know what he has," Teri warned, strutting away.

Dwight's face stung as though he'd just been slapped. The young woman gasped and looked from Teri to Dwight. "Aww, she's just another fan and she likes to joke around at my expense. Don't pay any attention to her," Dwight said, his voice hard and loud. "Now, what's your name, sweetheart?"

Several other women crowded around Dwight. Teri looked back and got even more pissed. Harrison was just a few feet away and had heard every word of her conversation with Dwight. He couldn't remember the last time he'd seen a brother get so verbally coldcocked and still be standing. He left the group he had been talking to and approached Teri.

"Something tells me that you are a passionate basketball fan," he said to Teri, his voice dripping with sarcasm.

"Not anymore," she replied in a serious tone.

"Or are you not into any games period?"

She gave him a thoughtful look before she responded. "Not anymore," she repeated.

CHAPTER 22

Dwight had double-zero chances of ever fucking Teri again. Harrison was the only man who did have a chance, but only if he approached her the right way, and at the right time. He grabbed two glasses of champagne off a passing waiter's tray and handed one to Teri.

"You look like you could use another one of these," he told her. She accepted the drink with a forced but weak smile. She had to keep reminding herself, whether or not she ever slept with Harrison again, that if she wanted him to keep showcasing the artists associated with Eclectic Records, she had to continue to be nice to him. However, she didn't want to overdo it. She mumbled a thank-you and nodded. "You know anything I do for you is my pleasure, Teri."

"I'm feeling that," she muttered, taking a sip from her glass. She had lost track of how many drinks she'd already had, but she promised herself that this would be the last one. She still had to drive herself home and the last thing she needed was a DUI.

"After just witnessing your encounter with Dwight, I know this is probably not a good time to ask you again, but I will anyway. Can I get in touch with you, uh, maybe sometime early next week?"

"I'll have to get back to you on that." Harrison didn't try to hide his disappointment. His smile faded within seconds. She had cooled off a little about seeing him acting so cozy with Mia, but she didn't want to look too eager about him calling her. Teri was glad to see Carla walking in her direction.

"Teri, can I talk to you for a minute?" Carla asked as she approached. She didn't even give Teri a chance to reply. She just took her by the arm and led her across the room near the front window. Teri had wanted to continue her conversation with Harrison, but she'd still let Carla whisk her away. When she glanced around and saw him still standing in the same spot with the same look of disappointment on his face, she knew she had to adjust her agenda if she really did want him to continue showcasing the artists she worked with.

Despite the fact that she felt as if she were about to burst out of her clothes, Nicole couldn't seem to stay away from the buffet table. Her thong panties were feeling a lot tighter than they'd felt when she'd slid into them a few hours ago. She had turned down the last three requests to dance, but men were still coming at her from all sides.

"Sister, I've been watching you for a while. I love to see a woman enjoy her food. I wouldn't even waste a minute of my time on none of these flat-butted, toothpick-leg skanks running around this city these days." Talking to her was a man in a plaid jacket and white pants, chewing on a toothpick. "You one of them catwalking supermodels or something?" he asked. He had a folded white handkerchief in his hand. When he lifted it to wipe sweat off his shiny forehead, Nicole noticed coarse, scraggly hair on the back of his hand. It looked like a brown cat's paw. She leaned her head back when he reached toward her face with the same napkin. "You got a few crumbs on your jaw," he told her.

"That's all right. I'm fine." She blocked his hand with hers.

"Like I said, I love a woman who loves to eat. My mama would love to meet you," the man told her, still chewing on that toothpick.

It was a shame that men didn't have better pickup lines these days. No man in his right mind would mistake a woman her height and weight for a supermodel—unless he meant a plus size model! It was an even bigger shame that people as classy as Carla and Reuben knew people this tacky.

"Sorry, but I'm married," she lied. She still wore the cheap ring that Greg had given to her on the day they got married. She had stopped wearing it for a while, but when she told men who she didn't want to be bothered with that she was married, the first thing they did was look for a wedding ring. She held her hand up and wiggled her ring finger in her admirer's face, making him look at her as if he wanted to bite her hand and her head off.

"Well, your man must not be doing his job! Not with all the skinning and grinning and dancing and booty rolling you been doing since you walked up in this place." The man sniffed, leaned back, and looked Nicole up and down.

"That's none of your business," she advised, one hand on her hip. "I am a married woman and that's that."

"I hope you stay married!"

Not a minute later, Nicole heard the same man using the same supermodel line on another woman. It must have been what that woman wanted to hear because from that point on, he was the only man she danced with or talked to.

Dwight was still enjoying all the attention he was getting from some of the other women. He was totally ignoring Mia. But she didn't care. Her roving eyes had settled on Harrison Starr and he seemed to be more than a little interested in her. When she asked him to dance again, he wrapped his arm around her waist and practically skipped to the dance floor as if he were Fred Astaire or Michael Jackson. What Mia didn't know was that the only reason Harrison agreed to dance with her was because he was beginning to feel that he would never be with Teri again.

Surprisingly, Harrison enjoyed dancing with Mia. She felt nice and warm and soft in his arms. And he was glad that it was a slow song, one of Luther Vandross's most sensuous tunes. He closed his eyes and moved with her body.

"Be careful with that gun in your pocket," Mia whispered, happy to know that she'd aroused him. "Don't hurt anybody with *that*." She nudged his crotch with her hip.

"Sorry," he said, chuckling. "This is kind of embarrassing," he admitted, stopping. "You want to sit down?"

Mia shook her head. "I don't want to sit down and . . . I want you to keep doing what you were doing," she told him in the most seductive voice she could manage. "I am not complaining."

"I'm glad to hear that," he said with relief, grinding against her some more.

"I'm a woman who speaks her mind. I want you to know that."

"Oh? Is there something on your mind you'd like me to know right now?"

"There is, but I'll save it for later. Maybe in a more private setting?"

With this vague promise of some possible action, Harrison gave Mia the kind of look that made her even more aggressive. From her actions and movements, he could tell that she was ready, willing, and able to do whatever he wanted her to do. What was that they said about one bird in the hand being better than two in a bush? And since he didn't have much luck getting any kind of commitment from Teri, it looked like Mia was going to have to be his bird tonight.

He looked toward the door that he'd seen Teri walk through with Carla a few minutes earlier. Had she walked back into the room before Mia could secure her hooks in him, it would have made all the difference in the world. But Teri didn't return to the room in time.

CHAPTER 23

While Harrison and Mia were practically dry fucking on the dance floor, Teri was in the same room where Carla had read for Nicole. She was crying softly, wiping her tears with a napkin.

"It's your mother and father. They weren't around long enough for you to get to know them," Carla said, holding Teri's hand across the desk. She reached for a tissue from a box next to the speakerphone on the corner of her desk and handed it to Teri. "That's what's bothering you. They are on your mind all the time." Carla dipped her head and gave Teri an encouraging look.

Carla sucked in her breath and sat up straight as soon as Teri started to talk. "They died in an automobile accident when I was eight. I've been with my grandparents ever since," Teri stated.

"I know," Carla said with a nod and a sigh. "I knew it long before you ever told me."

Teri snorted, rubbed her nose, and let out a sharp laugh. "Of course you already knew! Why do I even bother telling you anything? You know just about everything there is to know about me anyway." She blew her nose into the tissue and started to wipe her eyes with it when she realized it was soaked and about to tear. Carla handed her another tissue and Teri wiped her eyes until

they ached. They stung when she looked at Carla, who was looking at her with an annoyed expression on her face.

"Listen, I know that some of my methods are unconventional,
but I am serious and compassionate when I tell you that I already
know something about you, Teri. Please don't take it lightly."

"I'm sorry, Carla," Teri said with her head bowed submissively.

Carla stifled a yawn and continued. "Just know that I know the
kind of pain you feel when you think about your parents and
what happened to them."

Teri pressed her lips together and gave Carla a guarded look.
The last thing she wanted was for Carla to think that she didn't
respect her abilities. "Carla, I believe everything you tell me and I
really do appreciate it. And just to let you know, I've experienced
other things that were *unconventional*."

"Such as?"

"Something I experienced a long time ago that was really weird."
Teri wrapped her arms around her chest and shivered, even though
the room was too warm, if anything.

"Do you want to talk about it? I'd love to hear about it, if you
don't mind."

Teri blew her nose and slumped in her seat. "My grandmother
is the only other person who knows what I'm about to tell you. I
haven't even told Nicole, or anybody else." Teri's eyes darkened
and she blew her nose again before she continued. She was taking her time and that irritated Carla.

"Well, are you going to tell me what it is *this week*?" Carla asked,
not even trying to hide her impatience. She leaned forward and
rested her chin in her hands.

"The day my parents died, we'd been at the park having a pic-
nic. It was just them and me, and my dog Snoopy. A pit bull, if you
can believe it. He was so docile our cat used to chase him around.
Anyway, a tractor broadsided our car on the way home. Snoopy and
I managed to crawl out the back window with just a few scratches
before the car exploded. One of the few things that survived the
explosion was the camera that we'd taken a lot of pictures with
that day. About a month after the funerals, my grandmother got
the film in the camera developed. Out of twenty-four shots, only
one came out fully developed. All the others were blank, totally

blank. It was a picture of Snoopy and me walking away from the wrecked car." Teri shivered every time she recalled the strange incident. Carla gasped and felt a sudden chill.

"Holy shit . . ." Carla said, blinking so hard she saw two of everything. She rose and rubbed her eyes, mumbling under her breath. She gave Teri a hard look before she returned to her seat. "I'm sure . . . I . . . that's one of the most haunting stories I've ever heard," she admitted. "And I've heard some doozies! I am baffled," she said, shaking her head and wringing her hands. She narrowed her eyes and looked at Teri as if she was still seeing double. "Maybe . . . maybe one of your parents took the picture . . ."

"Carla, like I said, the picture showed me walking away from the crash that my parents had *died* in. Just me and my dog."

Carla was so stunned she was speechless. All she could do for the next few moments was sit there with her hands on top of her desk, staring at Teri.

"Don't ask me who, or *what,* took that picture. All I know is that it was not something normal. My grandmother made me promise I'd never tell my grandfather or anybody else in the family about it. To this day . . . well, you're the only other person who knows about it. So you don't have to worry about me not taking you seriously when you tell me something from an unconventional point of view."

"You've been holding this inside you."

"I have, and if you don't mind I don't ever want to talk about this again. It's enough for me to deal with the loss of my parents."

"I see. Well, you don't have to worry about me bringing it up again. You, um, you're still angry with your parents for leaving you?" Carla couldn't remember the last time she'd felt so uneasy.

"No, I am not angry," Teri insisted, shaking her head. "I'm just . . . so alone. I love my grandparents to death and I've got some great friends, but sometimes my life feels so . . . empty."

"And it's because of that emptiness that you are fighting with yourself," Carla suggested. She closed her eyes and mumbled what sounded like gibberish to Teri. What Teri didn't know was that Carla was doing everything she could to divert her attention away from the eerie secret Teri had just shared with her.

Carla slowly opened her eyes, feeling somewhat more at ease now. For a brief moment, she seemed so much older than her actual age. Her eyes looked heavy and tired. She seemed to hold so many secrets and knowledge about other people that she never asked for in the first place. That had to be a burden on some level, Teri decided. She didn't know why, but she suddenly felt sorry for a woman in Carla's position.

"What do you have to prove to others? Trying too hard pushes you further away from what you want." Carla paused and then muttered more gibberish. "You need to reacquaint yourself with love, Teri. And you need to share that love. Don't run away from the man who wants to share that love with you."

"What the—what do you mean by that? Who is he?" Teri asked, her eyes shifting from side to side as if she expected the man in question to crawl through one of the windows.

"I know, and I know you know," Carla said with a harmless smirk. "Don't play games with me, Teri. We've been friends too long for that."

"What brought this on? I was really interested in hearing more about my future."

"You just did," Carla said, rolling her eyes.

CHAPTER 24

"The future I meant was my job."

"Your job?" Carla lifted her chin and gave Teri a critical look. "Teri, it's a sin and a shame if you feel that the only important thing in your future is your job."

"I didn't say that. I've never said that . . ."

"You didn't have to," Carla exclaimed, giving Teri an incredulous look.

"You're talking about Harrison Starr, aren't you?" Teri asked in a gentle voice, looking at her fingers. When she looked up, Carla was sitting with her hands folded on the desktop, looking like a sphinx.

"It doesn't take a psychic to know that. Stevie Wonder could see that that man is crazy about you."

"We tried to have a serious relationship last year but it didn't work out. I really don't know if it's worth another shot . . ."

"So what? If I had a dime for every woman who gave up on the man she loved because 'it didn't work out the first time' I'd be on the cover of *Fortune* magazine. You're different, Teri. You usually know what you want and you don't stop until you get it. You've proved that with your job."

"So you're saying I should use the same approach with Harrison?"

"Why not? I would, and I am sure half the women in this house would, too. I know I am older than you, but you are still old enough to know that good men are getting harder and harder to come by."

"I do care about the man . . . Harrison. He makes me nervous and he knows it. Like tonight. Every time I bump into him I want to run out the door. It's just that sometimes I get so afraid."

"Afraid of what? What is there for you to be afraid of? The man is not a snake so he's not going to bite you. The man's a man!"

"Carla, in my case, relationships can cause just as much pain as pleasure. You know how hurt I was when Dwight and I broke up."

"Harrison and Dwight are from two different planets. You shouldn't even be mentioning those two men in the same breath. Dwight is a hound dog."

"Some women feel that all men are dogs," Teri offered with a casual shrug. "My grandmother even says that."

"That's true. Men are dogs. Some are pit bulls." Carla paused and nodded toward a picture on the wall of her and Reuben. It was the first picture they'd posed for at their wedding so many years ago. "Some dogs are faithful, obedient, and dependable. I wouldn't trade that mutt of mine for Prince Charles."

Teri gave Carla a stunned look. Carla had never spoken so openly about her own relationship before. "Just be patient with Harrison, but don't let him get away. What you are feeling is normal, Teri, so you shouldn't be afraid."

"I really don't know where all this is coming from or where it's going," Teri said. There was a hint of a smile on her face, and despite the fact that she was confused, she was curious.

"Wild women, they don't wear no blues. Now that's coming from my old granny, may she rest in peace until I get there," Carla said with a heavy sigh. "That's what you have to do."

Wild women don't wear no blues? Now what in the hell did that mean? Teri wondered. She was even more confused now, but not enough to ask for clarification. All she wanted was for this reading to be over so she could return to the party and possibly reconnect with Harrison. Just in case . . .

"Carla, you know I always appreciate these, uh, sessions. And to be honest with you, it's the unplanned ones like this that I enjoy the most. I know it's not what I pay you for, professionally, and it is something extra, but it means a lot to me. You and Reuben are like family to me. Especially now . . ."

"I know all that." Carla laughed. "And when we talk like this, it's on the house. I enjoy doing this, especially with subjects as complex and interesting as you."

Teri blew out a loud breath. "I'm going to have to be careful about what I do in the bedroom if I don't want to be embarrassed. With the right man, I might do things I don't want you to know . . ."

"You already have." Carla laughed again, rising. "Now let's get out of here before I tell you something you don't want to hear."

The party was finally coming to a close around midnight. Small groups of guests walked, some staggered, to their cars. Teri attempted to locate Harrison and invite him to have a cup of coffee with her, or something. She had given a lot of thought to what Carla had said in their session. If things didn't work out between them the second time around, she'd move on to someone else. But she could at least say that she tried.

"Did Harrison leave already?" she asked Carla.

Carla had already started to clean up the mess in the living room.

She gave Teri a sorrowful glance and then she looked toward the door. "They just walked out the door," she said, nodding toward the exit.

"They?" Teri was confused. "Oh." She looked at the floor, then at the door. "I'll call you tomorrow," she said, leaving. Nicole was right behind her.

They got outside just in time to see Harrison and Mia walking toward his car holding hands. Holding hands! What the hell? And Harrison was the man that Carla told her she needed to pursue. Mia? Harrison and Mia? He was not just a run-of-the-mill dog. He was a hound from hell! Well, if he wanted her, he had to come after her and she was not going to make it that easy for him now.

"Well, look who is taking Miss Black Saigon home with him," Nicole said as they strode toward Teri's car.

"Better her than me," Teri huffed, her eyes burning with red hot anger. She was horrified when she saw Harrison haul off and kiss Mia. And if that wasn't bad enough, that half-breed cow was in the driver's seat of his car! He was going to let her drive! The nerve of that motherfucker! How the hell did he expect to make amends with her by acting like a dog in heat with another woman? And in public at that, Teri wondered.

"I heard that," Nicole said, climbing into the passenger seat of Teri's BMW. She flipped on the radio.

"Spend your early morning hours with me right here at 98.6 on your FM dial. L.A.'s best . . ." Harrison's recorded promotional plug was the last thing she or Teri expected, or wanted, to hear. Especially since they could still see him and Mia *still kissing*! ". . . from six A.M. to one P.M., Monday through Friday, start your day with me, the Morning Starr."

"Correction—falling star is more like it," Teri said nastily.

Nicole sucked on her teeth and mumbled profanities under her breath. Teri got dead silent and was breathing through her mouth, thoroughly horrified. Watching the man she was supposed to be trying to resume and establish a relationship with kissing on another woman was excruciating.

She turned off the radio so fast she broke a nail. She cursed, shook her hand, sucked on the damaged nail, and then she started her car. She almost sideswiped Harrison's Jaguar as she shot out into the street. But Harrison was so busy with Mia, he didn't even notice.

CHAPTER 25

Harrison was in the studio sipping coffee and murmuring into the microphone. It had been a struggle for him to roll out of bed, shower, get dressed, and make it to work on time.

He regretted spending so much time at Carla Andrews's party the night before. But more than that, he regretted hooking up with Mia. "Damn," he muttered, rubbing the inside of his thigh where she had bitten him. She had bitten him in a few other places, too. How in the world had she managed to bite one of his big toes and he not remember it? he wondered.

He didn't understand women like Mia. First of all, she had manipulated her way into his condo, claiming that she couldn't take him to her place because she had houseguests. That was one thing. That couldn't be helped. After Teri Stewart had turned him on like a light switch, he wanted some so bad he would have fucked a stump—and he didn't care where he got it.

But as soon as Mia got her scheming ass inside his place, she immediately started talking all kinds of shit about how good she could be to him, what a striking couple they made, how much more class he had than Dwight, and how proud her folks would be of her for reeling in such a big fish. Like he would have been fool enough to start a long-term relationship with her in the first place! While he was in the bathroom, she even had the nerve to take her skanky ass into his kitchen and put on a pot of coffee. Naked at that.

Staring at her bare ass in his kitchen with his dick so hard he could hardly walk, his plan was to hit it as quickly and thoroughly as he could and drive her home. Then she had to say the wrong thing: "I can't wait to see that uppity Teri's face when she finds out about us," she'd said, cackling like the witch she was.

His erection had gone south so fast it made his head spin. Without giving it much thought, he immediately asked her to leave.

"What's wrong with you, man? What did I do?" she wanted to know, scrambling around his living room for her clothes. When he couldn't offer an explanation for his sudden change of heart that satisfied her, she bombarded him with such labels as "fag-ass punk" and "cheesy-ass motherfucker." Mia was so angry she refused his offer to drive her home. And when he escorted her to the cab he had called, she viciously slammed the cab door shut on his arm on purpose as he helped her in. Now he was sitting here with a throbbing shin, too. And he was still horny!

Harrison loved his job. In some ways it was more like an interesting hobby. He had some great coworkers, the pay was good, and he loved his hours. This was the advantage to working for a small independent black-owned radio station that operated by its own rules. And a popular station at that. In addition to nailing down a huge portion of L.A.'s black audience, a lot of white folks and Asians tuned in. Not only did they play all the latest hits, everything from hip-hop to reggae, they often interviewed black authors, recording artists, and a few people in other areas of the entertainment industry.

Last week he had interviewed a thirty-two-year-old former porn star who had offered a lot of sound advice to discourage young people, especially females, from contemplating a career in the adult industry. Harrison had been so impressed with the reformed actress that he invited her to lunch afterward. Over iced tea and ham-and-cheese sandwiches on rye, he learned that the woman had contracted HIV while engaging in unprotected sex in front of a camera. It made him profoundly sad to know that a woman his age would have a shortened life. And all because of her foolish choices and reckless behavior.

It never ceased to amaze Harrison what some people would do to get attention. Even though he had already agreed to "spend some time" with Mia the night before, she'd still offered to give him a blow job in his car that would "blow his mind" before they even left the Andrewses' property. He had been tempted. However, he was now proud of the fact that he had turned down her offer. He decided that he was not such a dog after all. Either that or he was lame as hell, like Mia had laughingly called him after the blow job rejection.

What impressed Harrison was when people like the former porn star admitted their mistakes and bad choices. He had made a lot of bad choices of his own.

Teri had no idea that she was on Harrison's mind that morning as she sat in her own office preparing for another painful staff meeting. Harrison was on her mind, too. But not in a pleasant way. She still could not believe that he had left Carla's party with Mia and that he didn't even try to hide it. Had he given up on ever resuming his relationship with her? It seemed that way. Well, it was his loss. Now all he was to her was Mia's leftovers. And some sloppy leftovers at that. She rose from her desk with a lump in her throat. Her eyes were still slightly red from the crying she had done in Carla's office last night. She kept telling herself that her tears were for the parents she never got a chance to know, not Harrison and her lackluster love life.

"I feel the way you look," Nicole said, peeking into Teri's office. "This is not going to be a pleasant meeting."

Teri cleared her throat before speaking. "Is it ever?" she asked. "The numbers for that new album we just released are not good."

Victor was his usual cantankerous self, grunting and growling under his breath like a wolf as he lumbered into the conference room. He just waved his gnarled hand when Teri spoke to him and he didn't even bother to look at her. When he did look up from the report that he had asked Miguel to prepare, it was just long enough to fire Miguel *again.*

Miguel didn't even wait for Victor to dismiss him from the meeting. While Victor was doling out wolf tickets about how he was thinking about selling or closing the business and moving to the Bahamas, Miguel let out a few grunts himself. Then he collected his copy of the report that had Victor in such a tizzy and stood up to leave the room.

Victor stared at him in slack-jawed amazement. "Excuse me, Miguel. This meeting is not over," he yelled, spit flying out both sides of his mouth.

"It is for me," Miguel announced with a casual shrug. There was no anger or sadness displayed on his face. He looked at Teri and gave her a wink. Nicole and Teri both gave Miguel a conspiratorial "thumbs-up" smile as he quietly left the room.

The meeting went even more downhill from there. While Teri was giving her report, which was well prepared as usual, Victor abruptly ended the meeting and rushed out so fast he left his BlackBerry behind.

Teri and Nicole were the last to leave the room. Nicole went quietly to her workstation to plow through a ton of e-mail and Teri headed for hers, instructing Nicole to hold her calls. As soon as Teri shut the door to her office, Nicole noticed that her line lit up and a few seconds later Victor's did, too. Less than two minutes later both lights went out.

"Do you have Miguel's cell number?" Teri asked, walking in Nicole's direction with her hands on her hips. She had that triumphant look on her face that had become so familiar to Nicole over the years.

Nicole gave her a puzzled look. "Yeah . . . what's up?"

"Get him back here. Get him back here right now," Teri ordered with a heavy sigh and fingers snapping. "And . . . tell him I need that Wilson piece for *Can Do Magazine* on my desk ASAP." She paused and massaged the back of her neck. "One of these days, girl . . . one of these days." Nicole didn't ask any more questions. She promptly looked up Miguel's cell number and called him.

CHAPTER 26

Miguel came strolling back in less than five minutes later. This time he had not even bothered to pack his personal belongings, collect his briefcase and laptop, or leave the building. This was the third time that Victor had "fired" him in less than two months and each time he'd rehired him. The last time Victor was in a firing frenzy, the victim had been John, his long-suffering secretary.

"I don't know how you put up with Victor's shit, Miguel," Nicole said to him, shaking her head. "The first time he fires me will be the last time."

"One of these days I won't come back. Believe me," Miguel told her with a serious look on his face.

"Want to have lunch?"

"Sure, *chica*. This time it's on me. You pick the place," Miguel said before he left to return to his office with a proud strut in his walk, whistling all the way.

Nicole's desk was busy most of the time, but like almost every other person in a position similar to hers, she always found time to manage her own agenda in the workplace. Teri was trapped in a midmorning sales meeting with Victor and other employees from the sales department. Miguel, one of the few people at Eclectic whom Nicole liked to interact with, was busy working on the report that Teri had requested.

Nicole looked around before she snatched up her telephone and made a few personal calls. She made an appointment to get her nails done, she returned a call to her cousin Wodell Scruggs in Compton who owed her fifty dollars, and she called her mother in San Jose.

Unlike Teri, Nicole didn't have a pleasant relationship with most of her family. For one thing, Wodell and the rest of her cousins usually called her only when they needed money or wanted to dump some sob story on her. Last month her cousin Lola Boone showed up at her door one night with her twin nine-year-old daughters, looking for a place to hide from a boyfriend whose favorite sport seemed to be slapping her upside her head.

The next day when Nicole got home from work there was Lola stretched out on the sofa that Chris slept on drinking and smoking like she didn't have a care in the world. But the worst part of the scenario was that the same abusive boyfriend that Lola had fled from was in her kitchen frying the last of her pork chops! And Lola's girls were all over the place and into everything— fucking with her makeup, making long-distance calls to their daddy's relatives in San Francisco, and jumping up and down on her bed as if it were a trampoline.

By the third day of Lola's presence, Nicole was ready to slap her upside her head herself. As soon as she put her foot down, Lola packed up and left in a huff. But a week later she apologized profusely in a voice mail message she'd left on Nicole's work phone.

Nicole dialed Lola's home phone number, expecting to get her voice mail. Despite her cousin's trifling ways when it came to men, she was one of her favorite relatives. Next to Teri, Lola was the only other sister she admired from afar for her accomplishments. Lola was not just another thirty-five-year old black woman walking up and down the streets of L.A. She had a lot going for herself, even though she often didn't make the most of her talents.

Anyway, Lola had a degree in journalism and a kicked-back job writing investigative pieces for *New Century L.A.* magazine. She wrote about everything from the city's gang problem to which L.A. hotels to avoid. Nicole hung up when the abusive boyfriend answered.

One thing she could not understand was how some women could put up with just about anything to have a man. It was even more baffling when the woman involved had as much going for her as Lola. Lola's excuse was always that she didn't like being lonely. Hell, yes, she was lonely, too, Nicole thought to herself. She knew she could have kept Greg in her life if she'd been stupid enough to put up with his infidelities and other foolishness. And from all the hints he'd dropped since their divorce, he'd come back to her in a heartbeat if she'd let him. She was not even going *there*. She realized now that that Korean heifer he'd married had actually done her a favor by taking him off her hands. She'd remain alone for the rest of her life if Greg Mason was the only man she could get.

Thank God she still maintained a couple of male friends that she kept on the hook to satisfy her biological urges. A wicked smile crossed Nicole's face. She was deep in thought, hoping she'd meet someone interesting that she could have a "regular" relationship with soon, when Teri's line rang. It was Eric, that fine-ass photographer who had caught her roving eye at the Andrewses' Valentine's Day party.

"Teri's in a meeting," she told him, her voice quivering. Something was wrong with this picture. No other man had ever made her this nervous. "Would you like to leave a message?"

"Just let her know I called," he replied. He had such a crisp, professional-sounding voice.

"Okay. And you have a nice day," she said, biting her bottom lip. She sniffed and pressed her lips together, listening with the telephone pressed against her ear so hard it irritated her earlobe.

"Sure," he said. He didn't hang up right away. She could still hear him breathing. "Nicole, you have a nice day, too," he added. He still didn't hang up.

"Uh-huh," she finally said. She had to move the telephone to her other ear and hold the damn thing with both hands.

"Bye, Nicole. I hope I see you again soon," he said quickly. His last comment made her heart skip a beat. Didn't he look at her like she was something good to eat at the Andrewses' party? How could such a smooth, polite, and pleasant brother like him be involved with a loud, matted, weave-wearing skank from ghetto hell like that Yvette? And now what in the world was he up to—obviously flirting with her? Well, she'd find out soon enough if it was the last thing she did. He had hung up but her telephone was still in her hand.

"I need to set up a meeting this week with Trevor Powell," Teri told Nicole. Nicole had been so deep in thought she didn't even know that Teri had returned from a meeting and was standing right in front of her desk.

"Huh?" She placed the telephone back in its place, blinking at it like she didn't know what it was.

"Nicole, are you all right? You look catatonic or something. And if I didn't know any better, with that glazed look in your eyes, I'd swear you just had an orgasm," Teri said with a dry chuckle. Then she gave Nicole an amused look that quickly turned to a look of envy.

"I'm fine." Nicole shook her head and started to fiddle around with the pens, pencils, and other knickknacks on her desk. "Uh, Eric called. That photographer." She coughed and cleared her throat.

"I'll have to call him back later," Teri mumbled, looking at her watch. "Grab your pad and pen. You and I have to talk to a blind rapper." Teri rolled her eyes and beckoned Nicole to follow her.

CHAPTER 27

"A blind rapper. Humph! I've heard everything now. I don't know what this world is coming to," Teri mumbled as she and Nicole marched down the hall toward the conference room. "I don't even want to think about what we'll have to deal with next."

They were caught off guard by the blind rapper as they quietly entered the conference room. He was talking to somebody on his cell phone, but as soon as he realized they were in the room, he turned his head in their direction, grinning like a player with twenty-twenty vision. "Hello, ladies," he said, his head rocking from side to side.

Nicole looked at Teri and said in a low voice, "I thought you said he was blind."

"He is. Victor told me he could smell pussy and fish from a mile away. Only thing is, he can't tell one from the other." Teri didn't tell Nicole that Victor had also said that whenever the blind man, whose name was Ernest Townes, passed a fish market he flashed his most flirtatious smile.

"Well, it sure looks like he knows what we are," Nicole mentioned.

"We could be two catfish standing here for all he knows," Teri insisted.

"I will be with you ladies in a minute," Ernest said, licking his bow-shaped lips. His dark glasses hid his eyes, but the rest of him didn't look half bad. It was hard to tell his age. He could have been anywhere from twenty-five to forty-five. Judging from his high cheekbones; smooth skin; and bone-straight, jet black hair slicked back in a duck tail, he had more than a few drops of Native American blood flowing through his veins. He returned his attention to his cell phone. Both Teri and Nicole were sorry that the man was blind and had been since the age of seven. But he was not to be pitied. Within a minute of their arrival he was fussing and cussing at the party on the other end of the line. "Fuck that shit! Hell no! Kiss my black ass!" he roared with his head and body rocking from side to side in the chair he occupied at the head of the conference table.

Marvin Woods, the rapper's manager who was also his stepfather, was just as crude. He entered the room and goose-stepped over to the rapper. "Get your blind ass off that phone!" he shouted, snatching the cell phone out of his stepson's hand. Marvin slapped the telephone up to his ear and started fussing and cussing at the same party on the other end, too. "Fuck you! Hell no!" Marvin looked enough like Ernest to be his real father, and according to the rumor mill, he actually was.

"Teri, exactly what are we supposed to do here?" Nicole wanted to know, speaking in a whisper.

"We need to set up his photo session with Eric. That's what Eric was calling about," Teri whispered back. Just hearing Eric's name made Nicole tingle all over.

"Oh?" she responded, turning her head so Teri wouldn't see the mysterious smile on her face. "Oh."

"My grandmother told me there'd be days like this. Well, this is 'one of those days,'" Teri decided, in a bone-dry voice.

Harrison Starr's granny had told him the same thing that Teri's had told her. He was having one of those days, too. His had certainly gotten off to a fairly bad start. He had forgotten to set his alarm the night before and had overslept. He'd opened his eyes just in time to take a quick shower and run out the door. He had taken a shortcut to work, only to get caught up in a traffic jam caused by a three-car accident on the freeway. He made it to work on time by the skin of his teeth.

He usually stopped at Starbucks to get his coffee and a muffin or a bear claw every morning. But this morning he had to settle for that deadly vending machine shit in the studio break room that looked more like pee than coffee. He had dressed in such a hurry that he didn't realize he had buttoned his shirt wrong until a coworker told him.

Now, after making what he considered a rhetorical comment about what he thought a woman should do to be a good mate, an irate female caller was giving him hell. This was something he should have been used to by now, but he wasn't. And that bitch— who should have had something better to do with her time at ten o'clock in the morning—was so loud he had to hold his earphone away from his ear to keep his eardrum from throbbing.

". . . and another thing, black boy, your whole notion of what a woman should do to be a good mate is ill. You got that?"

Chuck Irby, the perennially distressed station manager, rushed into the booth with a horrified look on his mulish face, rotating his arms like a windmill. Harrison tried his best to ignore him, but Chuck stood in front of him, making Harrison dizzy with all that arm action.

"Thank you for your comments, sister, but I must move on," Harrison said, trying to remain calm and diffuse the situation at the same time. "Thank you again, my sister. Have a nice day." He hung up, grinding his teeth before he spoke again. "Any other listeners like to make a comment?" The same wild woman who had just hung up called again.

"Nobody else was listening to your tired ass!" she barked.

"I have to call it the way I see it, ma'am."

"You ain't no Dr. Phil! You ain't even Oprah! You ain't *nobody*!"

Harrison wiped his brow with the back of his hand and held his breath for a few moments. Some people were like trees when it came to trying to have a rational conversation with them. The woman on the other end of the line was as pliable as a dead sumac.

"Are you finished this time?" Harrison asked, praying that he

didn't lose his cool and slide down to the same level as this difficult caller.

"Naw, I ain't finished! I bet you ain't even got no woman, and I
ain't surprised. Probably couldn't catch one with a fishhook! I
seen your picture and you look like a straight-up fag to me!"

"Hey! You hold on there, now. Don't go *there*, sister."

"I am not your damn sister! You sissified, suit-wearing punk!"

"Well, you are sure acting like it."

"You dumb, egotistical bastard."

Chuck pleaded with Harrison to hang up but to do it very po-
litely. Harrison knew that he was fighting a battle he had no
chance of winning and the best way out of it was to let his oppo-
nent think she'd won.

"Please accept my apology," he said. He hung up before the caller
could say another word. He expected her to call again, but after
five minutes had passed with no additional calls, he breathed a sigh
of relief.

Chuck left the booth, but he stood outside so he could watch
through the glass. Harrison shook his head and wiped his brow
again with the back of his hand. He glanced at Chuck and gave
him a weak smile and a nod.

The afternoon was much more pleasant than the morning for
Teri. She returned from another meeting shortly after noon. Nicole
was on the telephone, pretending like she was on a business call
until she saw Teri. Then she started talking the usual trash that
she engaged in with her cousin Lola. "Yeah, girl this; yeah, girl that."
Teri shook her head and rolled her eyes at Nicole as she collected
a stack of telephone messages from her desk.

Just as Teri was about to enter her office, something on the
radio on Nicole's desk caught her attention: Harrison Starr's
voice. Had he always sounded that sexy? she asked herself. Nicole
ended her telephone call, and Teri stood by the side of her desk
listening and enjoying the sound of that sexy voice . . .

CHAPTER 28

"I have to admit that I wasn't prepared for that kind of response. To all my listeners, I want to say that I am truly sorry . . ." Harrison's words puzzled Teri.

"Sure he is," Nicole said with a chuckle, sarcasm dripping from her lips like hot wax.

"What did I miss?"

"He was spewing some chauvinistic shit about how a woman's role was to always put her man very high on her list of priorities—if she wants to keep him out of the 'other' woman's bed . . ."

"Girl, you have got to be kidding!" Teri said with a profound gasp. She stood there in slack-jawed amazement. "Harrison? Has the man lost his mind?"

"No wonder you didn't stay with him . . ."

Teri gritted her teeth and considered Nicole's comment. "What's that supposed to mean?"

"I know you, and I know you do not put your man that high on your list of priorities. I'd say you put your shoes higher on the scale than your man."

A worried look crossed Teri's face. "Is that what you think? Nicole, you know that's not true. I work hard at my relationships," Teri said defensively. "And by the way, you haven't been in a real relationship yourself since last year," she reminded, unable to hold back a grin.

"Touché," Nicole responded with a sigh. She gave Teri a pensive look before she continued. "I still can't believe that Harrison chose that nasty-ass Mia over you to take home from Carla's party. I bet she's the kind of woman who would even put her man before the good Lord."

"Maybe she does, but that still doesn't mean a damn thing. You do remember that she had come to the party with Dwight. Whatever she was doing to hold on to him didn't work if she left with another man."

"Some men are so trifling," Nicole decided, throwing her hands up in the air.

"I won't argue with you there," Teri said. Harrison's seemingly sincere apology on the radio had not softened her.

Teri attempted to keep her mind on her work and off men the rest of the day, but a man like Harrison was hard not to think about. Despite the fact that they had not been able to maintain their relationship, she gave him a lot of high marks on her imaginary checklist of what she wanted in a man. In her opinion he was handsome, not *cute*. She hated that word when it came to describing adults. Babies, puppies, and dancing bears were cute. He was intelligent, sensitive, generous, dapper, and he possessed a fantastic sense of humor. He also loved kids . . .

She was glad when her line rang. To get her mind off Harrison she reached for it, but Nicole grabbed it on the second ring. With the door to her office open she could hear Nicole's end of the conversation.

"If that's not Trevor's producer, get him on the line," she yelled to Nicole. "And when you do get ahold of him, I want you to remind him that *I said*: we don't do business by a CP's time clock. This 'Colored People's time' bullshit does not sit too well with me." Teri muttered the rest of her comment in a low voice but Nicole heard it anyway. "That's why the rest of *us* have to work so hard to make up for that shit."

Nicole gave her a blank look and nodded her head in agreement. "Yes, this is Teri Stewart's office . . . oh, hello, *Harrison*," Nicole announced, looking through Teri's opened door with her eyes stretched open so wide she looked as though she'd just stepped on a live wire.

Teri blinked rapidly several times and tried not to look as goofy as Nicole. Just the mention of that man's name made Teri stiffen. That was bad enough. But she also felt like she had turned into a pillar of salt. What was even worse was the sudden warm itch in her crotch! With an amused look on her face, Nicole waved at Teri and pointed to the telephone. The timing was unbelievable. With Harrison on the telephone asking to speak to Teri, Eric, the man who made Nicole wet between her legs, suddenly strolled into the reception area.

Working the hell out of a denim jacket and matching jeans, he stopped in front of Nicole's desk. Like a robot, she turned her head to keep from looking at him right away.

"Hold on," she said into the telephone receiver, trying to sound as professional as she could. "Uh, Teri, it's Harrison Starr calling from the radio station," she reported. "Are you available to take his call?"

"I'll be with him momentarily," Teri said, her voice cracking. She bounced out of her office and rushed up to Eric and gave him a warm hug.

"Got it," Nicole told her. "Harrison, she will be right with you." As familiar as Nicole was with the features on the telephone on her desk, she hit three wrong buttons before she hit the hold button.

Eric was amused by this little exchange, but he managed not to show it. "I don't mind waiting." His eyes were on Nicole's face. His gaze was so intense she felt like a burning bush.

"That's all right, Eric. Harrison is not going anywhere," Teri decided. She gave Nicole a confused look and held up one finger. *Why the hell is that man calling me?* she wondered. She beckoned for Eric to follow her into her office.

Nicole removed a bottle of water from her purse. She didn't know who was more stunned, her or Teri. She took a few sips, then wet a tissue and wiped the back of her neck. She sucked in her breath and looked toward Teri's door.

Teri waved Eric to one of the two high-back guest chairs facing her desk. While Nicole was still staring at Teri's door, Teri came back out. She gently closed the door behind her and moved swiftly to the side of Nicole's desk.

"What the hell does Harrison want?" she asked. Nicole waited for Miguel and several other coworkers to pass by before she replied.

"He didn't say," Nicole muttered with a questioning look. "I was hoping you'd tell me . . ."

"Shit," Teri mouthed. "I certainly was not expecting a call from him."

"Do you want me to tell him you'll call him back?" Nicole questioned.

"No, I'll be with him in a second." Then, like she was talking to herself, she added, "I have to keep reminding myself that we don't want to get on his bad side. We'd be up a shitty creek with a broken paddle if his station ever decided to stop promoting our music."

Nicole took a deep breath and nodded toward Teri's office. "Uh, what about Eric?"

"What about him? Oh, he's only here to discuss a photo shoot. That blind rapper, remember?" Teri said, looking at the blinking red light on the telephone as if it were a ticking bomb. "We both need to get a grip. All we need is for Victor to strut up in here and see us both acting like a couple of schoolgirls."

"To *dick* with Victor," Nicole mouthed. "He don't sign my paycheck, you do," she added, speaking in an exaggerated urban street fashion and rotating her neck ghetto style for more emphasis.

"Well, as your supervisor, I demand that you get back to work," Teri said, knowing damn well that she didn't even know how to scold Nicole properly. Nicole knew it, too. Teri's words rolled off her back like water off a duck's.

"If you need me to take notes for you and Eric, buzz me," Nicole told Teri. *"Please!"*

Teri glanced at Nicole and gave her a wan smile. But then she sucked in a deep breath and shook her finger at Nicole. "You—

you behave yourself! Go stick a tampon in that crack of yours if you've got to have something in it." Nicole just blinked and shrugged. Teri exhaled and returned to her office, gently closing the door behind her.

"My budget estimate for the next shoot," Eric began as soon as Teri returned to her desk and composed herself.

"Yes, uh, do you mind if I take this call before we get started?" she asked, already reaching for her telephone. Before Eric could respond and before she could pick up her line, the red light stopped blinking. "Harrison?" she said, hearing only a dial tone. She hung up and looked at Eric with a smile. "I guess it wasn't that important if he couldn't wait."

"I guess it wasn't," he agreed with a shrug. He cleared his throat and removed his paperwork from his battered briefcase.

CHAPTER 29

Unlike some of Carla Andrews's other patients, who didn't care one way or the other, Harrison Starr didn't want anybody to know that *he* was seeing her on a professional basis, too. A big, strong, strapping brother like him would never admit to his homeboys that he had problems he couldn't deal with on his own.

He recalled his uncle Ed who had had an emotional breakdown when his wife Vera left him for another man. Instead of getting the professional help he needed, he'd turned to his church. It had been ten years since Uncle Ed's breakdown and so far nothing Reverend Spencer had told him had done any good. He was as depressed as ever. And what good did it do to just talk to a preacher? Most of the old people that Harrison knew were just as qualified to offer as much psychological advice as any preacher he knew. Some even more so. Ninety-five-year-old Aunt Bessie, still living on her own, could put Dr. Phil to shame.

The last time he did try to get some useful advice from Reverend Spencer was a couple of years ago when he thought he was going to lose his job due to budget cuts. All the good preacher did for him was tell him to go home and read his Bible and drink some hot toddy or some tea. Aunt Bessie had not even been able to pull him out of the doldrums that time, either. A few sessions with Carla had done him a world of good. Her advice gave him more confidence and the initiative he needed to take care of his business. Even though he'd sent his resume to other broadcasting institutions, he prepared himself for the worst. He had even obtained the address of the nearest unemployment office. Fortunately for him, everything regarding his job eventually worked out in his favor. He refused to talk to anybody but a professional these days. What if he needed some type of medication for the rare times he experienced depression? Other than suggesting a hot toddy or some warm tea, preachers and old sisters couldn't help him. Besides, Carla was so much easier to deal with.

"Well, are you going to talk or do you plan to spend the entire session wearing out my new carpet?" Carla asked. She leaned back in her chair as Harrison paced back and forth in front of her desk like a panther. He had been in her office for ten minutes and this was as far as he'd gotten.

"I'm trying to get my thoughts together," he explained. He plopped down hard in the chair facing Carla. Behind the chair he occupied was a black vinyl couch that was available if a patient wanted to stretch out during or throughout his or her session. It was rarely used. As a matter of fact, it was used more as a trampoline by Carla's kids than it was for anything else. For some reason, Carla's patients seemed to prefer to sit in the chair and face her, pace back and forth, look out the back window, or all three.

"I feel like a punk coming to talk to you after so long. After things got straightened out at work that time, I didn't think I'd ever need to talk to you again," Harrison said, looking embarrassed. "Especially not about . . . a damn woman."

Carla looked so regal and wise sitting with her arms folded across her chest. He never knew what to expect from her. "A damn woman that you happen to be hopelessly in love with." That was not exactly what he wanted to hear, but she was the psychiatrist.

"I don't know about being 'hopelessly in love' with her, or anybody else for that matter," Harrison replied, his hand held up in a defensive gesture. "I've been with a lot of women. I know a lot of women. Beautiful, successful women! I could pick up the telephone right now and call any one of them and they'd be glad to hear from me."

"Every one of them except Teri Stewart," Carla said with a shrug. Oh, this sister was enjoying every moment of this! It was times like this when she almost wished she didn't have psychic abilities. She already knew how the situation between Teri and Harrison was going to play out.

Harrison shot Carla a sharp look. "The last time I called her up, she brushed me off like I was a piece of lint! She had Nicole put me on hold, and she never did come to the phone." He didn't even attempt to hide the bitterness in his voice.

"How long did you wait?"

"I waited long enough, that's how long I waited. Like I said, I know a lot of other women. I don't have to run after one . . ."

"I know you don't. But if you want to be with the woman you love, or think you love, you have to put forth some effort. Securing a relationship takes a lot of effort. You have to let her know you want her."

"That's what I've been trying to do! I've been trying to get back with her for weeks. You saw how hard I tried at your party. What do I have to do to make her see that?"

"Well, for one thing, you can stop taking other women home with you right up under Teri's nose."

Harrison gasped so hard he started to choke on some air. Carla quickly leaned across her desk and slapped him rapidly on his back; he had to do some deep coughing to clear his windpipe. After he'd composed himself, he looked at Carla like she had slapped his face, too. "You . . . how . . . Teri knows about that?" A confused look crossed his face. "That was nothing," he insisted. "There was nothing to that."

"That's not what it looked like."

"No, I am serious. Nothing happened. I didn't do anything with Mia. I mean, we kissed a few times before we left your party, but that was all."

"Where did you go after you left my party?"

Harrison looked even more confused. For a moment, to Carla it looked like he couldn't or didn't want to answer her question.

"My place." He held up his hands. "But nothing happened."

"Why did you take her to your place? What did you expect from her? I know Mia well enough to know that she doesn't follow a man home from a party to watch a movie on the Lifetime channel."

"I did not fuck that woman, but I wanted to. I am not going to lie about that," Harrison admitted, scratching the side of his cheek. "But I didn't."

He didn't know that Carla was psychic and she didn't want him to know. That was the only reason she didn't tell him that she knew he had not slept with Mia.

"Hmm," Carla replied, looking at him from the corner of her eye.

"Look, whatever I planned to do with Mia was only for recreation."

"Did Mia know that?"

Harrison twiddled his thumbs. "Carla, I don't want to spend my session talking about Mia. That woman didn't mean a damn thing to me that night, and she never will. Yes, I paid her some attention at your party, she made sure of that. Yes, I took her home. Teri had made it clear that she was not interested in going home, or anywhere else, with me. And I had been drinking . . ."

"Harrison, how do you think Teri felt when she saw you leave my house with a known slut like Mia?"

"I wouldn't know. She didn't tell me. As a matter of fact, I haven't spoken to Teri since your party. I tried to, but like I told you, she didn't take my call." Harrison gave Carla a guarded look. "I think she thinks I'm playing games with her feelings."

Carla nodded. "I can see why."

"Excuse me?"

"Teri Stewart is nobody's fool. She is one of the most level-headed women I know and she's not one to make foolish choices. You know her well enough to know that. She's been through a lot for a woman her age. Not only did she lose her parents at a young age, but now she's in a position where she's assumed a similar role herself."

"Where are you going with this?"

"I know your relationship with Teri didn't last that long, but did you meet her grandparents?"

"I did. We spent our first Sunday together in church with them and later that same day we had dinner at Roscoe's House of Chicken 'n Waffles, one of her favorite restaurants. I've never been to the elder Stewarts' home, though."

"Did you notice how she interacted with them? They took care of her when she needed it, now she's taking care of them. Emotionally at least. And from what I can see, she's doing a damn good job. Here is a sister not even thirty yet. She's got a job that most people twice her age couldn't land, or handle. She's got herself together in every other area. The fact that she has not been in a relationship for several months now says a lot about her. She's not one to jump into anything too quickly. And if she does, she jumps out in time to avoid too much conflict. From what you've told me, Teri is not going out of her way to resume her relationship with you. She must have given it a lot of thought. Maybe she feels that she's better off without you in her life."

"That's the way it looks to me, too. And maybe I should forget about her," Harrison said, raising his voice. He was beginning to feel hot under the collar. "She's not doing a damn thing to help restore our relationship."

"But she still interests you anyway? Have you considered the fact that since things have not worked in your favor so far, you should move on?"

"That's my next move, I guess." Harrison looked at his fingers, then twiddled them again for a few moments before he looked back up at Carla. "I've run into her several times since our breakup. That party on New Year's Eve at the rapper's house. Your party. And even before that. It seemed like no matter where I went, there she was."

"How did she react when she saw you those other times?"

"She didn't."

"Excuse me?"

"If she even saw me, she didn't let me know. And each time I was with somebody else."

"Well, under those circumstances, how else could she react to seeing you?"

Harrison held up both hands again and waved them above his head in surrender. "You got me! I can't argue with you because I know I can't win." There was a weak smile on his lips.

"Harrison, *why* are you here?" Carla asked, making a sweeping gesture with her hand. She paused and dipped her head, eyeing Harrison in a way that made him nervous, something most women couldn't do.

"I needed to talk to somebody," he said with a shrug. "I couldn't think of a better person than you." He leaned back in his seat and winked at her. "And since I can't afford Dr. Phil . . ." Harrison sucked in his breath and got serious. "I always feel better after I talk with you. Maybe you should change your name to Dr. Feel-good." He laughed sharply. Carla's face remained straight. She did not see any humor in his comment.

"Maybe I will," she told him as she rose and looked at her watch, indicating that the session was over.

One thing that Carla Andrews would never have to worry about was running out of business. The truth of the matter was, she had been referring potential clients to some of her colleagues. She laughed to herself every time she thought about all the times her parents had told her she was "crazy" for considering a career as a psychiatrist. "Black folks ain't crazy—they don't need that kind of mess," she had been told. Not just by her parents, but by others as well. But she had made up her mind years before she'd ever told anybody what she wanted to do. It pleased her to know that half of her clients were not black. The brassy blond woman who had stumbled in before Harrison had admitted to her that she felt more comfortable sharing her feelings with a black person. She'd been raised by a black nanny and according to her, "black folks are naturally more insightful than white folks." Carla didn't agree or disagree with that assessment, but she had more than a little confidence in her abilities. The fact that her clients kept coming back said a lot about her.

After Harrison's departure just after one P.M., three more sad sacks shuffled in.

CHAPTER 30

"**M**y annual pap test last week is the closest I've come to having sex in a whole year."

Teri's words didn't surprise Carla. Nothing she said did anymore. "And that's a damn shame. It's been a whole year now since your breakup with Harrison, right?" Carla said in a gentle voice.

Teri nodded. "A year and three days actually."

"So, other than your gynecologist, no man has touched you in more than a year?"

"Not unless I can count the hugs I get from Grandpa Stewart and Reverend Upshaw on a regular basis . . ." Teri didn't have a problem being so frank with Carla. She felt comfortable sharing information with her that she couldn't even share with Nicole. However, she didn't like the fact that Carla had a notepad in her hand and was busy scribbling something after every comment she made.

"So how does that make you feel?"

"I'm horny as hell, and if I don't get some soon, I won't be responsible for my actions," Teri admitted with a weary look on her face.

"Well, you can always invest in a few sturdy sex toys." One thing that Carla's patients liked about her was her sense of humor. But Teri did not find Carla's bold suggestion the least bit amusing.

"Yeah. I just might do that," she snapped, clearing her throat and looking away from Carla. She was too embarrassed to tell Carla that she'd already worn out a couple of vibrators. But Teri had a feeling that Carla already knew that. Especially after the conspiratorial look Carla gave her after the sex toys comment. This was one of the few times that Teri wished she didn't know about Carla's psychic abilities. She was so embarrassed her face felt as if somebody had stuck a match to it.

While Carla paused to write on her pad, Teri rose, stretched, and strolled to the large wall-to-wall back window. She parted the ivory-colored blinds and shaded her eyes with her hand. The early June sun was almost as bright and warm as it would be by the middle of August. Even with her eyes shaded, Teri still had to squint to see the backyard that the Andrews were so proud of. The kidney-shaped pool was still covered. Some of the lawn furniture was also still covered, but Pepe—the eager and thorough young Salvadoran who did landscaping chores on the Andrewses' property—was busy mowing the lawn.

"You haven't talked about work in a while. I assume that's because everything is going well there," Carla commented, talking with her back to Teri. Teri sniffed and returned to her seat, glad to see that Carla had stopped taking notes.

"It's a job," Teri said with a heavy sigh. "I'm working on a new album project right now." She paused and gave Carla a thoughtful look. "I am worried about the recording session scheduled for tonight. These artists are difficult."

"What artist isn't difficult?"

"I'm waiting to hear if we've booked the right group they want to use to do backups on a couple of songs and the right models for the publicity photos. You know, almost every male artist—and a few of the females—want to fuck me at some point in the relationship."

Carla drew in her breath, then scribbled furiously. "Oh? And how do you feel about that?"

"It's kind of difficult to tell you this, but my first year at Eclectic, I spent more time fucking than a porn star. I am happy to say that that got old real fast." Teri shuddered just recalling her wild youth.

"When did you stop enjoying sex? Being abstinent more than a year is a long time for a woman like you."

"A woman like me?" Teri gasped and looked at Carla with her eyes stretched wide open. "What do you mean by that?"

"Calm down," Carla suggested, holding up a hand. "You're young, you're beautiful, and you work in an industry that oozes sex. I've known you long enough to know that you are a sensuous woman. Well, you used to be." Carla picked up her pen again and started tapping the top of her desk.

"I'm still a sensuous woman," Teri said, her voice faltering. "I just got tired of jumping in and out of bed with the wrong men. Dwight's got too much action going on in his life. I know I could never resume my relationship with him. And I feel sorry for any woman who thinks she can tame a professional athlete. Especially one as popular as Dwight."

"What about some of the single men you work with?"

"*Sssss!*" Teri hissed, waving her hand as though she were shooing a fly. "Most of them are in the same boat with Dwight. The only single man that I work with who is worth his jockstrap is Eric. But our relationship is strictly professional. Not only is he a fantastic photographer, I am sure you'll agree, but he's also a great guy. I enjoy working with him, but that's all." Teri paused and rubbed the tip of her nose. "Besides, Nicole's had her hungry eye on him and from what I've seen so far, he's been eyeballing her, too."

"What about Harrison?"

"In a perfect world, he'd be perfect for me," Teri said with a dry laugh. "I don't know what he thinks, though."

Carla gave Teri a mysterious look, wondering what she would say if she told her how important she was to Harrison.

"Tell me the one thing you think contributed the most to your breakup with Harrison."

"The fact that he was, and probably still is, so fucking high maintenance. And he had the nerve to tell me that I was high maintenance." Teri chuckled. A somber look swept across her face like a veil. "Men like him need a woman around twenty-four seven. Like a mama or something."

"That's because when it comes to the opposite sex, men will be boys. And *baby* boys at that. They need to be taken care of. And as far as they are concerned, that's what their women are for. First their mama, their sisters, and any other females in the family. Then as soon as they come of age, their needs become the responsibility of the girlfriends, wives, and mistresses. It's been that way from the dawn of time. I laugh when people say that prostitution is the world's oldest profession. The world's oldest profession is just being a woman. Our work is never done."

"Carla, I just want to be happy," Teri lamented. "I want what every other woman wants. I'll be thirty soon. Once my grandparents are gone, I'll be virtually alone."

"You've got other relatives," Carla reminded. "They are scattered all over the place."

"And I hope that's where they stay." Teri laughed. "I can do bad by myself, if you know what I mean."

"I do. I do know what you mean," Carla assured her.

CHAPTER 31

Teri was still thinking about her session with Carla the next morning when she arrived at work. She had two meetings scheduled before lunch and a conference call with the blind rapper and his diva of a manager. She had no idea what they wanted to demand or complain about this time so she was not looking forward to the call.

Another disturbing issue she had to keep on the front burner was her boss. Victor was all over the place, fussing and cussing up a storm. The rumor around the office was that his latest wife wanted to leave him to be with another man and wanted to take a huge chunk of his money with her. So in addition to acting like a scalded rooster, he was looking like hell these days, too. Since he was already homely, a lot of people didn't even notice a difference. But to the more observant people like Teri and Nicole, they noticed how bad their boss was looking. The heavy blue bags he'd had removed from underneath his eyes a couple of years ago had returned and this time with a vengeance. He looked ten years older. His dyed, black hair, with the gray roots of every single strand showing for the first time, looked thinner. His ponytail resembled a beaver's tail—flat and stiff.

"Keep as far away as you can from Victor today. He looks like hell and I don't want you to get caught up in the crossfire," Teri told Nicole with some concern as soon as Nicole arrived.

"I take it he's in a bad mood this morning?" Nicole asked casually.

"What's that dragon's name that breathes fire?"

"What are you talking about? Some *Harry Potter* shit? What the fuck has a fire-breathing dragon got to do with Victor?"

"Victor is that dragon this morning." Teri lowered her voice and leaned closer to Nicole's ear. "I heard his wife is leaving him for another man," she reported.

"No shit?" Nicole said, cursing under her breath. "He has my sympathy because I know how that feels. Well, thanks for the warning."

"Have you spoken to Barry Conover about his boy Trevor?" Teri wanted to know. There was a grave look on her face. "I tell you, some of the agents and tour promoters and managers are just as much trouble as their artists. Barry's a major thorn in my side. And I thought that blind rapper's manager was a bitter pill to swallow. Sheesh!"

Nicole nodded as she turned on her computer. "I told Barry to make sure Trevor is on time for the meeting. He has a nasty habit of missing planes. I saw another meeting on your Outlook calendar for this morning that I don't remember setting up. Didn't say who with, though. What's up with that?"

"I did that before I left the office last night. It's with—well, look who's here," Teri said, revealing one of her warmest smiles as Eric entered the reception area, lugging one of his cameras and a briefcase that had seen better days, and approached Teri. "I hope we didn't have a meeting scheduled for this morning that I forgot about or that someone forgot to tell me about," she said, rubbing Eric's shoulder and looking at Nicole at the same time.

"I don't have an appointment with you this morning, but I was passing by and was hoping I could catch you free. All I need is five minutes." Eric grinned as he gave her a brief embrace. Then he turned to Nicole and smiled. She grinned so hard she bit her tongue. She had not seen him since his last visit to the office a week ago. "Nicole, how are you doing?"

"I'm fine," she managed.

Teri bit her bottom lip and glanced at her watch. "Well, if I don't meet with Trevor Powell soon, the shit is going to hit the fan big time. I was going to have to talk to you about him anyway. His album cover bid is too high."

"You're telling me *now*," Eric said, his smile gone.

"Come on, Eric. Work with me," Teri pleaded, folding her arms. She wore a navy blue skirt and a bright yellow blouse. Not only was the blouse just a little too snug, it was low-cut. It was difficult for Eric to keep his eyes on her face. And that was another issue. He often wondered how the men that Teri had to work with could continue to maintain their composure when they had to deal with her face to face. He liked Teri, but he liked Nicole even more. She was more his speed. Teri was too ambitious and way too high maintenance for a simple hot-dogs-and-beer dude like himself.

Now Nicole was a different story. Eric didn't know that much about her, but he knew enough to know that she was more his speed than Teri. The way she looked and acted around him revealed a lot about her. If only he didn't have that loud-ass bitch Yvette in his life!

"Wasn't the bid approved already?" Eric questioned, shaking his head. He glanced at Nicole, then he turned back to Teri. "Do you want to continue this in your office?"

"I wish I could," she replied. "But it would take more than a few minutes and that's more than I can spare right now. Look, why don't you work with Nicole and get on my calendar as soon as possible, later today or even this evening after hours. If you can't come to me, I will come to you."

"Cool. But before I leave I just want to know one thing—wasn't that bid approved already?"

"Yes it was, but only if it can be cut by 5 percent." Teri held her breath as Eric thought this over.

"That's not the way I do business, Teri," Eric said, looking thoroughly disgusted. "That's not what we agreed to."

"I approved your budget, Eric. The changes were made over my head. I can't do anything about that. You know I love working with you and I want to continue doing so. I enjoy it, and I know you need the work. But—and I know you don't want to hear this—but my hands are tied. Victor made it clear that if you didn't agree to this, he'd go with another photographer. Nicole, did Barry finally settle on what model he wants featured on the album cover with Trevor? I want Eric to shoot her."

Nicole responded, "Yeah, but I just found out a few minutes ago that she violated parole. Something about her slapping a waiter at McCormacks. But we've got her look-alike sister to fall back on."

Teri rolled her eyes and slapped the side of her head. "That's one less headache I have to deal with." She released a huge sigh of relief.

"And I'm sorry to be one of the headaches that you do have to deal with. But this is not fair, Teri. I've worked with Trevor before. His last album went gold and I shot the cover for that album. If anything, I should be getting more money this time, not less! Where is the logic?"

"This isn't about logic. And honestly, it's not even about Trevor. It's about power, who has it and who doesn't have it." Teri was silent for a few moments. "Enough said. You do me a favor and go with this, and I will pay you back."

"I see," Eric said. From the look on his face, he was through with this conversation. Nicole was glad to see that he was a man who knew when to quit. But as far as she was concerned, he was still in a good position. How many other struggling photographers, with just a few credentials to their credit, got to work with some of the top recording artists in the business? And Eric didn't seem like the kind of person to push his luck. She liked that because she wasn't, either.

People often asked her why she'd settled for being "just a secretary" when there were so many other opportunities available these days. But she was happy being a secretary. She was already where she wanted to be. She wouldn't trade places with Teri for all the money in the world. Or her cousin Lola. That magazine that Lola wrote for had just about sent her screaming to the nuthouse. She was always stressed out about one job assignment or another. Last year after she'd interviewed a group of rowdy Hells Angels, she'd had to take the next two weeks off to recover. No, Nicole had gone as far as she wanted to go. She had a steady job, a son she loved, and almost everything she needed to be happy.

Now if she could just get herself a do-right man like Eric she wouldn't have to die to find out what heaven was like.

"Can I call you later in the day to set up an appointment?" Eric asked. Nicole didn't realize he was talking to her until Teri cleared her throat and shot Nicole an impatient look.

"Oh! Yes, please do that," Nicole chirped, looking and acting flustered. She started straightening papers and pads on her desk, but her eyes were still on Eric's face.

He handed her his business card. "If I don't call you, would you please call me?" he asked.

Teri excused herself, rushed into her office and shut the door.

"I'll do that," Nicole said, blinking.

CHAPTER 32

"Your 'Morning Starr' is going to face you from the skies over this great city of L.A. for the rest of the day. I will be back tomorrow morning at the same time, and I hope you will all join me again. Up next right after our news break is my favorite lady DJ, Sister Beverly Blue. God bless and remember, where you go, there you are. Peace and blessings." Harrison brought up what had become his signature sign-off music, anything by Miles Davis.

He closed his mike as Beverly Blue entered the booth, huffing like a sumo wrestler. Why this woman chose to hide her pretty face behind a pair of saucerlike sunglasses all the time was a mystery to Harrison and everybody else. She had big, beautiful brown eyes. They went well with her nut brown complexion and her soft, attractive features. She also had a nice firm body that she usually hid somewhere within the folds of a voluminous, floor-length skirt and a baggy sweater like today. But she was the only female DJ at the station and she wanted to be admired for her ability, not her looks. Ironically, the men she worked with rarely tried to hit on her. Even though her friends had warned her to use every weapon she had at her disposal. If she had to get over, "use your booty and your beauty" she'd been told. But she didn't have to flirt with or fuck anybody to get or keep her job. She was one of the most dignified and straitlaced women Harrison knew. And he meant it when he referred to her as his favorite lady DJ.

"BB, my DJ," Harrison greeted, kissing her gently on the lips. "Have you met Trevor Powell?"

Trevor, an artist who was the source of a lot of Teri Stewart's recent frustrations, stood backed up against the wall in the booth. Trevor was a highly talented singer with millions of fans. He was also a man whose greatest love interest was himself. He and Harrison had been friends for several years, but a lot of people didn't know that.

"Not in person, but I was at your last concert," Beverly told Trevor, shaking his hand. "Only believe the good stuff that Harrison tells you about me," she joked.

"So far it is all good," Trevor told her, still holding on to her hand. When he started to squeeze it, she gently removed it.

Trevor, a month from his thirty-sixth birthday, was good looking and he knew it. He had known it all his life and had used his pretty-boy features to his advantage. He knew that a lot of women went for men like him with light brown skin and wavy black hair, even if the man was ugly. His brother Errol looked like a flying monkey, but women never looked past his high yellow skin and that head full of thick, wavy brown hair he possessed. Trevor knew that he didn't have to do much to get a woman. Just looking good was enough, but being a major recording artist had earned him a spot on a pedestal that was so high he knew that if he ever fell off, he'd break every bone in his body. And if that didn't do it, his long-suffering wife probably would. But as long as she kept her ass on the grounds of their lavish estate in Atlanta, raising their three sons like she was supposed to, he didn't have anything to worry about. He also owned a townhouse in London. But the condo he owned in L.A. was where he could be found most of the time when he was not on tour.

Trevor and Harrison spent a lot of their quality time visiting inner-city schools speaking to the students, encouraging them to stay in school and avoid the gang activity that had become such a thorn in L.A. culture. Despite his reputation as a difficult, self-centered womanizer, Harrison counted Trevor among his most important friends.

Beverly loved Trevor's music, a soft blend of reggae and jazz, and she knew that half of the women in L.A. would love to be standing where she was right now. They would have stripped down naked right in front of Trevor if he had asked them to. But she wouldn't. Other than his music, which was some of the best, there wasn't a damn thing he could do for her. She'd been in a serious relationship with the same man for four years, and so far the only other man in the industry that she would consider fucking was Diddy, Doody, Puffy, or whatever the hip-hop bigwig *Sean Combs* was calling himself these days. With other women and babies coming out of his ear, it was unlikely that a relationship between him and her would ever develop. Hell, she hadn't even met the man in person yet. Anyway, she was happy with what she had in the meantime.

"Well, I guess I'll hit it if you brothers don't mind," Beverly said, plopping down hard on the high chair that Harrison had just vacated. "How did you two meet?" she asked, looking from Harrison to Trevor.

"We met in London about five years ago," Trevor told her.

"Is that right?" Beverly said, looking at Harrison. "You've known each other that long. Harrison never said a word . . ."

One thing Harrison didn't do was exploit the relationships he had with a lot of well-known performers. Early in his career he had been bombarded with requests from friends and relatives for him to get autographed CDs and pictures, free concert tickets, and even dates for them. And he had tried to accommodate as many requests as he could. He did until the details of an after-hours liaison that he'd set up between a casual female friend and an up-and-coming rapper ended up on the Internet. That would have been bad enough, but it had included a video that she'd secretly taped with a hidden camera tucked into the folds of her cap—her sucking dick like it was going out of style. From that point on, Harrison was very closemouthed about the relationships he had with celebrities.

"Uh, I'd like to stay so you and Trevor could get better acquainted, but we've got to roll," Harrison told Beverly with a wink. He knew from the way Trevor was looking at Beverly that he wanted to mount her right then and there. To avoid a potential nauseating situation, Harrison ushered Trevor out of the booth and they went straight to the garage.

Harrison ignored the stares they received from the people entering or leaving the parking area. But Trevor loved it. He grinned and waved and would have done more if Harrison had not rushed him to his car.

"Say, brother. I heard you were dealing with Miss Teri Stewart over at Eclectic," Harrison said, pulling out into traffic.

"Unfortunately," Trevor said with a groan. He sniffed and adjusted the rearview mirror to check his hair. Then he had to make sure that nothing like a bacon bit or a sliver of bell pepper from the omelet he'd eaten for breakfast was stuck between his pearly white teeth. Satisfied with his flawless appearance, he let out a loud breath and reared back in his seat.

"Oh? You don't get along with her?"

"Man, Jesus couldn't get along with that woman for longer than a minute. She's a bitch! Do you know how long me and my people have been trying to work out some minor details regarding my upcoming album cover? Shit!"

"I disagree with you, brother. I've heard some good things about Teri," Harrison said defensively. "She's very focused."

"So was Idi Amin. What's your point?"

"I like Teri. As a matter of fact, I like her a lot . . . if you know what I mean." Harrison gave Trevor a mysterious wink.

"Come again?" Trevor said with a jaw-dropping gasp. "That woman is too stone cold for me, man. She could freeze a ball of fire into a block of ice with one of her mean-ass looks. I wouldn't go near her without one of those flame-throwing gadgets. That's what it'd take to thaw that heifer's pussy out. I bet there's an ice cube where her clit ought to be! I'd like to shake the hand of just one man who has even made it into her bed, bath, and beyond in the last five years."

"Be my guest," Harrison said. He began to steer with his left hand. Then he extended his right hand to Trevor.

CHAPTER 33

Trevor whirled around and looked at Harrison's outstretched hand, then his face. He stared at him for a few seconds with his mouth hanging open so wide that Harrison could see the wad of Dentyne parked on top of his back teeth. "You? Teri Stewart let *you* into her 'no parking' zone? No shit." Trevor closed his mouth for a moment, then he guffawed in a way that reminded Harrison of a scene from the old movie *Francis the Talking Mule*. His friend, who was one of the most handsome men he knew, now looked like a laughing mule with his teeth bared and his tongue flapping like the soles on a pair of cheap shoes. Trevor slapped the dashboard so hard it made Harrison swerve. "You and Teri? Aw man, you have got to be kidding me! *Why?*"

"Why what?"

"Why would a man like you get involved with a woman like Teri? You can do a whole lot better. I've seen you do it."

"Better? Better than what?" Harrison asked, glaring at his friend out of the corner of his eye. "What's wrong with Teri?"

"Nothing is wrong with that sister if you're a robot or Superman. I bet she's got computer wires and telephone cords where her brain ought to be. Other than that, there is nothing wrong with Teri." Trevor sniffed. "As a matter of fact, I like the woman. After all, *she is pretty.*"

"I guess you don't know the Teri I know," Harrison offered.

This gave Trevor something to think about. He wiped the tears of laughter from his eyes and gave Harrison a thoughtful look. "I guess I don't, huh?"

"See, there's a side to Teri that she doesn't let too many people see, my man. Oh, she's good at her job and she's admired and respected by a lot of people, and she is pretty. But she's also one of the most sensitive and passionate women I've ever met. She's also funny, and witty, and a great conversationalist."

A dumbfounded look crossed Trevor's face. "What about all this other action I've seen you with lately? Like that former Miss Jamaica with a butt that would bring the pope to his knees? And that light-skinned sister from Frisco? Does Teri know about them?"

"Oh, Teri and I are not together anymore. I was with her about a year ago."

Trevor looked amused again. But he suppressed his laughter this time by pressing his lips together and caressing his chin. "Oh? What happened? How come you are not with her now if she's so sensitive and passionate and witty and all the rest of that shit?"

"That's a good question. We started with a bang, but we both had so much going on in our lives at the time, we didn't invest enough time and energy in our relationship. I've been trying to get back with her, but it doesn't look like it's going to happen."

"*Hell no,*" Trevor told him, putting so much emphasis on his words that it sounded as if he were speaking a foreign language.

"You don't think so?"

"Well, I know for a fact that she and you have more going on in your lives now than ever before. If that was the reason you couldn't make a relationship work in the first place, what makes you think you can do it this time? Get a grip, brother, and use your head for more than a hat rack."

"I don't think we were ready that other time," Harrison admitted, defeat in his voice.

"But you're ready now?"

Harrison nodded. "I am, but I don't know about her."

"Well, all I can tell you brother is that if you really want to get back with her, don't give up on her too soon. Good black women, good women period, are hard to find."

"Tell me about it," Harrison mumbled, slapping the side of the steering wheel.

"Me, I lucked out when I found Debra. I'm glad I married her when I did while she was still a young virgin and didn't know shit! True, she can't fuck worth a damn, but that's all right. I got that covered. I've always had more pussy than I could handle, anyway. Marriage didn't change that. Me, I don't care what Dr. Phil, Dr. Ruth, Dr. Doolittle, or any other doctor says, a man getting him a strange piece of pussy now and then has nothing to do with his marriage. What I do outside my marriage is only about biology, nothing more," he decided. "But Debra's clean, she can cook up a storm, she's quiet and sweet, she's cute—and she'll do anything I tell her to do. She's got everything she needs, and she belongs to one of the most sanctified churches in Atlanta to boot. I can do whatever else I want to and not worry about her acting a fool about it. Leaving me and shit then writing a tell-all book! What more could a man ask for? Shit. Man, do you mind if I smoke?" Trevor didn't even wait for Harrison to respond before he whipped out a package of Newports and flicked on his lighter. But Harrison had stopped listening to him anyway.

Harrison and Trevor visited an old friend who was now a bartender at a popular jazz club in South Central. This was where they spent the next two and a half hours. It had been a long day for Harrison and all he wanted to do now was relax.

It had been a long day for Nicole, too. She had managed to set up a meeting for Teri with Eric. But because it was after hours and because Eric had a problem getting a babysitter for his daughter, Teri had to meet Eric at his loft. She didn't have a problem meeting with Eric at his place, even though it was in a fairly rough neighborhood in a semi-industrial area near a vegetable-and-meat-packing plant on Baylor Street. Nicole had even offered to go with Teri to "take notes," but Teri had jokingly scolded her and told her that she needed to come up with a better plan if she wanted to get in Eric's pants.

Teri had lived in a loft once so she knew what to expect when she entered the big brooding building Eric called home. The hallway to get to the elevator was long, dark, and deserted. And it was spooky enough for her to make sure that the can of mace she kept in her purse was easy to get to.

When Teri got out of the elevator on the third floor, Eric was waiting for her. He wore a pair of jeans torn at the knees, a shabby plaid shirt, and sandals. He looked so bohemian and comfortable with himself. It was no wonder Nicole found him so irresistible. His front door, directly across from the elevator, was wide open.

"I hope you didn't have any trouble finding this place," he said, greeting her with an embrace.

"I used to live around here. I still know my way around," she explained, following him inside.

"I won't take up too much of your time. I know how busy you are, Teri." Eric had no way of knowing that the only thing left on Teri's agenda for the day was to pick up some take-out soul food, then go home and see what movie the Lifetime movie channel had to offer.

"Don't worry about the time. I can stay as long as you want me to," she said. She immediately wished she had not said that. Yvette leaped up off the floor in front of a large leather sofa with the same scowl on her face that Teri had seen the last time she saw her at the Andrewses' party. "Hello, Yvette," Teri said, forcing herself to be cordial.

"Eric, I wish you would stop leaving that damn door open when you expecting somebody. We got enough flies and other flying creatures up in here already." Yvette paused and gave Teri a crooked smile. "Hi, uh, Teri is your name, right?" Yvette blew on the nails she'd just painted candy apple red.

"Teri is my name," Teri said, putting a lot of emphasis on her words.

Yvette gave Teri a prolonged critique, staring her up and down determined to find a few flaws. "I'm glad I'm not the only one having a bad hair day," she said, patting her matted braids. "It must be windy as hell out there. Girlfriend, you ought to wear a cap or something when you go out." Yvette's unflattering comments didn't even faze Teri. Yvette was what she was, and that wasn't saying much. She was consistent if nothing else, so Teri always expected a chilly reception when she encountered miserable people like Yvette.

Eric's five-year-old daughter, Akua, entered the room from behind a curtain with an iPod in her hand, shaking it. "I'm Akua. I know who you are already, Teri. My daddy told me all about you and how much he likes working with you."

"Hi, sweetie. I'm glad to finally meet you."

"Do you help them dudes make records?"

"Not exactly. All the recording is done in a studio in Encino and I rarely go out there. I work in the administrative end of the music business. But I get to hang out with a lot of stars," Teri said, speaking in a childish tone of voice.

"You know Bow Wow or Romeo?" Akua wanted to know. She stood in front of Teri, grinning like a Cheshire cat.

"No, I'm afraid I haven't met those young brothers yet. But when I do I'll let you know." Teri's face was all smiles despite the fact that Yvette was staring daggers at her.

Teri knew that Eric had a daughter, but she had never met the girl until now and she'd never even seen a picture of her. Akua looked exactly like Eric, and she seemed well mannered, despite the fact that she had an oafish bitch like Yvette in her life.

"Oh, okay." Akua shrugged then turned to Eric. "Daddy, it still doesn't work," she whined, shaking the iPod so hard it rattled.

"Eric, if this is not a good time we can get together tomorrow or a later date. There's really no real rush for me to see the prints we discussed or to talk to you about your bid."

Yvette plopped down on the couch and began to paint her toenails, which were almost as long and curled as her fingernails.

"This time is as good as any," Eric insisted, cutting her off with a wave of his hand. Right after he said that, Yvette whirled around.

"Boogie Dawson is on her way over here to do my hair. She couldn't find a babysitter so she's bringing all her kids with her," Yvette announced with a smirk. "I didn't know you had planned no meeting here tonight and I can't change my appointment."

"Eric, we can go to my office so I can look at the prints," Teri suggested. She caught the glare that Yvette cast in her direction, but that didn't bother her, either.

"Well, if you don't mind, I don't mind," Eric said. Teri could tell from the look on his face that he was in a situation that he was no longer happy with. Why that was the case was a mystery to her. "Just let me get my gear and we can be on our way. Honey, now that Yvette is going to be home with you, you'd better mind her while I'm gone," he said to his daughter, offering her a weak smile.

"What?" Akua shrieked. "I want to go with you!"

Yvette let out a croak of a gasp that was probably heard by residents in the next state. "Oh no, you ain't going there! Just because I'm going to be home, that don't mean I feel like babysitting, Eric. I already told you that. If you are not taking her with you, you'd better call somebody else up and get them over here," Yvette told him, not looking up from her toes.

"Teri, I'm sorry. It looks like I'm going to have to reschedule after all," Eric muttered, a sharp pain shooting through his chest. This was one brother who knew that he had to make some serious adjustments in his life. He loved his daughter and he loved his work so there was nothing he could do about that. And, in his own strange way, he still had feelings for Yvette. Whenever she acted a fool, which seemed to be all she ever did anymore when it came to his friends and associates, he thought about the good times they had had early in their relationship. But the memory of the good times was getting dimmer and dimmer and he knew he had to make a change.

CHAPTER 34

Teri kicked off her pumps and slid out of her pantyhose as soon as she got inside her front door. She poured a glass of wine as she stood over the counter in her kitchen to listen to her voice mail messages. She deleted the first one before it even played all the way through. She didn't need a copy of her credit report. She listened twice to the next one, which was from her grandmother, just calling to say hi and to ask if she wanted some bread pudding. Since it was almost nine o'clock, she decided not to return her grandmother's call. She didn't want any bread pudding, but she'd call her from work tomorrow and visit on her way home from work. Even though she had just done that two days ago. Her grandparents loved seeing her and she loved seeing them. But she had other reasons for wanting to see them again so soon. Ever since she had diverted that potential scam that they'd gotten involved in, she discretely monitored their actions more closely.

Teri glanced at some travel brochures on the telephone stand next to the answering machine. Mexico, Belize, and Jamaica were beckoning her, but she knew that she was way too busy to answer them with a visit. With a heavy and hesitant hand, she dropped the brochures back onto the stand.

The third message, which was so long the machine had cut it

off, was from Lola, Nicole's long-winded cousin. Lola had interviewed Teri for a piece that she had written for her magazine
about women who worked in the music industry. She wanted to
know if Teri wanted her to mail her a few copies of the magazine
with the interview in it, or if she wanted to meet her somewhere.
Lola offered to treat Teri to dinner and drinks and some girl talk.

Teri liked Lola, but Lola ran a little too hot for her tastes. The
few times she'd met Lola for drinks, Lola had spent most of the
time yip-yapping about how great her life was. "Girl, you need to
let me hook you up with some fresh meat," Lola told her during
their last encounter. "Nicole told me you weren't involved with
anybody." She had declined Lola's offer and reminded her that
none of the men she'd hooked Nicole up with had worked out
anyway.

She decided that she'd look at those travel brochures again
soon and figure out a way she could get away for a week or two.
That thought didn't stay on Teri's mind long. She knew that her
time was severely limited. She told herself that even if she had a
man, when would she have time to spend with him? She answered her own question: *Now.* Instead of devoting her time and
energy to her job and other people's needs, she could be with her
man tonight, if she had one.

Victor had left the office early that day to spend some time with
his wayward wife so they could work on their faltering relationship. Less than an hour after he'd left to go home, he called up
Teri on her cell phone and told her that he was taking the next
two weeks off to spend with his wife in Paris. Not Paris, Texas,
where Victor was from, but Paris, France, the most romantic city
on the planet. Shit! If a workaholic like Victor could put everything on hold at the drop of a hat to run off to Paris to work on
his personal life, why couldn't she? Teri wondered.

The last voice mail message made her heart skip a beat. It was
from Dwight. As soon as she realized it was him, she stopped it
and played it from the beginning, leaning over the machine as if
she were half deaf. "Teri, this is Dwight. I've been thinking about
you a lot lately and I'd really like to see you. Nothing heavy, just
drinks, if that's all right with you. I miss you . . ."

She listened to his message three more times before she finished her wine and went to bed. She was flattered that Dwight was *still* trying to get back with her. And even though she had no desire to resume their relationship, she was still glad he'd called. Having drinks alone with him was tempting, but scary. She knew that she was losing her grip. Just the thought of him and the way he had handled that big stick between his legs when she was in bed with him was too much for her to think about.

She had a dream that night that she was embarrassed to think about the next morning. The dream had been so sexual that she'd experienced a climax so intense, it woke her up. She was throbbing between her legs and juice had soaked clean through her thong panties onto her silken sheets. All she could remember about the man who had shared her erotic dream with her was that he'd had no face.

Various parts of Teri's tortured body were still humming when she got to work. Victor's sudden departure was an undisguised blessing. It wiped out half of the meetings on her calendar for the next two weeks. The first thing she planned to do today was call up Eric and invite him to lunch or dinner, her treat. She would have Nicole reschedule the only other meeting she had on her calendar. Then she would lock herself in her office and kick back. Maybe she could finally read the last three issues of *Ebony* and other magazines stacked up on her desk. After that, she'd sneak out the back way, go get her nails done, and get a facial.

"See if you can reach Eric," she told Nicole as soon as Nicole got in that morning. Nicole called up Eric right away and transferred him to Teri's line. A few minutes later Teri pranced out of her office, grinning. "I wish every day could be like this."

"If I didn't know any better I'd swear you finally got you some," Nicole teased.

"Why would you think that?"

"Well, you're glowing for one thing," Nicole said, looking toward the hallway that led to the elevator. "Either you've had a few drinks to prepare you for your meeting with Victor this morning or you've had a nervous breakdown."

"Neither." Teri proceeded to tell Nicole about the phone call she'd received from Victor last night.

"Victor's going to be on the other side of the planet for two weeks?" Nicole was not Catholic, but that didn't stop her from crossing herself and swooning as though she'd just seen the face of God. "We all need to celebrate!" she hollered. "I suggest I go to lunch with you and Eric."

"I don't need you along to take notes. And you know I don't believe in mixing business with pleasure."

"You don't, but I do," Nicole said firmly.

"Listen." Teri slid her tongue across her bottom lip and moved closer to Nicole's desk. Nicole didn't know what was coming, but she had a feeling it was something she didn't want to hear. She was right. "Yvette is still living with him. She's got a good thing going. She's not going anywhere anytime soon."

"What are you talking about, woman?"

"Girl, don't clown me. I know you better than you know yourself. I see the way you look at Eric and I see the way he looks at you. But the timing is off."

"So what are you trying to say, Dr. Phil?"

"I'm not *trying* to say anything. I'm saying it. I don't want to see you get hurt again. If and when Eric wants to be with you, he will do it after Yvette is out of his life. He's not a player. He's not the type to juggle two women at the same time."

"You know Eric that well?" Nicole asked, suspicion clouding her face.

"What? Oh no, it's not what you are thinking. I know him just well enough to know that he's not like a lot of the men we know. He's among the last of the, uh . . . good ones," Teri allowed, with a wan smile on her lips.

"Well, since you are such an authority on relationships, I won't argue with you. By the way, I put a brochure in your in-box from some dating outfit called eHarmony. Did you see it?" The smirk on Nicole's face was brutal.

"You can keep it for yourself." Teri chuckled, shaking her head. "Make a lunch reservation for two at Mr. Chow. Then call up Eric and give him the address and time. And make sure you request a table in the back. I can't stand to sit near the entrance and watch all those egomaniac celebrities prance in and out, doing everything but standing on their heads to get attention." Teri cleared her throat and glanced at her watch. "That's all for now," she said.

*   *   *

"How was your lunch meeting with Eric?" Nicole asked when Teri returned to the office at half past two that afternoon.

"Perfect. Eric's happy with the numbers, I was happy with his sample prints, and I am sure that Trevor is going to be happy. Life is good," Teri said, strutting toward her office. "Any messages?"

"None you have to worry about."

"Good! I can concentrate on my e-mail this afternoon. Remind me to call my granny and your cousin Lola. You can call Lola yourself and tell her my whole afternoon is free if she wants to drop by with my copies of the magazine piece she interviewed me for."

"Uh, I don't think so," Nicole informed Teri, rising.

"What?" Teri had her hand on her door and was about to go in.

"There are some people in the conference room waiting to see you."

She stopped abruptly, giving Nicole an impatient look. "Oh? Well, are you going to tell me who those people are and why they need to see me?" Before Nicole could respond, Trevor and Harrison strolled into the reception area.

CHAPTER 35

"Trevor, it's so nice to see you again. I thought you were in London," Teri squealed. She gave Trevor a bear hug.

"It's always nice to see you, baby," Trevor said, planting a wet kiss on her lips, more to taunt and tease Harrison than anything. "I was out chilling with my man here and we decided to pay Victor a visit. I was disappointed when I called John and was told that Victor's out of the office! But I didn't want to waste up such a nice afternoon so I decided to drop by anyway and check you out. Besides, you and I need to sit down and discuss my album cover bid. I hope you don't mind me dragging my boy Harrison along with me . . ."

"Uh, how thoughtful of you," Teri mumbled. "Just let my secretary know when you're available." Then she glanced at Harrison. "It's nice to see you again, too, Harrison." Harrison just nodded and grunted. But from the eager look on his face, Teri knew that he was glad to see her, too. That was nice because she really was glad to see him. Just as she was about to speak again, she glanced at Nicole, who was waving her hand at her and blinking hard. "Yes, Nicole? What is it?"

"Teri, I couldn't reach Young Rahim in time to cancel his meeting with you this afternoon," Nicole said. "He and one of his people are in the conference room."

"Well, it looks like this is going to be a very busy afternoon after all," Teri said with a dry laugh. "That Rahim. His last CD is still so fresh some folks haven't even heard it yet, but he wants to talk about his *next* project already," she explained. "These rappers sure don't like to stand still long enough to let the grass grow under their feet. They like to move fast."

"That's the key to success," Harrison offered. "And just to let you know, I've been playing Young Rahim's latest on my show every hour on the hour; it's just that popular with my listeners." Nicole noticed how Teri tried not to look Harrison in the face. Instead, she kept her eyes more on Trevor. "If you don't stay on the ball, the ball will roll right past you."

"I heard that," Trevor added. Teri got a whiff of the alcohol and weed on his breath. Harrison stood even closer to her and as far as she could tell, he had not been drinking or smoking anything.

"Well, if you gentlemen don't mind, I need to get into the conference room. I know Young Rahim doesn't like to be kept waiting," Teri said, moving toward the door. She still had on the light blue suede jacket she'd worn to work over her navy blue pantsuit.

"Don't mind us," Trevor said, following Teri. Harrison was right behind him.

"Uh, Nicole, can you get Sandy or one of the secretaries to cover your desk. I'd like for you to be present in case we need to take some notes," Teri said, folding her arms.

"Sure," Nicole said. She took Teri's jacket from her and hung it on a hook across from her work station. "Why don't you all go into the meeting room and I'll be there in a few minutes."

Teri's legs felt like rubber as she walked toward the conference room down the hall. She didn't like the fact that Trevor and Harrison were walking behind her. Knowing Trevor, she knew his eyes were on her butt, watching it bounce, jiggle, and wiggle as she walked. But when she glanced at the mirrored wall outside the conference room, she saw that it was Harrison's eyes that were looking her ass up and down. Why in the hell did she wear the tightest pair of pants she owned today of all days?

It got worse once she entered the conference room. With more than a dozen chairs available, Young Rahim was sitting on top of the long, oblong-shaped table, reared back like he was in his own home, and smoking at that!

"I'm sorry but you can't smoke in here," Teri said firmly, fanning smoke.

"I smoke everywhere I go. Ain't nobody never had a problem with it before," Young Rahim said. From the glassy look in his eyes, cigarettes were not the only things he'd been smoking today.

"That's fine. But it's against the law and that law is strongly enforced here," Teri said. She was no longer nervous now. With Victor out of the office she was in charge and she didn't put up with any mess that Victor didn't put up with. This was why she was always put in charge during Victor's absence because he knew he could count on her.

"You heard the lady," Harrison said.

"Let's not have any heart attacks up in here," Young Rahim said with a sneer, putting his cigarette out in a half-empty cup of coffee sitting next to him on the table.

"And if you don't mind, please don't sit on the table. You can sit in any one of these chairs if you want, but not on the table," Teri said, hands on her hips. She saw Trevor jab Harrison in the side with his elbow.

It was not much of a meeting in the traditional sense. Young Rahim's manager, Freddie Spivey—a pinch-faced man in his midthirties—and Trevor tried to outtalk each other. Trevor boasted excessively about his latest work. Freddie, his puckered lips looking like somebody had screwed them onto his face with a pair of pliers, gritted his teeth and gave Trevor a dismissive wave. Then he took the spotlight and boasted about Young Rahim's latest work, reminding Trevor that Young Rahim was still fresh and *young*. Therefore, he had more time left to develop his career even further. "That's life, old man," Freddie said, patting Trevor on the shoulder.

"That's bullshit," Trevor said, removing Freddie's hand from his shoulder. "Being young didn't do much for Sisqo and Vanilla Ice, wherever they are these days . . ."

Knowing that his manager represented him well, Young Rahim left to go outside to smoke a cigarette. After Harrison answered a lengthy call on his cell phone, he moved closer to Teri. She stood there idling, looking at her watch, and wondering how in the hell to whip these assholes into shape. Freddie and Trevor were going at each other as if Teri had disappeared into the wall.

She cleared her throat and turned to Harrison. "I don't know about you, but I have more important things to do than just stand around here waiting for I don't know what."

"I thought you had a meeting with Rahim and his man," Harrison said, giving her a sympathetic look.

"I thought that same thing myself," Teri replied, rolling her eyes and looking at her watch. "Could you do me a favor?"

"Anything," Harrison replied.

"I'm going to return to my office and return a few phone calls while I'm waiting. Tell everybody I said—" Teri didn't get a chance to finish her sentence. Nicole rushed into the room with a wild-eyed look on her face. Young Rahim was a few steps behind her.

"I don't appreciate this motherfucker pinching my breast or any other part of my body. If he touches me again, he is going to be sorry," Nicole yelled, looking directly at Young Rahim's manager. Freddie couldn't understand why Nicole was so upset. She had been around performers often enough to know what to expect by now. He decided to let his client climb his own way out of this hole, since he was the one who'd dug it

"I didn't do a damn thing," Young Rahim hollered with his hands up in the air and his eyes bucked.

"What's going on here?" Teri asked, looking from Young Rahim to Nicole. "Nicole, are you all right?"

"He comes up to my desk asking if he can make a local call. While he's on my phone, he reaches over my desk and fondles me!" Nicole shrieked, waving her arms.

"All I was doing was reaching for a pen to write down a phone number," Young Rahim insisted.

"Did you see any pens anywhere near my fucking titties?" Nicole asked, shaking a finger in his stunned face.

"I don't have to hang around here and get insulted by some pooh-butt secretary! Don't you know I could buy this damn place and you in it! Wait until I see Victor again!"

"Hold on," Teri said calmly, her face just inches away from Young Rahim's. "Victor would tell you the same thing I am about to tell you. This is a place of business and if you can't treat it as such, you are not welcome here. I know about all the fooling around you do in the recording studio, but you can't do that here. Until you can treat the employees in this company with some dignity and respect, I advise you to vacate the premises before I call security. Sexual harassment has never been tolerated around here and never will be as long as I'm here."

Young Rahim stared at Teri with his mouth hanging open. He turned to his manager, who looked totally embarrassed, and then he returned his attention to Teri. "I have never met a bitch that had enough nerve to get up in my face like that," he said calmly.

"Well, you can't say that anymore," Teri told him with a firm nod. "Nicole, go call security," she added, pointing toward the door.

CHAPTER 36

"What the hell are you talking about—sexual harassment? I have never harassed a woman for sex! I get more pussy than I can handle! What I need to be sexually harassing some dumb little secretary for? People all over the world know me! I got women from Japan to Timbuktu lined up waiting to be with me!" Young Rahim was talking so loud his voice cracked. He turned to Freddie. "You better talk to this woman!"

Freddie, with an irritated look on his face, was about to speak, but Harrison spoke first.

"Brother, can I say something?" Harrison asked in a gentle voice. He decided to position himself between Young Rahim and Teri. "A real man wouldn't treat a woman like that."

"And whose side are you on, dude?" Young Rahim hollered, looking Harrison up and down as if he was inspecting him.

"I'm on nobody's side. But it wouldn't hurt if you apologized to these sisters and do what you really came here to do," Harrison said. He was so close to Teri she could smell his aftershave. She liked his smell. It brought back some warm memories. "Come on, man. These ladies have to work here. This kind of activity can make a person not want to be here. They have to be here, you don't."

"Look, I'm sorry!" Young Rahim said, glaring from Teri, to Nicole, to Harrison. Trevor stood off to the side, watching in amazement. Despite his arrogant ways, he was glad that he had enough sense to conduct himself in a more gentlemanly manner than this obnoxious rapper. Yes, he flirted with the ladies everywhere he went. But that was all he did in public. He knew where to draw the line. He did his other more intimate business behind closed doors. He had seen so many talented performers rise and then fall flat on their dumb asses. And it was all because they thought their shit didn't stink and that they could conduct themselves any way they wanted. On one hand, he was glad they did. It made serious artists like him look even better.

"Now if you said it and meant it, I am sure that Teri and Nicole would both be more inclined to accept your apology," Harrison advised. He was speaking in a low but firm voice.

"Shit!" Young Rahim snarled. Then he waved his hands above his head and started to laugh. "All right. I am soooo sorry I got loose up in here." He paused and turned to Nicole. "I really didn't mean any harm out there, but beautiful women bring out the worst in me. You know how we can get." He grinned, looking at Harrison for confirmation. "Right, man? Tell these foxes how hard it is for us bad boys to be good boys around lovely ladies."

"Do you still want me to call security?" Nicole asked Teri. Harrison couldn't have been happier that Nicole spoke when she did. The last thing he wanted to make a comment on was what Young Rahim had just said. The truth was, Harrison was just as overwhelmed as this uncouth rapper. It was hard for him to stand so close to the woman he loved and not grab her.

"I don't think that'll be necessary now," Teri said, looking directly at Young Rahim. "What do you think?"

"This 'meeting' is over and I'm out of here," he said. He whirled around so fast he almost fell to the floor. "You folks have a blessed day."

"Damn!" Trevor said, his eyes still on the door after Young Rahim and his manager had departed. "I hope you don't have to deal with shit like this too often."

"We don't, thank you," Teri said, turning to Harrison. "Thanks for having my back. I don't think anybody could have handled that situation as well as you just did. I owe you."

"You sure do," Harrison said, pursing his lips.

"Uh, Teri, Eric called a few minutes ago," Nicole announced. "He said he left some paperwork in your office the last time he was here and wanted to know if it's all right for him to stop by on his way home to pick it up?"

"I don't see why not," Teri said with a shrug, knowing damn well that if she'd said no, Nicole would have pouted like a two-year-old.

"I'll call him back," Nicole said, looking as eager as a child who had just received a new puppy. She left the room in a flash, and as soon as she made it to the hallway, she trotted back to her desk. She couldn't dial Eric's number fast enough. Even though nobody was close enough to hear, she practically whispered into the phone when Eric answered. "Eric, what time did you want to come by?" Her voice had never sounded this husky. For a moment, Eric thought it was a man.

"I can be there in twenty minutes," he told her, hoping she'd still be there when he arrived. "If you have to leave, you can leave my property on your desk. It's just a few sheets of paper in a manila folder with my name on the front."

"I'll be here," Nicole assured him, speaking in her normal voice now. *I'll wait here all night if I have to,* she thought to herself.

Teri was still in the conference room with Trevor and Harrison. "Would either of you like some coffee or something cold to drink?" she asked.

Harrison was about to speak, but Trevor beat him to it. "You ready to roll, man?" He started moving toward the door before Harrison could reply. "Thanks for the offer, but we've got a few more stops to make," Trevor explained, looking at Teri.

As much as Teri was enjoying Harrison's presence, she was relieved to hear that they were leaving. With Trevor in the way, the timing and location were not in her favor. What could she and Harrison talk about in front of Trevor with his self-centered self? She knew that no matter what Harrison tried to talk about, Trevor would steer the conversation back to himself.

"Sure," Harrison mumbled. "Teri, you take care of yourself," he said, gently tapping her on the shoulder. "I'll see you around?" he said with a hopeful look on his face. She was glad that he had made it a question.

". . . Yes," she replied slowly, trying to prolong the bliss she was feeling at the moment. She decided that he deserved one of her biggest smiles before he left.

"What a day," Teri said, walking up to Nicole's desk. She had just returned from escorting Harrison and Trevor to the elevator. She glanced at a large stack of telephone messages for her on Nicole's desk and moaned.

"I hope you don't mind me leaving a little early today," Nicole said with a sniff. She was straightening up her desk with both hands. It took Teri a few moments to realize that Nicole was shutting down for the day.

"Of course not. I don't even want to think about all the hours you've stayed late without getting paid overtime," Teri replied. "Do you have an appointment or something like that?"

Nicole took her time responding. She sat up straight in her chair, clasped her hands, and looked Teri in the face. "Something like that."

"Uh-huh. Well, just be careful." Teri turned to go into her office.

"Why did you say that?"

"You know what I mean. You're going to meet Eric, right?" Teri stopped and faced Nicole with a concerned look on her face.

"He called again and invited me to meet him for a drink. He didn't want to come all the way back down here just to pick up his papers," Nicole said, almost with a pout. "Look, this was his idea. If Yvette meant that much to him, why would he be inviting another woman out to have a few drinks?"

"He is a man, Nicole. That's what they do," Teri reminded.

CHAPTER 37

"Thank you for your advice, again. Now if you don't mind, I need to run to the little girls' room to freshen up my make-up," Nicole told a subdued Teri with a smug look on her face. She then proceeded to remove her purse from a drawer. "I hope you don't plan on working late again."

"No, I'm going to close up shop in a little while myself. I've got plans, too," Teri mouthed, forcing a smile.

Nicole gasped. "It's about time. I wondered what you and Harrison were talking about in that conference room after I left!"

"It's not what you think. I'm spending the evening with . . . my grandparents, not Harrison," Teri admitted, looking embarrassed. She immediately felt guilty about feeling embarrassed. She loved spending time with her family. "Grandma saved some bread pudding for me." Nicole gave her the most pitiful look she'd ever received before in her life.

"Oh," Nicole said. "Well, I hope you have a good time. With Victor being out of the office, I hope you take some time to catch your breath."

"I will," Teri assured her. She closed the door as soon as she got into her office. Then she sat at her desk staring at the wall in front of her for the next twenty minutes.

Teri focused on things in her office that had been present for years. Things that had never bothered her before but did now. Especially some of the large, framed color photographs on the wall facing her desk. There was one of Young Rahim standing with his legs spread slightly apart, his hand gripping his bulging crotch. Two half-naked young women were in the picture with him. The two women looked as though they wanted to kiss his feet. He had a grin on his face that made him look like a shark.

But the picture that bothered Teri the most was one of Victor posing with Ike and Tina Turner. She had always thought that it was hideous and would have been more appropriate on display in a rock museum. She didn't know how old the picture was, but from Tina's long, straight wig and miniskirt, Ike's bell-bottom pants and Beatle wig, she knew it had to be old. Hell, if she remembered correctly, Tina had left Ike's crazy ass decades ago.

She could have removed the pictures and other things in her office that irritated her, but most of this shit had already been in place when she got hired. She kept it around as a reminder to herself of how far she had come. Besides, she had her large live plants in every corner, her own water cooler, and a mini-fridge that Victor had given to her two Christmases ago; on her desk were pictures of her beloved grandparents, and one of Nicole and her son.

She picked up the telephone to call her grandmother to let her know she was coming over. But before she dialed the number Miguel quietly opened her door and leaned in. Peeping over his shoulder behind him was John, Victor's secretary.

"It's kind of slow. Do you mind if I shut up shop?" Miguel asked with a pleading look on his face.

"No problem," Teri said, dismissing the two men with a casual wave.

"It's my dad's birthday," John said anxiously. "I need to pick up the cake."

"Good night, you two. I'll see you tomorrow," Teri said with a light chuckle, dismissing them with an impatient wave. "When the cat's away, or in this case, the lion, the mice will play," she said to herself. "Well, since I can't beat 'em, I'll join 'em." With that, Teri grabbed her purse and briefcase and practically ran out of her office. Two other people had suddenly gotten "sick" and had

to leave work an hour ago. Teri didn't even know about the folks
in offices on the floor above her. But half of them had fled early,
too. That was what happened whenever Victor was not around.
Under normal circumstances, she did not condone this type of
behavior. But with Victor for a boss, she felt it was justified, as
long as everybody got their work done and as long as it didn't
happen too often.

Teri called her grandmother from her cell phone as she navi-
gated her way through the heavy commuter traffic. "I meant to
call you earlier," she said as soon as her grandmother picked up.
"I'm on my way. I should be there in about ten minutes. If I ever
get out of this mess on the freeway." She knew, and had known
for years, that I-405 was to be avoided like the plague during this
time of day. "Keep a plate warm for me."

"Don't rush. I didn't have time to cook dinner today. I've been
packing for the past hour," her grandmother told her, sounding
cranky. The tone of voice concerned Teri.

"What's the matter?" she asked, her heart thumping like a
beaver's tail on a log.

"Nothing is the matter. All this packing is nerve-racking, that's
all. I better make sure I pack my Dentu Grip . . ." the old woman
mumbled.

"Packing for what? Are you and Grandpa going somewhere?"

"We'll be on the red-eye when it leaves LAX tonight. I don't
know why in the world they call it a 'red-eye' flight. It would make
more sense if they called it the 'midnight flight' because that's
what it is."

"Sure enough." It was the voice of Teri's grandfather in the
background.

"When I talked to you yesterday morning you didn't say anything about going anywhere." Teri didn't like to talk for more
than a minute or two when she was driving. "Let me call you right
back." She took the next exit and stopped in front of a Chevron
station. She redialed her grandparents' phone number and this
time it was Grandpa Stewart who answered. "What's going on?"

"Nothing's going on. Me and Mother are just going out of

town for a few days," he mumbled. Teri waited for him to continue, but he didn't. A full minute passed in silence. This not only annoyed her, it gave her something to worry about. The way her grandparents liked to run off at the mouth, she was surprised that they were being so closemouthed now.

"Going where? And why didn't you tell me before now?" she demanded. An Asian attendant inside the gas station was peeping at her out the window. There was a frown on his face that Teri found disturbing to say the least. The last time she had stopped in front of a place of business to make a call from her cell phone, the merchant had called the police, claiming she'd been "casing the place."

"Can you hold on for a few minutes?" Teri didn't wait for a response. She pulled her BMW up to the pump closest to the station. She had filled her tank on her way to work that morning so she didn't need any gas. She went inside the station and started to randomly grab merchandise. She'd donate the Fritos, bottled water, gum, and a small bottle of Rémy Martin to the first homeless person she encountered.

Something told her that she was going to need a drink or two when she got home so she would probably keep the alcohol for herself. By the way the clerk was grinning and nodding, the fact that she'd made a purchase seemed to satisfy him. As soon as she walked out the door, he returned his attention to a small black-and-white TV on the counter featuring something in a foreign language.

"Where are you two going?" she asked as soon as she got back on the phone.

"Sister Etienne Conroy passed away this morning," Grandpa lamented. "Me, her, and Mother all grew up together. We all had the same godmama."

"Oh, I'm sorry to hear that. She's the lady back in Louisiana, right? The one with the lazy eye that played with my ears so much that time you took me back there for a visit when I was fourteen?"

"That's her. Been gooch-eyed all her life. Born and raised in Slidell. I swear to God, Sister Conroy just about died when we up and moved to California. If she didn't call us at least once a week after we got here, we called her. She was more like family than some of our family. You'd have loved her to death."

"I'm sure I would have. And isn't she the lady whose husband died two months ago?"

"Uh-huh. We didn't make it to his funeral on account of I was down with the grippe, remember? But grippe or nothing else could keep us from missing out on saying bye to Etienne. You know where we hide the key. Come by and water the plants and take the mail out the box. Don't worry about the newspapers. I've already taken care of that. Now you go on and don't worry about us. I'm sure one of your friends would love to spend this evening with you, doing whatever you young people do these days. You got a boyfriend?"

"No, I don't have a boyfriend. Uh, I'm going to swing by anyway," Teri said, starting her motor.

"Well, you'd better hurry. Brother Pickett is driving us to the airport and you know how he is. We don't need to be there until ten, but he drives the way he walks, slow as a snail. We'll be lucky if we don't miss that red-eyed plane."

"I'll take you to the airport," Teri insisted. She hung up and sped back onto the freeway.

CHAPTER 38

Teri loved her grandparents and would have been willing to walk through fire to accommodate them. But sometimes they were as fractious and unruly as toddlers. By the time she dropped them off at LAX she was a nervous wreck.

All the way to the airport, her grandfather had complained about her driving. No matter what speed she drove, it was either too slow or too fast. "Can't this thing go any faster? I told you to get a Buick!" A few minutes later it was, "Slow down, girl! You almost ran over that squirrel crossing the street!"

Her grandmother was no better. "I hope I locked all the doors and all the windows. I hope I didn't leave the oven on. I hope those Donaldson boys don't break out my front window the way they did the last time we left the house for a few days," the old woman whined. On top of everything else, both grandparents looked like they were going to church. Grandpa had on his best navy blue suit and fedora; Grandma had on a flowered dress with a white collar and a wide brimmed hat with a feather on the side. She had on enough rouge to coat a bus.

"I'll go back to make sure you locked all the doors and windows and turned off the oven," Teri volunteered.

"Lord, I hope we don't have to deal with a terrorist situation on that plane tonight," Grandpa complained, shaking his head.

"I doubt if any terrorists will be on a plane to Slidell, Louisiana," Teri said with a mighty sigh.

"Well, if they had enough of the devil in them to get on a plane going to San Francisco, then hijack and crash it, not to mention all the rest of those planes they crashed up that September, what's to stop them from doing the same thing on a plane to Slidell?" Grandma asked, leaning forward from the backseat.

Teri didn't even bother to respond to that last comment. Unless she agreed with her grandparents, having a conversation with them was usually a no-win situation.

"Don't forget to take your pills. Both of you," Teri reminded in a tired voice. She was thoroughly exhausted by the time she dropped them off and left the airport.

She took her time going home from checking her grandparents' house. She stopped at a Chinese takeout next door to a Cat's Paw shop. Even though everything on their menu was greasy she picked up some egg rolls. She started nibbling on the way home, driving with one hand, eating with the other. By the time she entered her living room the container was empty and her greasy lips were shining like new coins.

She saw the light blinking on her answering machine. Before listening to any of the messages, she called Nicole, assuming at least one was from her.

"Did you call?" she asked when Nicole answered on the sixth ring.

"No," Nicole told her, speaking in a low voice. Teri groaned and rolled her eyes around like marbles. From the sound of Nicole's voice, she was up to something that Teri did not want to hear about.

"Oh. Well, I won't keep you on the phone long." Teri told Nicole about the episode with her grandparents and how worried she was about them. "I know that when one of them goes, the other won't be that far behind. It seems to happen to all elderly couples. Girl, that is one thing I am not looking forward to. I could be planning two funerals in the very near future and that is not something I want to think about."

"Then don't." Nicole didn't even try to hide the impatience in her voice.

"I . . . you know you are sounding kind of strange tonight, even for you. Did I call at a bad time?"

"I have company," Nicole whispered, confirming Teri's suspicions.

"Humph. I figured it was about time for one of your maintenance men to pay you a visit. I'll let you get back to whatever it was you were doing. Get enough for me this time. I could sure use some." Teri chuckled. She sat down on the arm of her couch with the remote in her hand. "How did you manage to get away from Eric in time to get home for your little rendezvous?"

Nicole took her good old time responding. "I didn't . . ."

Teri gasped. "Oh shit! It's Eric?"

"Uh-huh. I really do have to go now. Are you going to be in the office tomorrow?"

"As far as I know," Teri said, speaking slowly. It was a struggle for her to suppress her disappointment. On one hand she was glad that Nicole had finally got Eric alone in her apartment. And despite his relationship with Yvette, she hoped that things would eventually be more serious between him and Nicole. From what she'd witnessed in Eric's loft between him and Yvette, she had a feeling that Yvette's days were numbered.

She had plenty of alcohol in her living room minibar, but she popped open the Rémy Martin that she'd purchased at the gas station as soon as she got off the phone with Nicole. She took a few sips before she pushed the Play button on her answering machine. The first call was from her hairdresser, calling to confirm the appointment she had scheduled for Saturday. The second message was from someone who had dialed her number by mistake. The third message was from Harrison. It was brief and to the point. He had just called to say how he'd enjoyed seeing her that afternoon and that he was sorry she had to put up with Young Rahim's antics. Then he hung up. He didn't ask her to return his call and he didn't say anything about wanting to see her. Again, she felt that "can't beat 'em, join 'em" feeling. She used to know Harrison's telephone number by heart but had recently forced herself to forget it. She stumbled across the room to the stand by the door where she'd left her purse. She dumped out the contents to locate her palm-size address book. She had written his number in red ink. But it was no longer his number. As soon as she heard the recorded message indicating that the number she had just dialed had been either disconnected or changed and was now unlisted, she got tears in her eyes.

"I guess it's not meant to be," she said, dragging herself into her bedroom. "Shit!" was the last thing she said before she finished her drink and turned in for the night.

Teri slept like a baby that night and didn't wake up until after eleven the next morning. She fixed herself some toast and made herself a tall mimosa. She had used only a splash of orange juice and a lot of champagne. She got an instant buzz, and it was a lot smoother and milder than the one from the Rémy Martin the night before. She was admiring the granite-top counters she'd recently had installed during a home improvement frenzy last month when the telephone rang. She grabbed the cordless off the counter.

"Teri, are you all right?" It was Nicole, calling from the office.

"I'm taking a day or two off," Teri replied, looking at the wall clock above her stove. "If I have any meetings, reschedule them for next week in case I don't make it in tomorrow or Friday . . ."

"Okay. What did you do last night after I talked to you?"

"The same thing I usually do. I hope you had a good night," Teri commented, rubbing the back of her head. She made a mental note to avoid that potent-ass Rémy Martin shit from now on and stick to wine, margaritas, and mimosas. She returned to her bedroom and crawled back into bed with the telephone.

"I did . . . and I plan to do the same tonight."

"I see. Well, you can tell me all about it when I see you."

"Listen, you just got a call . . ."

"And?"

"I didn't know if you wanted to talk to Harrison. He said he left a message at your home number last night but that he hadn't heard from you yet."

She was back on her feet in a flash. An earthquake couldn't have jolted her out of bed any quicker. She got so tangled up in her sheets she stumbled and inadvertently plopped back down on the side of her bed.

"I tried to call him back, but he's got a new phone number and he didn't leave it. What did he say? What time did he call?"

"He called just a few minutes ago. Here's his work and home numbers," Nicole said.

Teri wrote Harrison's numbers down on the back of a dog-eared *TV Guide*. She couldn't get Nicole off the telephone fast enough.

CHAPTER 39

Harrison was on the air, so Teri got his voice mail when she called him back at his work number. She didn't want to sound too eager, so all she said was that she'd received his message and was returning his call. She sat there for the next ten minutes hoping he'd take a break and call her right back. He didn't, but she knew he would.

She took the telephone with her into the bathroom when she couldn't hold her bladder any longer. He returned her call an hour after she'd left him a message.

"Teri, I know you're probably busy, but I wanted to ask you anyway," he began. "I read the magazine interview you did, and I was wondering if you'd be interested in letting me interview you on my show."

"When did you see it?" she wanted to know. Damn that Lola. She hadn't even dropped off a copy of the magazine for Teri. And she couldn't buy it because it wasn't on the newsstands yet.

"While I was out with Trevor last night we ran into Lola. She had a few copies with her."

"She was supposed to have delivered me some copies by now."

"So she told me. Anyway, you'll be proud of how she showcased you. She devoted half a page to you, and just a few lines to the other four women."

"Is that right?" Teri was not a boastful or arrogant woman, but she was human. She knew she was good at what she did. Was it possible that she could eventually be in as high a position as Suzanne de Passe was over at Motown? Victor had even told her that she'd probably be running his company when he retired because she was the only person who could do his job as well as he could. How could she not pat herself on the back every now and then? It pleased her to know that so many other people thought the same thing.

"Hearing about your success, as if I didn't know about it already, was so refreshing. I think it would be a big inspiration to a lot of young folks out there. You and I both know that most of them need all the help and inspiration they can get. I can work around your schedule as long as we do it within the next three weeks. I'd like to do this before the story gets stale. Like, before the next issue hits the stands."

"An interview?"

"And you don't have to worry about me taking up too much of your time. I know how busy you are. Ten minutes max is all I'm asking for. But I'll settle for whatever I can get. The last interview I heard Donald Trump do lasted only two minutes, but he kicks so much ass when he speaks, the less he says the better. It keeps him fresh and it makes people want more of him. Same with you . . ."

"Oh. Thanks for the compliment. You just made my day. Well, how about this Friday morning? I could stop by the station on my way to work."

"Hold on, let me check the calendar." Harrison put Teri on hold, and she had to suffer through half a minute of the tail end of Young Rahim's latest tune, then another minute and a half of Trevor's latest before Harrison returned. "I—hello? Are you still there?"

"Uh-huh."

"I thought you'd left me there for a moment. Look, you sound tired and I hope this is not a bad time for you. But if it's all right with you, I can come by your office again or you can call me when you get to your office. I'd really like to get this set up ASAP."

"We can talk now. I decided to take a day or two off," Teri muttered. She cleared her throat and scratched her chin. She wanted to laugh at the turn her life had taken. An *interview?* The one man on the planet that she had finally decided she wanted to be with and now all he wanted from her was a damn interview. Was it finally too late for her? She'd been turning down requests for dates left and right. Not just from Harrison and Dwight, but from a lot of other men. She had no reason to believe that the invitations would stop coming! Hell, she wasn't even thirty yet and nobody had to tell her that she was still one of the most beautiful black women in L.A. But had she played her last hand and lost? Was life going to pass her by after all?

Teri couldn't control her thoughts as she sat waiting for Harrison to respond to her last comment. Two of the things that she always had to fall back on—her grandparents and Nicole—didn't seem so secure anymore. Her grandparents could outlive her, but the reality was that they wouldn't be around too much longer. And she was not that close to any of her other relatives, so it would be as though she was an orphan all over again.

If Nicole's relationship with Eric did go somewhere, she'd have to find other things to occupy her downtime because that sister's time would become severely limited. Nicole was the kind of woman who liked to spend as much time as possible with her man when she was in a serious relationship. When she was still married to Greg, Teri wouldn't see or hear from her for weeks at a time. And as treacherous as women in her age group were these days, cultivating another close relationship with one was something she didn't even want to think about, let alone do. With a job like hers, what heifer could she trust? She couldn't count the number of women she'd met who had tried to use her to get to some of the artists she worked with. Her hairdresser had been hounding her for months to hook her up with any available rapper she knew. Her teenage she-devil of a cousin Cynthia, and some of her she-devil friends, had gone behind her back and used her name to get free concert tickets and invitations to all the star-studded after-parties. It never ceased to amaze her how low some women would stoop just so they could suck dick or fuck some arrogant-ass performer who only wanted to use them like a receptacle.

"Nine-thirty, Friday morning. Can you make that?"

"I'll be there," Teri said.

"If you could get here at least fifteen minutes early that would be nice. We could have some coffee and I can go over my interview questions beforehand. Most of my subjects prefer to do it that way. It makes them feel better prepared and more relaxed."

"I'll be there between nine and nine-fifteen," she said firmly.

"Thank you, Teri. Oh, before I go, I want to apologize for all that drama you and Nicole had to go through yesterday."

It took Teri a moment to clear her head. She had been doing that a lot since this phone call came in. "You don't need to apologize. You didn't do anything crazy. Besides, I'm used to Rahim acting a fool. I don't expect him to behave any other way."

"Does he clown like that when Victor's around?"

"He's worse. The last time he came for a meeting before Victor left for his vacation, Victor said something Rahim didn't like and he called him a motherfucking bastard."

"I am surprised that Victor is still working with this dude."

"Oh, we deal with shit like that all the time. These Rastas are coming by next week. Straight off the island of Jamaica, ganga and all."

"They bring their own shit with them? How do they get through customs?"

"I don't know what in the world those fools do. All I know is whenever they show up, they are already stoned out of their dreadlocked heads and then they still light up some more of that shit right in front of me, and Victor, and everybody else. And that's some secondhand smoke that does not need to be discussed. It's so potent, we all get an immediate contact high. Even more so than I did during my wild youth in college." Teri laughed. Harrison loved to hear her laugh.

"Teri, I hope I am not being too forward, but I won't know unless I ask you."

"Ask me what?"

"Now that business is out of the way, we can talk on a more personal level. Just for a few minutes. I have to get back on the air in five after the news break."

She hesitated before she replied. "What else did you want to talk to me about?"

"You and I had a few good times together and I know you don't want to go there again with me, but can we at least be friends?"

"We are friends, Harrison. Despite everything that happened between us, we are still friends. At least that's what I thought."

"Then as friends, can we have dinner and drinks every now and then? I really miss talking to you."

"Aren't you involved with . . . somebody right now?"

"The only person I'm involved with these days is myself. Yes, I do date from time to time, but there is nothing going on in my life that would prevent me from seeing you or any other woman." She didn't like hearing the part about him and "any other woman."

"I see," she said with hesitation.

"I heard that Dwight was trying to get back with you," he told her in a stiff tone of voice.

"Well, it's not going to happen," she said quickly. She knew that Harrison considered Dwight to be his biggest rival. "He was one of my biggest mistakes." She'd ended her month-long fling with Dwight two weeks before her tryst with Harrison.

"So he didn't mean anything to you then?"

"I didn't say that. And just so you know, I didn't love him at first, but I eventually did. I cared a lot about that man. Why I did, I don't know. I just know I did. But like I said, he was one of my biggest mistakes."

"He's still calling you," Harrison stated. His voice sounded gruff and distant.

"How would you know that?"

"Guys talk. Gyms are the new barbershops. I hear things."

"Well, you can't believe everything you hear. But just so you'll hear it from me, yes, Dwight is still calling me. I am not interested in getting back with him. I don't want to have dinner with him, drinks or anything else because he . . . he comes on too strong. And believe it or not, most women don't like to be hit over the head with a dick. Not that he'll be lonely. A relationship with him would be too crowded, and you of all people know I don't go there."

"After the interview on Friday, can you hang around until I finish my show or do you have to go to work?"

"I'm taking Friday off," Teri revealed, her heart pounding against the inside of her chest so hard she could hear it. The loud thump-thumping made her think of a gothic piece she'd read in high school. She couldn't even remember the story behind *The Tell-Tale Heart*. But she remembered how it had frightened her. She was frightened now. If she wanted to get back with Harrison, it was now or never. "I've got an even better idea. Why don't you come over to my place after you finish your show? I'll thaw out some salmon steaks."

"Do I have to wait until Friday to see you?"

"I think it would be better if we waited until Friday. I really want to do this interview and I want it to go well. If you come over here tonight and things don't go well . . . well, you know. Doing a live interview on Friday might be kind of awkward."

"I see. Well, I don't want to lose out on that. I'll see you on Friday."

"Yes," she replied, her voice so low he could barely hear her. "Bye, Harrison." She didn't wait for him to reply. She hung up the telephone and made herself some more mimosa.

CHAPTER 40

The interview lasted only six minutes, and during that time the switchboard lit up. Ambitious young schoolgirls called the station to ask Teri to come and speak to their classes. The president of a book club called to invite Teri to her next book club meeting. An older white woman called in and congratulated her for being such a "credit" to the "Negro" race.

Harrison had asked some good questions, like how she'd gotten her foot in the music industry door. How she managed to deal with all the ups and downs she encountered. And what it was like to interact with famous musicians on a business level. Despite the fact that he'd wanted to go over the interview questions beforehand, she'd been more than prepared. She was sharp, intelligent, and witty. She was easy for the callers to talk to. She laughed along with them and Harrison when she said something funny.

Harrison knew he had hit on a good thing by the way his boss, Chuck, was standing outside the booth with his arms folded and a huge smile on his face. Most of the interviews that Harrison conducted usually went without a hitch. However, being that there were so many fools out there, every now and then one took a notion and called up to say something stupid.

"Hey, bitch, how would you like to suck my dick? I—" Harrison cut the obscene caller off before he could say anything else.

"That wraps things up with this session, and I'd like to thank Teri Stewart for taking time away from her busy schedule to join us this morning. Miss Stewart is the Publicity Director for Eclectic Records located right here in the great city of Los Angeles. This is your Morning Starr, Harrison Starr, signing off for a short break. Stay tuned for our news break because you know you need to know what's happening in the City of Angels. And remember, if you don't know where you've been, you don't know where you're going." He cut off the mike, slipped on some Miles Davis, and turned to Teri. "You were great. Thank you so much for doing this. I know we'll probably get more calls, not like the last one I hope," he said, rolling his eyes, "but more like the others."

"It was my pleasure," Teri said. They locked eyes for a few moments.

"Teri, you were wonderful," Chuck said as Teri exited the booth. "You're everything Harrison said you were and then some." Chuck gave Harrison a conspiratorial smile and a wink.

"I enjoyed doing this," she said, hands on her hips. She looked so regal standing there in her cream-colored suit, Harrison decided. He couldn't wait to get his hands on her again.

"If you have time, would you allow me to treat you to lunch?" Chuck asked, with an exaggerated grin that allowed him to show off his recently capped teeth.

"Thank you so much, but I'll have to take a rain check this time. I have another important appointment this morning and I don't know if I'll be done by lunchtime." Her appointment was to get her nails and toes done, and that was important to her. Her flawless appearance played a major role in the image she projected.

"Well, I'm going to hold you to that, and I know Harrison will make sure you keep it," Chuck said, squeezing Teri's hand. She didn't like the fact that this man's face was just inches away from hers. She had never been able to figure out why some men thought it was necessary to get that close up on a woman who they knew only on a casual level. And to make matters worse, the Altoid melting on Chuck's thick tongue was not doing its job. The stench oozing out of his mouth from the breakfast garlic burrito he'd gobbled up was unholy. Teri had to hold her breath to keep from inhaling the hellish fumes.

She turned to Harrison and exhaled. "Do you have time to walk me to my car?" she asked him, releasing a mild cough. She could still smell Chuck's bad breath and was afraid that if she didn't get some fresh air soon, she'd have to be carried out. Harrison didn't even answer. He just draped her shoulder with his arm and followed her out the door and down to the parking garage beneath the building.

"So I'll see you tonight?" Harrison asked as Teri slid into her BMW and lowered her window.

"Five works for me, but you can come later if you'd like."

"I'll see you at five," he told her. Just as he was about to lean over and kiss her, Chuck came trotting across the lot waving his hands like an orchestra conductor.

"Teri, wait!" Chuck yelled. He looked from Teri to Harrison as he approached her car, his thick belly shaking like Jell-O beneath his shirt. He was out of breath by the time he stopped next to Harrison. "You are so awesome!" he hollered, looking at Teri as if she were something good to eat. Chuck looked as nervous as a high school nerd trying to make time with the homecoming queen. "Uh, Teri, would you think I was being too forward if I asked if it was okay for me to call you sometime? Dinner and a movie, maybe?" There it was again. Men couldn't stop hitting on her! Chuck was not only Harrison's boss, he was also some woman's husband! And apparently he didn't know that Harrison was not just interested in doing interviews with her.

"Harrison's got my number," she said as casually as she could. Then without warning she pulled Harrison toward her, holding his head in place with her hand. When she kissed him, he was more stunned than Chuck. His legs almost buckled when she slid her tongue inside his mouth. Harrison felt so lightheaded when she released him that he had to lean against her car.

"Oops," Chuck said, his face burning with embarrassment. "Why you dog you." He chuckled and slapped Harrison on the back. "I should have known you wouldn't let a gem like Teri get away." Chuck let out a deep sigh and looked at Teri. "Be good to him and he'll be good to you."

"I know," Teri said, her eyes on Harrison's face. "Five o'clock," she told him. She turned to Chuck with a warm smile and an apologetic shrug. "Sorry, Chuck. You take care." And then she drove away.

"Damn!" Chuck snapped. "Harrison, I didn't know you and she were, you know, *that* serious."

"I didn't either," Harrison admitted, blinking. He slid his tongue across his bottom lip, hoping to prolong the taste that her lips had left on his. "That's something I just found out myself." He stood in the same spot until Teri's car was no longer in sight.

After Teri's appointment at Marie's Nail Shoppe near Westwood, she stopped at the liquor store and picked up some more wine. And, recalling that Harrison preferred the harder stuff, she picked up some more Rémy Martin, a small bottle because she didn't know if he'd be around long or often enough to finish it.

"Now I'll tell you the same thing you told me the other night, 'get some for me.'" It was Nicole on the other end of the line. Teri had waited until last night to even tell her about the interview. And today to tell her about her upcoming date with Harrison.

"Don't you go there now. This is just dinner and a few drinks. That's all."

"That's all, my ass. Like my countrified cousin Lester would say to that flimsy shit you just said, 'if that's true, pig pussy ain't pork.' Woman, you are way way overdue to get yourself a doggie biscuit. How you've managed to go without it this long is a mystery to me."

"Well, we can't all be as lucky as you. I am very particular about what goes inside my body. Very particular. You know how picky I am even when it comes to tampons."

"And that's why you have such bad muscle tone. If you don't use it, you lose it," Nicole warned, giggling as she said it.

"Is that another one of your countrified cousin Lester's sayings?"

"No, that's coming straight from me. Seriously now, I hope it works this time."

"Aren't you getting a little ahead of yourself? He's the one who told me that he just wants us to be friends. I don't think our relationship will go beyond that this time. I'll probably never sleep with that man again." Teri didn't believe the words coming out of her mouth, and Nicole didn't either.

"You can tell yourself that shit if you want to. But if you don't get you some more of that prime beef, *pig pussy ain't pork.*"

"Girl, please!" Teri yelled, trying to sound angry and exasperated, which she was not. She just didn't want Nicole to know that what she was saying was getting to her. She knew damn well that Harrison would not resume a relationship with her and not want to sleep with her. And the way she had practically swallowed his face before she left the station earlier that day, there was no telling what she'd do to him in the privacy of her own home and with the assistance of two bottles of Chardonnay. She wasn't fooling Nicole or anybody else, not even herself. "How are things between you and Eric?"

"Eric and I are heading in the right direction, I think."

"You don't sound too certain."

"He's got to get that heifer out of his life before we can go public. You know I don't want to end up being somebody's backstreet piece."

"Oh? What about what's his name? Your married standby? Does he ever take you out in public?"

"That's different. I don't want to be seen in public with him. Sex is the only thing we ever had in common. That dumb-ass punk has never read a book, and his idea of a classy drink is that Mogen David shit that all the senior citizens drink." Nicole laughed. "I'm going to be honest with you—all I want from him is his body."

"You always know how to make excuses, don't you?"

"*Pfft!* Who, me? I am not making excuses, I am telling you like it is. What about Harrison? Is he, how can I say this, uh, available?"

"He's not living with anybody if that's what you mean. And, according to him, he's not seriously involved with anybody right now."

"Well, I can't say for sure, but I've told you before, I doubt if Harrison's been sitting around getting all his pleasure from self-service. He doesn't even have to go looking for pussy. It comes to him. What woman could resist a man with a big dick?"

"You nasty thing, you!" Teri said with a horrified gasp. "How would you know what that man's got in his pants?"

"Well, unless that's a sock he's got stuffed down in the crotch of his trousers, or unless I'm delusional, my guess is he's hung like a jury."

"Nicole, you need to behave yourself," Teri scolded. "We are both old enough, unfortunately, to know that that size thing is a myth. The size of a man's dick doesn't matter."

"No, the size of a man's dick doesn't matter," Nicole agreed. "But it matters when you're fucking him."

CHAPTER 41

Harrison had arrived at four, not five like she had suggested. But he had sat in his car two blocks away from her building for an hour before he rang her buzzer. He was in a fever of anticipation as he awaited her response.

She had on a pale yellow hostess gown when she opened the door. "Right on time," she said. Her smile was so radiant her face glowed. Her freshly painted toenails called attention to her bare feet. And she smelled like a rose, which he knew was one of the fragrances that Vera Wang endorsed because he was the one who had given her the perfume.

"I meant to ask if you wanted me to bring something. Like a bottle of wine." He felt like a schoolboy about to get his first piece. She felt like the Whore of Babylon.

There was no time for games so she cut to the chase. "Fuck a bottle of wine. Did you bring some condoms?" she said bluntly, with lust about to consume her.

Her question and eagerness caught him off guard. Had he known it was going to be this easy, he would have rung her buzzer an hour earlier. *"What you say!"* he mouthed, using a well-worn phrase that the elders used when they got excited about something.

"Did you or did you not bring some condoms?" she demanded.

"Uh, yes, I did," he told her. "But I *always* carry them with me. Habit from college . . ."

"Good!" she whispered in his ear, licking it for good measure. She was in the mood to get loose and she wanted him to know that. Like with everything else she did, she would leave no stone unturned. Right after she licked the tip of his ear, making him tremble and moan, she massaged his dick with both hands.

Before he knew what was happening, she had him by the arm, leading him to her bedroom, and that was where they remained for the entire evening.

She couldn't get enough of him. She felt safe in his long, muscular arms, and he loved the way she wrapped her legs around his waist. She thought her body would break in two when she arched her back and lifted her pelvis to make it easier for him to get as deep into her as he could. And he did. He slid both hands beneath her butt and pulled her even closer to him. He slammed into her so hard, the head of the bed banged against the wall. He could tell from how tight she was inside that she had not been with a man in a while. That was a damn shame. She felt almost like a virgin.

He had been with somebody just a week ago but the way he was jackhammering into her, she was convinced that he hadn't been intimate in a while himself. That was what she wanted to believe and that was what she did believe. But she didn't want a confirmation, so she did not ask.

They came together, and for her it seemed to go on for so long she was afraid that it would be fatal. Finally, when it was over for her, too, she slid from beneath his body, breathing so hard it made her lungs hurt.

"It's been a while for you, huh?" Harrison asked, still gasping for breath. He leaned off the bed and scrambled around on the floor for his pants.

"Uh . . . yeah. It's been a little while," Teri admitted, breathing through her mouth.

"Do you mind if I smoke a joint?" He had already lit up and taken a few hits.

"No, I don't mind," she said, reaching for it herself. Smoking weed was something else that she hadn't done since her last time with him.

"Omph! Baby, that was pure ecstasy. It was well worth the wait," he told her, turning onto his side. He propped himself up on his elbow and looked at her. "Woman, you are amazing and you know it, don't you?"

She smiled demurely. "It's tacky to brag, but what the hell. I'm hot." She laughed, pinching his arm. Then a serious look slid across her face. "Harrison, we really need to talk. I don't know where this is going this time, but it's something I need to know before we get too carried away."

"I want you to be my lady, Teri. I can't think of a woman in this city I'd rather be with more than you." He looked at her with so much affection, she shivered. "I am so proud of the way you turned out."

His last remark made her giggle. "You make me sound like a table leg," she told him.

"I mean, I am proud of the woman you are. You were at the top of your game when I first met you. And to be honest with you, back then I didn't think there was anyplace left for you to go but down. You are still at the top, and that's where you are going to stay, lady."

"Would you mind explaining yourself, please?" she said, sitting up. Her face was so close to his, his hot breath stung her eyes. "I'm the same woman I was a year ago."

"Uh-uh. For one thing, you are more beautiful now than you were then. And that body, girl, if you get any hotter I will have to turn a hose on you."

"You say all that now. But what will you say tomorrow?"

"Teri, all kidding aside, you are a beautiful woman, inside and out. You are strong and successful and smart. And, you got balls. Other than Rosie O'Donnell I've never seen a woman kick ass the way you do. Where do you think Eclectic would be without you?"

"Everybody is replaceable, Harrison. If and when I do leave Eclectic, I am sure that the company won't go out of business."

"Do you ever think about leaving?"

She shrugged. "It's crossed my mind. Recording artists aren't

the easiest people to deal with on a regular basis. Then there's
Victor, vying for the 'boss from hell' title. I will admit that my job
gets on my last nerve from time to time and sometimes I wish I
was back working the counter at Burger King. But, to be honest
with you, as far as a job, I am where I want to be. Why do you ask?"

"Because I'd like to know if a job is all you want."

"No, that's not all I want, Harrison. I want a whole lot more
than a job." She paused and let out a heavy sigh. Then a thoughtful look appeared on her face. She shared that thoughtful look
and a smile with him before she spoke again. "I want to be a stay-
at-home mom someday." This was the last thing he expected to
hear from her.

He was practically speechless. But after he cleared his throat,
he revealed what was on his mind. "I see. Well, some guy is going
to be a very lucky dude someday. I'm jealous already." This was
the *last* thing she expected to hear from him.

"I can tell," she said, a touch of melancholy in her voice.

Was this his way of telling her that that "lucky" man wouldn't
be him? That was what it sounded like to her. Damn him to hell!
What had she gotten herself into? Suddenly, she felt profoundly
sad and was sorry she had behaved like a video vixen. What did
he think about her now? They hadn't been together in more than
a year, and the first time they did get together again she practically raped him. What kind of woman was she? She knew how the
men she worked with talked about women who came on too
strong, or who were too easy. If she ever got married it would be
to a man who didn't know how nasty she really was. Why would
Harrison want to marry a woman like her? As far as she was concerned, she had a royal mess on her hands now.

They didn't talk for a few minutes. When Teri finally spoke
again, he didn't answer.

"Harrison, I just asked if you wanted a drink or something,"
she said. He still didn't answer. She nudged his leg with her foot.
His response was a resonating snore.

The broiled salmon that they had not even touched was still on
the platter on the counter in the kitchen when Teri rolled out of

bed the next morning. But the Rémy Martin was gone. The wine was gone. And Harrison was gone.

She found a neatly written note from him stuck on the front of her microwave in the kitchen. I had a great time. Will call you . . . the note said. She scratched her head and bit her bottom lip. This was not what she had wanted to wake up to. Not after all she'd been through the night before. Was this what she had "saved" herself all this time for?

"What did I get myself into?" she asked herself out loud.

CHAPTER 42

She had slept soundly and hadn't heard him leave. She didn't know if he'd eased out in the middle of the night, just before dawn, or what. Had she become just another piece of hit-and-run pussy like the women she regarded with such contempt? Like that Mia and Yvette? She felt like a fool. And she was the one who was always telling Nicole not to let any man make a fool out of her. Well, Nicole would get the last laugh on her. Maybe not. If Nicole ever heard about her getting played in such an avoidable way, it wouldn't be from her.

She threw out the trash, then took a shower. While she was still drying herself off, she called up Carla.

"I need to see you ASAP," she told her psychiatrist and close friend. Teri adored Carla but she knew that as long as Carla was happily married and had so many other wonderful things going on in her life, she could never have the same type of relationship with her that she had with Nicole. Teri doubted if she'd ever be Carla's equal. An attractive, happily married, successful woman—with two great kids thrown in the mix—was the goal of almost every woman Teri knew. It was hard enough to hold her envy at bay when she socialized with Carla. She would never tell Carla how she felt about her. How could she? But in her heart she knew that Carla probably already knew she harbored a spark of harmless jealousy. And even though she was a psychic, she didn't need to be one to know that.

"Well, I haven't heard from you in a while," Carla told her. She could tell from the tone of Carla's voice that she was glad to hear from her. She was just sorry that she had waited until she needed professional help before she called her friend. "I've been so busy," she lamented. That much was true.

"And things must be going well for you, too," Carla insisted. "I've got a pretty full schedule for the next two weeks. Is this serious?"

"Carla, I'm a damn fool! I am a low-down, stupid, black-ass slut! I am nothing. Do you hear me? I am a piece of dog shit!"

"Hmm. Is that all?"

"No, that's not all! There is a lot more and it's not pretty. Since I'm being honest and up-front, one of the reasons I haven't called you is because you're everything I want to be. I'm a little jealous! I love you to death, but I'm still jealous of all you've got! You've got it all. Me, I am nothing but a damn fool." She couldn't believe what she'd just confessed. After she'd promised herself she wouldn't! But she was glad she finally did. If nothing else, she felt liberated. It felt as if a huge monkey had been removed from her back.

"I know all that," Carla said calmly. "I know a lot more than I want to know."

"And that's another thing—I can't keep a damn secret from you." Teri laughed. "I'm glad I'm not your husband! I bet you don't even have to worry about him screwing around. And your poor kids! Their teen years are going to be hellish with you knowing practically every move they make." Teri stopped talking and started laughing. Carla laughed with her. "I'm sorry. I'm upset."

"I can tell. Listen, I'm really sorry that I can't talk to you more right now, but I'm expecting a seriously distraught client any minute. She's on her last leg."

"Well, I already passed that point. I'm on my knees begging you to squeeze me in within the next day or so!"

"Baby, you know I would if I could, but I have a responsibility to all my patients. Hey! I've got an idea that might work for both of us. If you don't mind skipping church this Sunday, I can give you an hour, but it has to be before noon. I have a hot date later in the day."

"A date? A *hot* date? *You?* Woman, I know what you do is your business, but you are the last person on this planet that I expected to . . . uh . . . get jiggy with another man. I guess if a shrink can't walk the straight and narrow, the rest of us don't have a chance."

Carla laughed and tried to imagine the kind of horrified look Teri must have on her face. "Don't let your mind run wild. My hot date is with my husband. After I give him a foot massage, I am going to treat him like the king he is. I've reserved a suite at the Beverly Hilton."

"You need a suite at the Hilton just so you can make love to your *husband?* That's where the stars stay."

"Well, my husband is a star to me. And I'm not going to make love to my star, I'm going to fuck him. Being his whore keeps him from going out and buying one."

Teri was at a loss for words. "I'll see you Sunday morning at ten?" she managed after a few moments.

"If you really think it's necessary, yes. I don't expect to see you, though."

"What do you mean?"

"I don't know all the details yet, but the information is still coming to me. I could see it more clearly if you were in my presence."

"You know about Harrison and me, don't you? You know he spent the night at my place last night?" Teri didn't allow Carla to answer her questions because she already knew the answers. "If you do, then you know he slipped out of here like the Frito Bandito while I was still asleep."

"Like I said, I don't know all the details. But I do know that he was with you last night."

"I'll see you Sunday morning," Teri mumbled. She hung up and moped around for about ten minutes.

Other than the empty Rémy Martin and wine bottles and her sore pussy, there was no other indication that Harrison had even been in her residence. His hit-and-run had left her feeling like roadkill.

Teri didn't even bother to call Nicole after her conversation with Carla. But an hour later, Nicole called her on her cell phone.

"What's up?" At first Teri didn't recognize Nicole's voice because she was whispering. And she sounded like a man. A few weeks ago Teri had received phone calls from some horny men who were trying to make dates with a call girl named Wendy. Come to find out, her cell phone number was the same number that had been issued to this Wendy woman. And that hussy must have had some damn good pussy or she offered discount rates, because men claiming to be her regular customers were calling day and night, seven days a week. Teri had called Verizon a week ago and had them change her cell phone number and had not received any odd phone calls since. Until now.

"You've got the wrong number," she said, rolling her eyes and letting out a harsh breath. She was in her bathrobe and house shoes in her kitchen making a salad. She could still smell the salmon that she had prepared for Harrison the night before. She had left it in the broil pan, wrapped it, and shoved it into the refrigerator. She didn't like to waste food so she decided she'd warm it up for lunch and dinner.

"It's Nicole," Nicole said, still whispering. "You able to talk?"

"Yes, I am able to talk. Why wouldn't I be able to talk in my own home?" she asked, slicing off pieces of lettuce and tossing them into a wooden bowl on the counter.

"Is he gone?"

"That motherfucker snuck out of here like he stole something!" Teri hissed.

CHAPTER 43

"**D**amn! What the hell did you do to him, Teri? Bite one of his balls in two or bore him half to death? See there! I told you that shit like that happens when you don't stay in practice in the bedroom. Either you fuck up or you forget how to do certain things!"

"Girl, I don't even want to talk about it. I should have never let my guard down again with that Negro!"

"Then why did you?"

"Because he's a . . . he's a—he's a smooth operator, that's why. He knows how to work a woman. But it'll be a cold day in hell before I let my guard down again."

"You can do better than that. That's the lamest thing you've said since, uh, since yesterday."

"Maybe we should change the subject," Teri suggested, chewing her nails, something she had not done since high school.

"Change the subject, my ass. You know I am not going to get off this phone until I get the whole story."

"It just didn't work out, okay? Again."

"Well, I don't know what he did or didn't do. Or what the hell you did, and it's none of my business. I just don't want to be dragged into this mess and then left out in the cold."

"I'm not dragging you into anything, Nicole. As a matter of fact, I didn't plan on telling you anything about last night."

"So why is Harrison calling me this morning? Will you tell me that much?" Nicole demanded.

"What . . . what do you mean?" Teri stammered. "This morning? Why would Harrison be calling you this morning?"

"Because he couldn't reach you. He said he'd called several times and let the phone ring more than a dozen times. Your answering machine didn't even pick up the calls."

Teri's head felt as if the sky had fallen on it. It was only then that she remembered she had turned off her landline and answering machine! And so far, Nicole and Victor were the only ones to whom she'd given her new cell phone number. "Oh shit!" She dropped the head of lettuce into the sink and slapped the side of her head. "I turned off everything just before Harrison got here last night because I didn't want us to be disturbed! He's been trying to call me?"

"All morning."

"Shit. Well, the way he snuck out of here—"

"The man told me he had to get his car to his mechanic this morning."

"And he couldn't tell me that?"

"Teri, give the man some slack. Like everybody else, he's got a life. You can't expect to be in on every little detail of it. We have to do our part if we want our relationships to work. Look at me. I know I've got my work cut out for me if I want to make things work with Eric."

"This is a fine mess," Teri said. She moved across the floor to the wall phone and turned it back on. Still talking, she rushed into the living room and turned on the other telephone and the answering machine connected to it. "If Harrison calls you again, tell him to call me."

The first person Teri called from her landline was Carla. She was glad Carla didn't answer. She left a brief message, canceling the appointment she'd scheduled for Sunday morning. Then she called Harrison. Her breath caught in her throat when he answered on the first ring.

"Hi . . . it's Teri. You tried to call me this morning?"

"I did." He sounded tired.

"I forgot to turn my phone and answering machine back on this morning," she muttered. "I like to sleep in on Saturdays."

"So do I, but I usually leave my answering machine on regardless," he stated. "Did you get the note I left?"

"Uh-huh."

"I tried to reach you earlier to invite you to my place tonight. This time, I am responsible for dinner. And I promise you, we will leave enough time and energy to eat dinner." He laughed.

"I'd like that. I'd like that very much. What time do you want me to be there?"

"Dinner will be at six."

"Do you still live in the same place near the Long Beach border?"

"I do."

"I'll print out a map from MapQuest. I don't remember how to get there."

"You don't have to worry about driving, honey."

"Oh. Okay. Then you'll pick me up?"

"Be ready around five-thirty. I hate to rush you off the telephone but I need to go pick up my car and run a few other errands."

"Then I'll see you this evening."

"Teri, last night meant a lot to me. And even though all we did was have a few drinks and do the, *you know*, it was about more than just sex to me. I truly enjoy your company and I have a lot of feelings for you. I want you to know that you are not just another piece of tail to me."

Piece of tail? Did people still use that phrase? Teri wondered.

"You didn't have to make it sound so raw," she said with a forced laugh. "Piece of tail sounds so . . . old school."

"Sounds ghetto, too. But I'm still a homeboy to the bone and proud of it. I think that's why I can deal with all these youngsters who think they are going to set the world on fire with their one-hit selves. Like that Rahim. He's had just *one* major hit and a few minor hits along the way. But the way he carries on, you'd think he was Jay-Z or Kanye."

"Tell me about it," Teri agreed. "Well, I'd better get up and run a few errands myself if I want to be ready for dinner tonight. Is there anything you want me to bring?"

"Just yourself."

Teri's buzzer went off at five-thirty. When Harrison didn't respond after she'd hit the buzzer and spoke into the intercom, she got worried. She grabbed her shawl and overnight case and took the stairs to the ground floor, running as if she were being chased by a rogue cop.

She tried to be nonchalant when she saw a chauffer standing in front of her building holding up a sign with her name on it. She slid into the backseat of the shiny black town car like it was something she did every day.

Saturday night with Harrison was more than Teri could stand. The man was going out of his way to make a better impression on her this time around and his efforts were greatly appreciated. He was a gourmet cook, preparing steak and lobster like a pro, and he was just as proficient in the bedroom as he was in the kitchen.

The same chauffer that had delivered her to Harrison's condo had returned Sunday evening to collect her and return her to her address. But this time Harrison escorted her. The good-bye kiss at her door was so long she had to push him away so she could catch her breath.

"I'll call you," he told her, tapping his lips with his finger, then tapping her lips with that same finger. "And please do not turn off your phone and your answering machine."

Teri was so light-headed she sailed right past her answering machine and didn't notice the "message waiting" red light blinking like a traffic signal. But just before she crawled into bed she checked her messages. All five were from her grandparents.

"Girl, where in the world have you been? We called and called and called yesterday and couldn't reach you. We were just about ready to hop back on that airplane and come home to check up on you," her grandmother sobbed. "You know better than to worry us like this!"

"You stop that crying right now! I'm fine. I was just busy," Teri explained.

"Since when did you get so busy you had to turn off your phone and your answering machine? And you got your cell phone *disconnected?* Are you not paying your bills, girl?" Grandma Stewart sniffed.

"I had to change my cell phone number. I just forgot to give it to you."

"Whatever. You still didn't explain what kind of busy you were that you couldn't accept any calls or messages . . ." The old woman's tone had become accusatory. Teri remained silent for a few moments, and this irritated her grandmother even more. "If you don't answer me I'm going to give up in about forty-five minutes, then hang up . . ."

"I'm sorry," Teri replied, her tone soft and contrite. "I had company and I didn't want to be disturbed. It won't happen again." A mysterious smile crossed Teri's face and stayed there.

CHAPTER 44

"Company?" Grandma Stewart asked, mumbling something unintelligible under her breath. She cleared her throat before she spoke again. "Is that what you just said?"

The next voice Teri heard belonged to her grandfather.

"Teri, you got company?" He spoke in a hurried tone of voice, as though he was afraid he'd forget what he wanted to say if he didn't release the words fast enough.

"Not now. But, uh, a friend was with me. That's all."

"Well, it must be more than just a friend if you didn't want to take calls or even get messages. Who?"

"Who what?"

"Who was your company? We know all of your friends."

"I'll tell you all about it when you get back home. How was the funeral?"

"The funeral is tomorrow. Mother helped pick out the burial dress—sky blue. Sister Conroy's favorite color," Grandpa Stewart said with a cough. "And let me tell you something, girl. These kin-folks of hers have already looted her house like those devils did after Katrina struck. I hate to think of how those stooges in our family are going to behave when me and Mother cross over."

"Well, as long as there's a breath in my body, you won't have to worry about a thing. I'll make sure of that," Teri vowed.

For the next ten minutes, Teri's grandparents took turns beating her over the head with mundane information she had absolutely no use for. What in the world made them think she'd want to hear the details of Brother Broadnex's gall bladder surgery? Before they released her, they gave her an updated report on their own health. Had she believed everything they told her, she would have started planning their funerals as soon as she got off the telephone.

When they paused long enough for her to speak, she jumped in and said, "I think I hear somebody knocking on my door . . ."

"Sweetie, anybody lucky enough to have you in their life is blessed tenfold. I hope all your friends appreciate you as much as me and Mother do. Bye, baby."

Monday morning when Teri returned to work, she was surprised at the stack of mail in her in-box. There were the usual industry magazines; several postcards from Victor, who was having an "awesome" time on vacation with his wife; and battered interoffice envelopes bulging with a lot of office riffraff that went no further than her trash can or shredder. At the bottom of the heap was a small envelope with no return information. She quickly opened it. It was an invitation to another party from Young Rahim and a scribbled "apology" at the bottom for his recent crude behavior in front of her and Nicole in the Eclectic conference room. His writing looked like that of a five-year-old, big and blocky.

Nicole arrived a few minutes later. She immediately peeked into Teri's office. "Well, now. The prodigal sister returns," she teased. "Things were pretty quiet while you were out so you don't have to worry about cleaning up any messes."

"Did Victor call? I received a few postcards from him."

"Haven't heard a peep from him, thank God," Nicole said with a look of relief on her face. Then she added in a hopeful tone of voice, "If we're lucky, the airline will go on strike and he will be stranded for a couple of weeks . . ."

"I doubt if we'll ever get that lucky," Teri said with a snort. "Hey, what are you doing this coming Friday night?"

Before Nicole replied, she held her breath, tilted her head to the right, and gave Teri a cautious look. "Why?"

"Rahim is having another party and the invitation says I can bring a guest." Teri wanted to invite Harrison to go with her, but she thought it would be a good idea to take things more slowly. Now if he had invited her to go to a party with him, it would have been a different story. From her point of view, she didn't want to appear too clingy or make it seem like she was smothering him so soon in the relationship. She'd already decided that she would let him make most of the moves until she knew where the relationship was going. However, if and when he made a move she didn't like she would not hesitate to let him know, and in no uncertain terms.

"You would think that by now that numbskull would send me my own invitation."

"Maybe he doesn't think he knows you that well yet."

"He thinks he knows me well enough to fondle me," Nicole reminded.

"Oh, I forgot about that," Teri said, exhaling a loud breath. "Maybe he wants to limit his guest list by killing two birds with one stone. He knows I'll be bringing you as my guest, anyway."

"Not this time," Nicole announced. "I'm not available Friday night." She had a tight look on her face, and that told Teri all she needed to know.

"You and Eric are going to do something? Again?"

"Again." Nicole grinned with a sparkle in her eyes.

Teri wanted to wipe the look off Nicole's face with a dirty rag. But since she didn't want another friend to know that she was slightly jealous of her, all she did was smile and say, "That's so nice." Her voice was small and more than a little sad. She hoped Nicole didn't detect that and feel sorry for her. The last thing she wanted was pity.

"Eric and me, and Miguel and Louisa. And all the kids, of course." Nicole gave Teri a wan smile. "Eric's daughter, Akua, is a little doll, and she and Chris hit it off immediately. Miguel took the kids to Disneyland on Saturday and now I want to repay the favor. I'm cooking dinner for us all this Friday. If you don't go to Rahim's party, you can join us."

"Oh, I don't think so. I wear a lot of hats but I never wanted to wear the same one worn by the 'man who came to dinner.'"

"The who?"

"It's an old movie," Teri said waving her hands. "It's not important. Okay," she mouthed. "I'll go by myself."

"Aren't we forgetting somebody else? I'm sure that that somebody else you know would probably love to go to Rahim's party."

"Your cousin Lola? I don't think so. She's been bugging me for months to bring her to some of the parties we go to."

"I was talking about Harrison," Nicole said, her tongue snapping brutally over each word. There were times when Teri exasperated her to the point of no return. "And you know damn well who I was talking about."

"Hmm. Well, he probably received his own invitation, but I'll mention it to him anyway."

Harrison did have his own invitation to Rahim's party, but he had other plans. That's what he told Teri when she broke down and asked if he wanted to be her escort. He didn't reveal to Teri what those plans were and she didn't ask.

To her everlasting horror, Teri ended up going to the party with Lola after all. Lola had finally come by her condo to deliver the copies of the magazine article that Teri had been waiting on for more than a week and when she saw Teri all dressed up, she made it her business to find out where Teri was going. As soon as she found out Teri was going alone but could bring a guest, she wasted no time inviting herself.

"I don't have time to go all the way back home to get cute, but I'm sure you've got something in your closet I can slide into," Lola had told her, gushing like a teenager.

She'd had fun at Rahim's party but she'd left early. She slunk out his back door and trotted across his spacious lawn to get to her car parked on a side street around the corner. Lola had already left with one of the musicians that backed up Rahim. Dwight had also been present, dressed like a tall penguin, with that oversexed Mia clinging to him like a grapevine.

Teri was glad to know that Harrison had not slept with Mia the night he took her home from the Andrewses' party after all. At least that was what he'd told her when she asked him that night at his place. And the only reason she'd brought it up was because he had asked her if she would ever get back into Dwight's bed. And of course she'd told him that she would not. As a matter of fact, she'd told him that she'd climb into a bed of nails before she got back into Dwight's. Hearing that had pleased Harrison so he'd dropped the subject.

Teri had danced up a storm with almost every man who asked her, but she had avoided Dwight like the plague. However, he'd still managed to corner her a few times, still trying to get her to agree to another rendezvous with him. His plea now included a "for old times' sake" enhancement, but that made no difference to Teri. She had no desire whatsoever to see Dwight again. Especially since Harrison was back in her life.

Yvette had come to Rahim's party alone, dressed like a low-rent hooker and sulking like a two-year-old. When Teri overheard somebody ask Yvette where Eric was, she said that Eric was at home in bed with a bad cold. Teri laughed to herself when she heard that and couldn't wait to tell Nicole.

When Teri got home around midnight, Harrison was sitting in his car in front of her building, lurking like a bounty hunter.

CHAPTER 45

When Victor returned to the office he was glad to see that everything was under control. However, he was disappointed when Teri admitted to him that he had not been missed.

"Are you always so brutally honest?" he wanted to know, glaring at her as she stood in front of his desk updating him. He had spent so much time in the sun that he was almost as dark as she was. And he looked like hell. Even more so than usual. Teri wondered how long it was going to take for white folks to get it in their heads that the sun was one of their worst enemies.

"Well, you asked." She grinned.

Victor gave her a dry look, then a smile. "I trained you well, didn't I?" He paused and cleared his throat. Then he got serious. "There are a lot of things I'd like to cover in the next few weeks. I hope you don't have a lot of plans because you are going to be working some long hours for a while."

"I don't have a problem with that," Teri told him, already wondering how this was going to affect her newly restored relationship with Harrison.

"I'd like to see the last two reports on the numbers for every artist on our roster." Victor shuffled a few papers on his desk. "Set up dinner for me, yourself, that blind rapper, and his people.

Something exotic as long as it's not Italian. That dago shit makes me shit," Victor said with a grimace. "And how are things with that photographer you were so determined for us to work with? Hmm?"

"Eric's been working out just fine. He accepted our offer and he's already signed a two-year contract. He's a great guy and an excellent photographer. And since he's just now cutting his teeth, he needs the work."

"His work is excellent," Victor agreed with a nod. "Are we getting a lot of play time on the locals?"

"Oh, yes. Harrison Starr is still one of our biggest supporters," Teri said eagerly, with her face glowing like a firefly.

"Well, let's keep him happy," Victor advised. "Now!" He rubbed his palms together and smacked his lips. "I don't want to be disturbed for the rest of the day. I've got hundreds of e-mails to plow through. Is there anything else?"

"Not at the moment," Teri said, grateful that Victor had decided to conclude this meeting so soon.

"Then you can go," he said. With that, he turned his back to Teri and faced his computer.

Nicole was on the telephone when Teri approached the reception area after she left Victor's office. Nicole pointed to the small clock radio on her desk, motioning for Teri to listen. With a puzzled look on her face, Teri stopped and leaned over the desk. Now that Teri was involved with Harrison again, she rarely listened to his show. She wanted them to have a real chance and that meant not spending more time than necessary with him, or on him. She knew from experience that "overexposure" could have a devastating effect on a relationship. However, she kept up with Harrison's shows anyway because it was the only show that Nicole and almost everybody else at Eclectic listened to during the morning.

Even with the mild static coming from Nicole's five-year-old radio from a dollar store, Harrison's voice was as smooth as silk. *"And coming up after our station break is Anita Baker with 'Caught up in the Rapture,' one of my favorite golden oldies. This one is a very special dedication to a very special lady . . . Teri, this is the Morning*

Starr, and I want you to know that you've got me caught up in the rap-ture, too . . ."

"No he didn't," Teri said, embarrassed. She looked around the reception area. "I hope Victor didn't hear that."

"If he didn't, he will. Harrison's been mentioning you quite a bit lately." Nicole turned her head to the side and gave Teri a look of approval. "In all the years that I've been listening to the Morn-ing Starr, you are the first woman he's showcased like this. Other than the artists, I mean."

"Well, I am flattered." Teri couldn't stop grinning. "Uh, listen. Victor's cooking up all kinds of shit for us. The way he talks, we are going to be attending back-to-back meetings over the next few weeks. We'll probably both have to do some serious overtime."

"Cool. I could use the money. Greg has been late with the last three child support payments," Nicole hissed. Then her face froze. "Oh, hi, Victor," Nicole said, turning toward the hallway.

He nodded at Nicole as he stopped in front of Teri waving a re-port in his sunburned hand. "Teri, I just read your comprehen-sive A&R report for black music," he said, holding the report up to her face. There was a grim expression on his face but that didn't mean anything. Victor was the only person Teri knew who could look that way and still be in a good mood. She was lucky this time. "Good work! I've said it before, but I'll say it again, you are bril-liant."

"Thank you, Victor," Teri said, trying not to sound too proud of herself. "I always set out to do my best."

"And you always do," Victor quipped, grinning through cracked lips. "How was Trevor's last session?"

"It was very strong. I was thoroughly impressed," Teri said, beaming.

"Good! I'm glad to hear you say that. I'd like to listen to the tracks myself later today. Which ones do you suggest?"

"Check out 'Breathless' and 'Favorite Flava,' please," Teri sug-gested.

"Flava?" Victor replied with his head tilted to the side and one eyebrow lifted. "And what rap lingo is that? What are we talking about here?"

"It means flavor," Nicole offered.

"Then why the hell don't they just say flavor?" Victor snapped. There was a hard look on his face but not for long. He sucked in some air, and then he laughed, braying like a mule. "These kids. I guess we can't all speak the Queen's English. I suspect that life would be pretty dull if we all did." Victor covered his mouth to muffle a belch and looked Nicole over as if she were up for inspection. "Nicole, that's a lovely broach you're wearing. It's good to see that your taste is improving," he said with a wink.

"So is yours. You brought this back for me from Paris," Nicole reminded him, giving him a wink back.

"Oh. So I did, so I did." Victor rolled his eyes and shrugged.

Nicole decided that whatever his wife had done to him on their latest vacation, it must have done the trick. He was a changed man. She and Teri had never seen Victor behave in such a frivolous manner. Even at the Christmas parties he usually wandered around looking like he was at a funeral. He was in a better mood than he'd been in in years, and he had every reason to be. His business was in good shape and his marriage was back on the right track. He'd been so frisky in the bedroom lately that he hadn't even had to rely on Viagra or any other sexual enhancement. "By the way, Teri, I hear that you've become quite popular. That is, if you are the Teri that Harrison Starr mentioned on his show this morning."

"Harrison and I have become very close," she confessed, blood rushing to her face. One thing she didn't encourage was mixing business with pleasure. At least not where she was concerned.

Victor gave her an amused look, leaning his head so far to the side he almost fell. "Aren't you a dark horse. I don't remember the last time you mentioned much about your personal life. As a matter of fact, I just assumed you didn't have much of one!"

"I've been so busy these last few months that I haven't had much time to date." Teri had to press her lips together to keep from frowning. The last thing she wanted to discuss with Victor was who she was sleeping with.

Victor got the message. From the look on Teri's face he knew that it was time to conclude this conversation. But he was compelled to end it on a "positive" note.

"Well, as long as you're happy that's all that matters. I've come to realize that as long as a woman is happy, she'll stay in her place. And since we're on the subject," he mused, looking at Nicole, "send a dozen red roses to my bride." He turned back to Teri and winked.

CHAPTER 46

Teri's grandparents returned from Louisiana the following Friday night. She was with them when Harrison called her on her cell phone. "Hey, baby, can you meet me at the Power Bass around eight?" he asked.

"Tonight?"

"Tonight," he confirmed, disappointment already creeping into his voice. This was the third time this week he'd invited her to spend some time with him at this particular club. "Can't make it again, huh?"

"Well, maybe later. My grandparents just returned from their trip, and I wanted to spend a little time with them. Would you like to come over here to get reacquainted with them?" Teri chuckled.

"What's so funny?"

"I won't go into detail, but they've been after me for the longest to find . . . a man. For some reason they think I'm going to grow old and die alone." Teri was disappointed when Harrison didn't respond right away.

"I don't think you have to worry about that," he said flatly. "Why would they even think that?"

"You know how old people are. I can't wait for you to really get to know them this time."

"Well, I'd like to. But not tonight. Why don't you check with them and see when it would be a good time for me to visit. I want to assure them that they have nothing to worry about. Their 'baby' is in good hands." His words made Teri feel warm all over. She exhaled and smiled so hard her face ached.

"They always have a big cookout on the Fourth of July and invite just about everybody they know."

"The Fourth sounds fine. You can count me in, baby."

"That's a month from now. Do you think you can make it? Don't you need to check your calendar?"

"As long as I'm not the guest of honor at the next funeral I attend, I can reschedule whatever else is on my calendar for the Fourth. Off the top of my head, the only thing I can think of is a little gathering with some of my folks. But I'd been hoping that something better would come along so I could get out of that. Don't you worry, I'll go with you no matter what. This is one time you can count on me, baby."

"All right now. I am going to hold you to that."

"Listen to me—I will be at that cookout. Now let's consider this case closed."

"Okay, but like I said, you can come with me tonight if you want to. Maybe we could go on to the club from there. Those two old nanny goats go to bed with the hens, so I won't be over there with them that late."

"Naw, that won't work for me. Trevor's riding shotgun with me tonight and we're supposed to hook up with some other industry folks there. These are some important people that it wouldn't hurt for you to know, too."

"Uh, if I can make it I will. Otherwise, let me take a rain check," Teri said casually.

"I see. You know, rain checks don't do me much good if I can never collect on them. And I've racked up quite a few from you these last few days. What's up with that?"

"Harrison, if I had my way, I'd be available every time you wanted to see me—"

"Please don't go there again right now. Let's end this conversation now and on a happy note. If you can make it to the club around eleven, fine. If you can't, don't worry about it."

"Keep your cell phone turned on so I can call you later," Teri advised. "If nothing else, I'd at least like to talk to you before I call it a day. I know I'll need somebody to talk to after a session with my grandparents. Flying makes them cranky and I'll have to hear a full report."

Harrison suddenly felt sympathetic. He was glad to see that Teri's devotion to her grandparents was still intact. "You sound tired, sweetheart. Maybe you should go on home after your grandparents. We can always go to a club some other time."

"Don't worry about me. I am fine. I don't care how tired I am now, or later. I would still love to spend some time with you tonight," she said, her voice dragging.

"I'll leave my phone on."

Harrison and Trevor had been at the club for about two hours when Yvette rolled in with June Mattox, one of her clonelike friends. June was a bug-eyed ex-stripper with platinum blond braids halfway down her back.

"I thought this was one of those uppity clubs that only let celebrities and such up in here," June whispered to Yvette as they sauntered in without having to pay the twenty dollar cover charge. The huge Latino bouncer guarding the door winked as he waved them into the club.

"It is," Yvette said, smiling at every man in sight. "I promised the DJ a BJ."

"Say what?"

"I promised the DJ a blow job. I do it all the time. Come on, let's try to find a seat near the VIP section. I'm hot tonight."

Yvette was hot in more ways than one. She was practically on fire because she was so angry. A few hours ago, she had come home from a jaunt to Tijuana and found that that punk-ass Eric had packed up all her shit and set the boxes by the door! If that wasn't bad enough, he took the key to his place from her and even paid a cab to haul her and her belongings to June's place. Well, she was glad to be rid of that limp-dick motherfucker and that mealy-mouth daughter of his.

"I was only with your cheesy ass because I felt sorry for you!"

she had told him before she left that shithole he called home.
She had also told him that she didn't appreciate him using her
up during the best years of her life. A woman was only twenty-
something once. Because of Eric and that little monkey he tried
to make her help him raise, she now felt like an old woman in her
forties. He and Akua, that nappy-headed, future Jezebel of a daughter of his, had aged her in a way that she would never recover
from. But she had news for him. He would be sorry that he had
played her. She wished that she could see his face in a few months
when he started receiving the bills for the four credit cards she
planned to open in his name. And if she was still this pissed come
Monday morning, she'd call the utility company, the cable company, and the phone company and have his service cut off. It would
take him days to straighten out all that mess. And that bitch Nicole's
butt was hers when and if she ever ran into her on the street.

"'Vette, look over there in the VIP section. Ain't that that radio
dude Harrison Starr?" June asked after a bored-looking waiter
had taken their orders. They had plopped down at a table across
the room from where Harrison and Trevor were holding court.
"You told me you met him at that Carla woman's Valentine's Day
party that Eric took you to."

"Yes, that is that butt-plugging, fag-ass motherfucker," Yvette
snarled. At the same table with Harrison and Trevor were several
musicians that Yvette had seen from time to time. And hovering
over them all were two half-dressed heifers looking like they
wanted to suck every dick in sight. "He's the one that's always on
the radio going on and on about that record company cow Teri."

"Is she the same one you told me was Nicole's homegirl?"

"Uh-huh. She is just as big a bitch as Nicole, maybe even bigger.
I'd like to coldcock her just as much as I'd like to get my hands
on that Nicole."

"And that looks like Trevor Powell sitting with Harrison."

"And he's just as big a punk as Harrison! Don't nobody but old
folks and sissies listen to that shit he sings. And if you ask me,
when he sings it sounds like somebody stepping on a moose's
tail." Yvette and June both roared with laughter at Trevor's expense.

June and Yvette didn't wait for the men to ask them to dance, they jumped up and danced alone or with each other. About an hour after they'd entered the club, which was now so crowded you could barely dance, Yvette moseyed over to Harrison's table and asked him to dance anyway. He was surprised to see her and even more surprised that she interrupted his conversation with Trevor to ask him to dance. The other women at his table wanted to jump up and take turns slapping Yvette. They decided that from the looks of this sister, she'd been around the block more than a few times so she had to know the club protocol: don't snatch food off another woman's plate until she stops eating. Especially in a club that catered to the hip-hop crowd.

"Maybe later," he told her, giving her a smile and a casual wave.

"Aw, come on," she said, pulling him up by the arm. The woman sitting next to Harrison could not believe her eyes! It was a good thing her friend held her back. Yvette went on about her business as if she didn't even see the two women at the table. "I'm going to be leaving in a little while, and as crowded as this place is getting, if we don't dance now there might not be enough room to dance later."

Even though it was obvious from the look on Harrison's face and his body language that he did not want to dance, he shrugged and rose. With Yvette still holding on to his arm, he followed her. It was one of the biggest mistakes he ever made in his life.

"I danced with you a few times at the Andrewses' Valentine's Day party, didn't I?" Harrison asked, trying not to show Yvette how bored he was with her.

"Uh-huh," she murmured, pulling his arm up and around her shoulder in a way so that his hand landed on her right breast. This crude gesture made him wish he had not agreed to dance with her after all.

He pretended not to notice where his hand was, but he discreetly moved it. "You're Eric's girl, right?" he asked as soon as they got out on the floor, moving to the rhythm of Kanye's "Gold Digger."

"I was until a few hours ago," she pouted. She proceeded to tell Harrison how she had come home from "visiting a sick relative in San Diego" and caught Eric in bed with another woman. He'd threatened to kill her if she didn't leave immediately. She'd packed her things and called June. Yvette was proud of the fact that she could concoct such a believable lie at such short notice.

"Shit. That's pretty cold. Well, you seem to be handling it all right, out here dancing and having a good time. That's a good sign."

"I'm only here because June had to meet her man here. I have to hang out somewhere until my uncle Buddy gets home tonight. He's on his way back from Vegas . . ."

"Well, I hope everything works out for you, Yvette. If there's anything I can do for you tonight, just let me know. If you need a ride or a few dollars, I've got your back. My little cousin Dana went through a similar situation a few months ago."

"A ride would be nice," Yvette said. "The car June's driving belongs to her man, and when we leave here with him tonight, I don't know if he'll be willing to drive me to my uncle's house in Compton."

"Well if a ride is all you need tonight, I can help you out. Just let me know when you're ready," Harrison said, giving her a gentle squeeze around her waist.

"Girlfriend, what are you up to?" June asked Yvette as soon as Yvette returned to the table and told her what she'd told Harrison.

"Nothing really," Yvette told her with a wicked smile on her face. "But I'll tell you this much. Just listen . . ."

CHAPTER 47

June went along with Yvette's elaborate ruse. She supported
everything Yvette had told Harrison. "If you can't get the goose,
get the gander. I hate Teri as much as I hate Nicole, and at this
point I don't care which one of those heifers I clown first," Yvette
declared.

"Girl, do you really think you going to hurt Nicole by tripping
out on Teri? I don't think so."

"You just watch me," Yvette sneered.

Since June's boyfriend was bogus, she had to hide in the ladies'
room until Yvette had lured Harrison out of the club and to his
car.

Once Yvette got into Harrison's car, she directed him down
one street after another until they came to a shabby house on a
dark corner in East L.A. He parked on the street but he left his
motor running.

"This is where your uncle lives?" Harrison asked. He checked
to make sure his door was locked. "I thought you said he lived in
Compton. Last time I checked, this neighborhood was 100 percent Latino."

"Oh! I forgot. He just moved here last week. He's married to a
Mexican woman . . ."

"Well, from the looks of things, nobody's home," Harrison said with some concern.

"Yeah, I guess he hasn't made it home yet. Uh, if you don't have time to sit here and wait with me, you can just drop me off at the corner next to that taco stand and I'll wait for him by myself."

"Yvette, look around you." Harrison gasped, his mouth hanging open. Right after he said that they heard gunshots. It was hard to determine which direction the shots came from. But a few seconds later, three shadowy figures darted across the street and accosted an elderly woman out walking her dog. Within seconds the shadows snatched the woman's purse and her dog and disappeared behind a dilapidated building. Harrison removed his cell phone from his inside jacket pocket and called the police. As soon as he'd reported the crime that he had just witnessed, he snapped the phone shut and laid it in the cup holder. "I wouldn't leave a dying dog outside in a place like this." He gave Yvette an incredulous look.

"It's not that bad," she whined. "This is all some people can afford."

"Don't you have any other place to go tonight? What about the girlfriend you were with? If her man is a man, he won't mind you hanging out at her place until your uncle makes it back from Vegas."

"I could," Yvette said, looking at her watch. "But they won't make it back to her place until around one she told me."

Harrison didn't want to be in this location any longer than necessary, and there was no way he was going to leave Yvette here alone. One thing he didn't do was kick a person who was already down. If only he had ignored her when she approached him in the club! Then he wouldn't be in this mess. But he *was* in this mess, and he knew that the only thing he could do now was get out of it the quickest and easiest way he could. And it had to be in a way that suited them both. He knew that if he left her alone on the street and something happened to her, he'd never forgive himself. There was only one thing left for him to do.

"I can't leave you out here. I can give you enough money for a room. I know some reasonable motels that you can stay in for a couple of nights, if you want to. That's just in case your uncle doesn't make it back from Vegas until then."

"Well, I could do that, but I don't want you to be out any money trying to help me. I mean, I've cost you enough just in gas. If it's all right with you, I can stay at your place until I can go to June's place. It's only an hour," Yvette said with a pleading look in her eyes.

For her sake, it was a good thing she was a pretty woman. Had she not been, the DJ would not have allowed her to enter that nightclub for free even if she'd promised him ten blow jobs. Her beauty didn't impress Harrison, but she thought it did. And she planned to use it to her advantage. It never occurred to her that he would have helped her regardless of what she looked like. She batted her eyes at him and sniffed.

"I promise I will never ask you for another favor again as long as I live. You don't know me that well, so if you don't want to do it, that's cool." When Harrison didn't respond fast enough, Yvette started to open the door on her side.

"What if I take you to my place and give you enough cab fare to get you to your girl's house? How's that?" Harrison asked, rubbing the back of his head, which by now was throbbing like a bad toothache.

"That'll work."

Harrison stopped at an all-night gas station to fill up his tank. While he was doing that, his cell phone, which he had left on in the cup holder, rang. Yvette picked it up, and what she saw on the ID screen made her flesh crawl: Teri Stewart. She had just enough time before Harrison returned to erase the message that that bitch had left.

Once they made it to Harrison's swank condo, which was a converted unit in a stately old building near the border of Long Beach, Yvette rushed inside behind him and made herself right at home, complimenting him on his good taste in décor. What she said was one thing, what she thought was another. His place looked like something out of a Tarzan movie. Who in the hell did this fool think he was, Shaka Zulu? She never could figure out why so many black Americans slapped some of the most loathsome African masks they could find onto their walls. That was bad enough. But this suit-wearing baboon had spears and other voodoo-looking shit displayed all over his place. There was just no telling what his bedroom looked like, but she planned to find out.

Just when she thought she'd seen everything there was to see, she looked at another wall and did a double take. Was that a picture of a witch doctor right next to a picture of Dr. Martin Luther King, Jr? Did Harrison, and others like him, think that doing shit like that made them more of a "brother" or more of a "sister" to the real Africans? If they really wanted to show some solidarity and human kindness, why didn't they send some money to those starving African kids they showed on TV all the time? Why didn't they go to Africa and adopt some of those little orphans like those white celebrities? As far as Yvette was concerned, Angelina Jolie and Madonna had done more for the Africans than any black American she knew, while the rich black Americans were spending their money on outlandish jewelry and gold teeth. She had always suspected that Harrison Starr was a confused jackass. The way he had decorated his place confirmed her suspicions.

While Harrison was in the bathroom, Yvette kicked off her shoes and wiggled out of her pantyhose. When he returned to his living room, he stopped in his tracks. He looked at her bare feet, then her face.

"What's all this?" he asked with his jaw twitching.

"Oh, my feet were hurting from all that dancing I did," she replied, rubbing the sides of her feet. "I hope my feet don't smell."

"Uh, don't worry about that. Would you like something to drink?" he offered, not too pleased to see her so kicked back on his couch, too.

"You got any beer?" she asked, still rubbing her feet. And they did stink. They smelled like stale vinegar, and Harrison could determine that from halfway across the room. He planned to spray his crushed velvet blue couch pillows with some Febreze as soon as she left.

"No, I don't have any beer, but I have just about everything else, though. How about some rum and Coke?"

"That'll work," she said, rising.

"Make yourself at home," he said, his voice dripping with sarcasm. But she was too dense to know that. "I'll be right back."

Yvette saw that Harrison had left his cell phone on a glass-top table by the door where he'd dropped his keys. While he was in the kitchen, the telephone by the couch rang. It rang four times before Yvette decided that Harrison couldn't hear it from the kitchen. She picked it up.

"Hello," she said, trying to sound as sultry as she possibly could. She did a good job, because on the other end Teri almost dropped her telephone.

"I'm sorry! I think I dialed the wrong number," Teri wailed.

"Are you calling for Harrison?"

Teri hesitated before she replied. "Yes, I am," she said firmly. "May I ask who you are?"

"Oh, I'm just one of Harry's good friends," Yvette cooed. *Harry?*

"If Harry is in, could you tell him that Teri is on the phone, please?"

Yvette was elated. This was going better than she thought it would! She took her time responding, knowing that that would irritate Teri even more. She cleared her throat and yawned.

"Hello? Is somebody still there?" Teri hollered.

"I'm still here . . ." Yvette cooed.

"If Harrison is there, will you please let him know that Teri Stewart is on the phone and I'd like to speak with him *right now.*"

"He's in the shower right now."

Teri hung up. She was stunned and frustrated, but optimistic. She had to give the man the benefit of the doubt. There had to be a reasonable explanation for what she had just experienced. There just had to be! But if Harrison had picked up a woman in the same club that he had told her to meet him in, he was a straight-up fool. And she would be just as big a fool as he was if she put up with that. He didn't answer his cell phone when she called him earlier, and he had not returned her call. Now here was a strange woman answering his telephone while he was in the shower! Oh, hell no. He had some explaining to do.

Teri had already left her grandparents' house and returned to her residence to change clothes. She was in no mood to go to the club, so she had decided to call Harrison to see if he wanted her to come over or if he wanted to come to her place. As soon as she heard a woman's voice answer his cell phone, she'd pulled into the parking lot of a convenience store near the Staples Center.

She'd snapped her phone shut and headed toward Harrison's neighborhood. She stopped her BMW so abruptly she almost jumped the curb in front of his building. His condo was in the front of the building. It looked like every light in his place was on. She took a deep breath before she rang the buzzer.

"Yeah," Harrison said, sounding like he was out of breath.

"Let me in," she ordered.

Harrison responded with hesitation. "Who is this?"

"You know who it is! Shit!"

"What? Teri? Teri, is that you?" Teri could tell from the way he spoke that he was surprised and disappointed to hear her voice. If what she suspected was true, he was dog meat.

"Who the fuck else? Or were you expecting another one of your whores?"

CHAPTER 48

"**O**h shit! Baby, I didn't know you were coming! Why didn't you call?!" Harrison shouted. "Damn! Damn! Damn!" His voice was so shrill and high pitched he sounded like a hysterical woman. Sweat had already started to slide down his face like molasses.

"I did, goddammit! That whore you picked up said you were in the shower! Now are you going to buzz me in or not?"

"Teri, I need to talk to you before I let you in here . . ."

"I bet you do!"

"Listen, baby—you've got it all wrong. I know what you're thinking, but this is not what you think!" Harrison said in a desperate and feeble voice. He turned to look at Yvette still kicking back on his sofa with a puzzled look on her face.

"Uh, what's going on?" she asked, rising. It was a struggle for her to keep a straight face. "I hope I didn't cause you any trouble." She had to force herself not to bust out laughing. Instead, she pressed her lips together and wrapped her arms around her chest, trying to look distressed. But Harrison hadn't seen anything yet. His goose was being cooked and Yvette was the chef that had shoved him into the oven.

"You just stay cool," he told Yvette, holding up his hands. "Let me handle this." There was a worried expression on his face as he looked toward the door. It was locked, but as angry as Teri sounded, it would not have surprised him if she kicked it down. "Listen, let me run downstairs for a minute and try to straighten out this mess. I'm sorry about all this. I know you've already got enough trouble; you don't need this, too. And I sure as hell don't need this shit!"

Harrison grabbed his keys and ran out the door. It didn't help his case that he was sweating like an ox and so nervous his hands were shaking. Even though he was innocent of what Teri suspected, he looked guilty as hell.

Teri had her face pressed against the window in front of the building lobby when Harrison got downstairs. "Baby, please calm down," he began as soon as he made it outside, holding the lobby entrance door open with his foot.

"What the hell is going on?" she demanded, trying to push him out of the way.

"Nothing is going on. I ran into a . . . uh . . . a young lady I know. She needed some help and I . . ."

"What kind of help? A mercy fuck?"

"No, nothing like that! It's Yvette and you probably know that Eric kicked her out. I was just trying to do her a favor."

"I bet you were and I bet you did. What is your problem? Are you so fucking sleazy that you couldn't wait a couple of hours for me? I can't meet up with you when you want me to, so you go off with another bitch? Is that the way it is?"

"That is not the way it happened. When I didn't hear from you by midnight, I didn't think I would."

"I left you a message on your cell phone!"

"I didn't get it! There was no damn message on my cell phone from you!" Harrison yelled.

"Get out of my way. I'm coming in."

Harrison stepped from side to side, blocking Teri. "Baby, please go home and cool off. We'll discuss this later." He looked toward the elevator, then the stairs. He was confused and flustered, and he didn't know what he expected Yvette to do. He prayed that she would not bring her ass to the lobby and make matters even worse.

"Motherfucker, move!" Teri used both hands to push Harrison

out of the way. She pushed him to the side so hard he fell and hit the back of his head on the mailboxes on the wall. He was dazed, and it took him a few moments to compose himself and get up.

"Teri, you . . . you're hysterical," he stammered, trying to reason with her even though it was obvious that she was beyond that point.

"You got that right!" The elevator was taking too long so she ran up the stairs two at a time. Harrison was right behind her rubbing his head, vigorously proclaiming his innocence.

"She'll tell you herself nothing is going on! What do you think I am?" he yelled.

He had left his front door ajar. The first thing Teri saw when she entered his living room was Yvette coming out of the bathroom with a towel wrapped around her naked body.

"Oh shit," Yvette said in mock horror. She covered her mouth with her hand to keep from laughing. It didn't take her but a few seconds to realize that there was nothing to laugh about. Harrison looked at her as though he wanted to strangle her, and it did cross his mind. Teri let out a muffled shriek and started stumbling backward until she hit the wall.

"What the hell are you doing, girl?" Harrison yelled, running toward Yvette. She was not prepared for his reaction. She backed up against the wall, with a look of pure terror on her face. "What the fuck is all this? Is this how you thank me for helping your trifling ass?" Harrison turned to Teri. "Baby, I swear to God, this is not what it looks like!" Teri stood against the wall looking like she'd just seen thirteen ghosts.

"You son of a bitch. You low-down funky black dog!" Teri screeched in Harrison's horrified face. She had yelled so much, her voice had begun to sound hoarse. She coughed to clear her throat. Then she turned to Yvette, who looked like a cross-eyed deer caught in somebody's headlights by now. "You low-life slut. You can have this hound from hell. You two deserve each other." She turned back to Harrison. "And I thought Mia was bad! The little comedy you played out with her was scraping the bottom of the barrel! Have you no shame? This time, with this oafish bitch, you settled for straight-up shit this time! I wouldn't let you fuck me again with a magic wand."

"Nothing happened between Mia and me! I already told you that!" Harrison hollered with his hands in the air. He looked from Teri to Yvette. "Yvette, get in your fucking clothes and get the hell out of my place before I throw you out!"

"You still going to give me the cab fare to get to my uncle's place?" Yvette whimpered, holding the towel around her body as tight as she could.

"Hell no! I don't give a fuck how you get to your uncle's place! You can crawl on your belly like a snake for all I care!" he roared, giving Yvette the disgusted look she deserved. Then it dawned on him what Yvette had tried to do. And from the looks of things, she had succeeded. Other than Eric evicting her damn ass, he wondered if any other parts of her story were true. "*You fucking set me up!* Why me?"

Yvette had done a lot of stupid things in her life that she lived to tell about. But she wasn't so sure she'd come out of this alive. The way Harrison and Teri were looking at her, she didn't know which one to fear the most. All she knew now was that she had to vacate the premises while she was still able. She stood in the middle of the floor with a wounded look on her face, looking like *she* was the victim of this evil prank.

"Yvette, don't you ever come near me again as long as you live!" Harrison was so busy chewing out Yvette he didn't even notice Teri leave. As soon as he did, he ran after her. He got downstairs just as she was starting her motor. He stopped her from leaving by grabbing the door handle on her side, banging on her window. "Teri, please let me explain."

"Explain my ass, motherfucker. Don't you ever fix your lips to speak to me again as long as you live!" she shrieked. "I am through with you! And *for good* this time!"

"Teri you know me better than that! You know I wouldn't be that damn stupid as hard as it was for me to get back with you! I was set up! Yvette set me up!" he insisted, giving Teri a pleading look, hoping she would soften. But Teri didn't get to be where she was in life by being soft.

"She sure did, motherfucker!"

Harrison didn't leave the spot where he stood in the street until Teri was completely out of sight.

By the time he made it back to his living room, Yvette had put her clothes back on and locked herself in the bathroom.

"Yvette, I want you to get the hell out of here right now," he ordered, slapping the bathroom door with the palm of his hand.

"I'm going," she hissed, slowly opening the door, rubbing lotion on her arms. "You don't have to worry about me."

"Why, Yvette? Why did you do this to me?!" Harrison boomed, grabbing her by the wrist. "What the fuck is the matter with you?!"

"Turn loose my arm, motherfucker, before I yell rape, too," she threatened. Harrison was so angry he was shaking. He wanted to slap that sneer off her evil face. Somehow, he managed to control himself. He released her immediately and stared at her with his mouth hanging open as she strutted back into his living room and plopped down on his couch with a groan, taking her time putting her shoes back on.

"I want you out of my sight. I want you out of my sight now," Harrison told her, stomping across the floor to the couch. He stood in front of her with his fists balled. When she didn't move fast enough, he lunged at her and snatched her up by her arm. She stumbled as he dragged her to the door. "If you ever fuck with me again, I will hurt you," he said in a voice so calm and low that she didn't hear everything he said.

"What did you just say?" she asked, struggling with him as he opened the door to push her out.

"I said, if you ever fuck with me again, I will hurt you," he repeated, this time loud and clear enough for her to hear every single word.

"You could go to jail just for threatening me," she snarled, smoothing down the sides of her dress as she backed toward the elevator.

"And it would be worth it," he told her before he slammed his door shut.

CHAPTER 49

Harrison locked his door and leaned against it for a minute, massaging his temple with both hands. He wanted to bang his head against the door, but it was already spinning like a top and throbbing on both sides.

"Fuck, fuck, fuck," he chanted, punching the wall with his fist, wishing that the wall was that no-good Yvette's empty-ass head. He sucked in some air and tried to make some sense out of what had just happened. A black man couldn't win for losing, he thought. He'd fucked up more than one relationship, but now that he was trying to walk the straight and narrow with his vision of a dream girl, another party took it upon herself to monkey wrench all his efforts! That bitch. That no-good homeless bitch! He slapped the side of his head with the palm of his hand, chastising himself for being so gullible. How many times had he heard stories from dudes at the gym and the barbershop about some of Yvette's antics? "If you lay down with dogs, you get up with fleas," one brother had warned him after he'd revealed how Yvette had rewarded him with a dose of genital warts. He rubbed his chin and nose and went to the window just in time to see Yvette flag down a taxi. He didn't leave the window until the taxi left with her in it.

He moved from the window and immediately called Teri's cell

phone number. He didn't expect her to answer once she saw his name on her caller ID. But he left her a message anyway. "Teri, please call me back when you get this message. I want to tell you what really happened. I . . . I love you and I wouldn't hurt you for anything in this world."

He called her home number and left the same message. Then he called Nicole, but he hung up as soon as she answered. She was indirectly responsible for this mess because she had taken Eric from Yvette and now Yvette had to take it out on whomever she could get to first. Because of his relationship with Nicole's best friend, Harrison had become a victim of Yvette's retaliation by default. But after thinking about it for a moment or two, he didn't want to drag Nicole into it until he had done enough damage control to get Teri to at least hear his side of the story. It wouldn't have done him any good anyway. While he was sitting on his couch in the same spot that Yvette had occupied a few minutes earlier, Teri was on the phone with Nicole, telling her all she knew.

"He did what?" Nicole hollered. "Girl, hold on. Eric's on the other line. Let me get rid of him." Teri sat in her car in the parking lot of a liquor store six blocks from Harrison's condo. This was something that couldn't wait for her to make it home to call Nicole. "I . . . I can't believe my ears! Oh, the man's got to be out of his mind. There is no other explanation! Yvette? Poor Eric. She's the worst thing that ever happened in his life. Did Harrison want some pussy that bad?"

"Tell me about it," Teri said with a painful sigh.

"There is just no telling what all kinds of activity have been going on inside that black hole between her thighs. If I were you, I'd make Harrison cover up with *two* condoms from now on before I let him stick his dick in me again. Eeyow!" Nicole made gagging sounds, and for a moment Teri thought she was going to vomit all over the interior of the beautiful car that she keeps as neat and clean as a pin.

"Ha! That's one thing I'll never have to worry about again!"

"Oh? What are you going to do?"

"What the hell do you think I'm going to do? Do you think I am going to go on like nothing happened? Do you think that I'd let him touch me again after this? I am not going to settle for a man who cheats on his woman, and I don't know why any woman with half a brain and some self-respect would, either. She's a damn fool if she does! All a woman is getting when she settles for a man who cheats on his woman is a man who cheats on his woman." Nicole remained quiet, so quiet you could have heard a pin drop. "Did you hear what I just said?"

"I heard you. I guess that includes me, too, huh?"

"Includes you how? What the hell are you talking about?"

"Eric cheated on Yvette with me," Nicole said in a flat tone of voice.

"So? He's not with her now and he's much better off with you than he was with her."

"But how is what he did to Yvette any different from what Harrison did to you?" Nicole asked.

This time Teri was the one who got so quiet you could hear a pin drop. Then she said, "I don't think I like the ugly direction that this conversation is going."

"I think it's already there," Nicole told her with a heavy voice. "I love Eric and he loves me. His relationship with Yvette was doomed from the start. She hooked him by claiming she was pregnant. A month after he moved her in with him and his daughter, she got her period. Then she claimed that the pregnancy 'must have been a false alarm.' By then it was too late for him to get rid of her. She had no place to go."

"Well, despite what I just said about men cheating on their women, I am glad things seem to be working out between you and Eric. He is a good man."

"So is Harrison."

"Girl, are you not listening to me? That 'good' man Harrison was with another woman. I caught him. I saw him with her with my own eyes! If he's what you call a good man, I'd hate to think of what you'd call a bad man."

"Oh, there are plenty of them out there. We don't even have to look hard to find them, they usually find us," Nicole said, impressed with herself for sounding so philosophical.

"Listen, I am going to go on home and pull myself together."

"Where are you?"

"Sitting in my car in a liquor store parking lot like a fool."

"Call me when you get home if you feel like it," Nicole suggested.

"This is one fucked-up night. I finally told my grandparents about Harrison and me being back together and they couldn't have been happier. The first thing Grandma did was pull out her address book to make sure it was current so that everybody would receive their invitations to my wedding on time. Grandpa was even worse. He's already made plans for him and Harrison to go fishing."

"Shit. Just tell them it didn't work out after all."

"Shit! I just remembered something." Teri slapped her steering wheel and let out a disgusted sigh. "I just remembered that I told them he'd be coming to our upcoming cookout on the Fourth," Teri whimpered. "Shit! Me and my big mouth!"

"That's still a month away. Maybe by then . . ." Nicole didn't have to finish her sentence. Teri knew what she was going to say and she didn't like that one bit.

"No way. I'm too through with that man. There is no way in hell I will let him get away with this."

"Teri, I know you look at life too critically these days. So do I. But no man, or woman for that matter, is perfect. Shit happens. We deal with it, try to correct it, then we move on. A strong, smart woman can find something positive in the worst situations when it comes to her man. But because she's strong and smart, and if that man is worth hanging on to, she deals with it. Look at Hillary Clinton. Do you think she'd be happier if she'd kicked ole 'I didn't sleep with that woman but I let her suck my dick' Bill to the curb? Most of the other high-profile women do the same thing Hillary did."

"Tina Turner didn't take Ike's black ass back." Teri hung up and snapped her cell phone shut.

CHAPTER 50

Harrison had never pursued a woman so vigorously in the thirty-two and a half years of his existence. But Teri Stewart wasn't just a woman; she was the only woman for him. He had not made that revelation clear to her or anyone else. He was compelled to make her see that now, if she'd let him.

It had been two days since the Yvette fiasco. He had lost count of how many messages he'd left on Teri's home phone, her cell phone, and her work phone. She had not returned a single call.

Harrison had a lot of male friends that he had bonded with over the years. He had always been quick to share some of his most intimate thoughts and secrets with his boys. But this was one thing that he wanted to keep to himself.

The only reason he didn't beat a path to Carla Andrews's office was because her calendar was booked solid for the next two months. It seemed like everybody in L.A. was in need of therapy. She had back-to-back appointments with some of her longtime patients and new patients were crawling out of the woodwork, some on the verge of suicide. Harrison wasn't *that* bad off, but he was at a point where he really wanted to talk to somebody about what had happened.

"If I get a cancellation, I will call you immediately," Carla told him. "But you hang in there. *Things are going to be all right.*" Harrison had not told Carla the source of his latest stress-induced condition, but he was hoping that if she had talked to Teri, she would know. However, with Teri believing the worst, her version of the events would make him look like the asshole she thought he was. Harrison couldn't imagine what was going through Carla's head about why he needed to see her all of a sudden. But he didn't care what she thought about him, as long as she was still able to give him the professional assistance he felt he needed.

He started to lose hope by the end of the week. He stopped leaving messages for Teri. When Carla finally did call him to tell him that another patient had just cancelled an appointment and that she could see him right away, he had too many other things going on to take her up on her offer. For one thing, it was too late for him to switch his broadcast hours with Beverly Blue or one of the other DJs. And skipping work to go see his shrink by calling in sick was something he would never do. One of the things he was most proud of was the fact that he had a work ethic that he didn't want to compromise.

By the second week, he was feeling much better. He had lost all hope of ever resuming his relationship with Teri. This was one personal situation that he chose not to discuss with his friends or coworkers but that didn't stop some of them from being nosy.

"Man, I've been meaning to ask you—what's going on between you and Teri? I haven't seen you with her lately, and you haven't even mentioned her," Trevor said with a suspicious look on his last visit to the station.

"Teri's fine, as far as I know. We're not as close as we used to be," was all Harrison offered, promptly changing the subject. "I've got some extra complimentary tickets to that jazz show at the Staples Center this coming weekend if you want to join me."

"Yeah . . . right," Trevor responded, giving Harrison a sympathetic look. But that didn't stop Trevor from pointing his nose in another direction. When he saw Teri at a small, private wrap party at Eclectic Records the next evening, he tried to get more information from her. "Uh, how is my boy Harrison these days?" he asked Teri, his sympathetic hand rubbing her shoulder. That little gesture alerted her right away. She knew Trevor already knew that she and Harrison had parted company.

"Why don't you ask him?" she asked, not facing Trevor as she stood in a corner nursing a flute of champagne. Despite her evasive behavior, she was as cordial and businesslike as ever. Victor had suddenly run off again with his wife. This time to Mexico for a few days to celebrate their wedding anniversary. Teri was glad to be in charge so soon again. The distraction helped her keep her mind off Harrison—and that was not easy. She saw him in her dreams, and several times she saw men on the street that looked so much like him it made her heart skip a beat each time.

The Monday after the wrap party a huge bouquet of roses arrived at the office for her. Despite the fact that roses were her favorite flowers, she was disappointed when she looked at the card and saw that they had come from Dwight. When she called him up to thank him, the first thing out of his potty mouth was, "The drums tell me that you finally ass-wiped that dickless Harrison. When can *I* see you?" Less than a minute after she declined Dwight's crude invitation he told her, "Lady, I don't know who you think you are, but you need a reality check. You know now that Harrison is a punk! I know what you need. You know what I can do for you, and I've been trying to give it to you again for eons. But all I get for my trouble is a runaround. Well, this is the last time I try to get next to you."

"Thanks again for the roses, Dwight," Teri said calmly, a dry smile on her lips. "You still know the way to a girl's heart."

"Fuck that shit. I want to know the way to a girl's pussy!" Dwight hollered.

"Dwight, I have to go now," Teri insisted. Nicole occupied one of the two seats facing Teri's desk. There was an anxious look on her face and she couldn't wait for Teri to end her phone call so they could talk trash about Dwight. "If things change, I might call you up again." Now she was teasing him. She had no desire or intentions to call Dwight again. At least not for the reason he wanted her to call.

"When?" Dwight asked, now sounding so humble it surprised him more than it did Teri. "You wait too long, you might not ever be able to reach me again," he warned.

"That's good to know," she told him. She hung up and shrugged her shoulders and let out a gentle laugh. She couldn't remember the last time she'd enjoyed some humor. Nicole looked like she had just swallowed a canary.

"That was cute," she told Teri. "It's good to see you laughing and having fun again. You've been too serious lately."

Teri knew where Nicole was going with this conversation so she didn't waste any time steering it in another direction. "I saw the sample shots for some of the new CD covers. Eric's getting so good we won't be able to afford him someday." Teri flipped a few sheets of paper, not realizing they were upside down. "Now all we have to decide is which covers we want to use for which artists . . ."

"Can I ask you something?" Nicole didn't give Teri a chance to respond. "And please don't get mad . . ."

"What is it?"

"Do you miss Harrison?"

Teri nodded and blinked hard.

"I've seen him at a couple of parties. Two nights ago, I saw him having lunch at The Ivy. I took Eric there for his birthday."

"It's good to know he's getting on with his life." Teri paused and restacked the same documents she'd already stacked up three times in the last five minutes. "Uh, how's he doing?" She couldn't believe her own words. The last thing she wanted was for Nicole or anybody else to know that she was even thinking about how Harrison was doing.

CHAPTER 51

"He was alone," Nicole stated. "Well, not alone as in by himself. Each time I saw him he was with one of his male buddies, not a female."

"I didn't ask you *that*," Teri snapped, glad to hear that anyway.

"He asked about you," Nicole reported. "Every time I see him he asks about you."

Teri blinked and cleared her throat, which felt like a fist-size lump was stuck in it. "Did you ever get that polycom machine fixed so people who can't come to the office in person can dial in and participate when we have staff meetings?"

"Fuck that polycom. If you want to change the subject, I know you can come up with something more interesting than that damn thing. And just to let you know, again, yes, I did get it fixed," Nicole said in a harsh tone of voice, crossing her recently slimmed-down legs. She had on a denim skirt that she had not been able to squeeze into for more than a year. Thanks to the vigorous bedroom workouts that she participated in with Eric, she had lost fifteen pounds.

"Teri, Eric saw Yvette a couple of nights ago," Nicole said, proceeding with caution. "They talked . . ."

Hearing this disturbed Teri. She leaned back in her chair and narrowed her eyes as she studied Nicole's face. She was surprised to see that Nicole didn't look as disgusted as she usually did every time Yvette's name came up.

"Oh? And you let him?"

"I didn't *let* him do a damn thing. The only person I have the right to let do anything is my son, and that's only because he's still a baby. Eric can do whatever he wants to do."

Teri looked at Nicole out of the corner of her eye. "What does all this mean? What could she possibly have to say that he'd want to hear? Or vice versa?"

"It means that now that enough time has passed and they've both cooled off, they decided to call a 'truce' so they could tie up a few loose ends. Eric had some concerns about certain things coming back to haunt him if he didn't take care of them now." Nicole paused and looked off to the side. She suddenly seemed unbearably uncomfortable.

"Please don't tell me that heifer is pregnant by Eric," Teri said, holding her breath.

"I don't think so. If she is, she hasn't said anything about it so far. Besides, I think that if she was, she'd get rid of it in a heart-beat. Just like the other three . . ."

"Shit. How in the hell did a man like Eric get involved with a woman like Yvette in the first place?"

"You'd have to ask him that. Anyway, he wanted to make sure that he left no stone unturned where she's concerned. Would you believe that they had a joint checking account? And that Yvette was authorized to pick up Akua from school?"

"I guess that once upon a time he didn't think she was that bad. But when he realized she was, it was too late. That just goes to show you what kind of man Eric is—too lenient for his own good."

"I don't think so. He's just being fair," Nicole defended.

"Whatever you say. I guess you know the man better than I do." Teri yawned and stretched her arms high above her head. "I suppose if worms can be tolerated, so can the Yvettes of the world." She let out a loud breath and gave Nicole a pensive look. "Since you've said this much, you may as well tell me the rest of what's on your mind."

"Teri, Harrison didn't fuck Yvette." Nicole paused long enough to let her words sink in. She didn't like the stunned look on Teri's face, but she continued talking anyway. "She ran into him at the club that night after Eric had kicked her out. She'd been drinking, Harrison had been drinking, and things got out of hand."

"Apparently," Teri scoffed.

"Stop! Let me finish," Nicole ordered, holding up her hand. "Anyway, she was hurting so bad that night, she wanted to hurt somebody. Anybody. Isn't that what Miss Cookson called 'displaced aggression' in our eleventh-grade sociology class? Harrison just happened to be in the wrong place at the wrong time. If it hadn't been him, she would have latched onto somebody else to torture that night. Harrison's only crime was his connection to Eric and me. And, as if you didn't know this already, you are not one of Yvette's favorite people. She wanted to hurt you and has for a long time."

"And you and Eric believed Yvette? Why should you believe her now?"

"She has no reason to lie about it now. She accomplished what she set out to do. But she didn't gain or lose anything. You and Harrison are the losers in this drama."

"Did we really have anything to lose?" Teri asked, a dumbfounded look on her face. "We tried to make a life together twice and both times we failed. If that's not a clear indication that it wasn't meant to be in the first place, I don't know what is. So I don't know what you think we lost."

"You lost each other," Nicole insisted.

Teri released a groan as she rearranged herself in her seat, sucking in her stomach. She wondered if she'd gained the fifteen pounds that Nicole had lost. She didn't know why everything seemed to taste so good these days. Last week when she went to purchase a new pair of leather pants, she was horrified when the clerk informed her that the size 10 she had struggled to try on was actually a size 12! In addition to working longer hours, she killed time shopping everywhere from Rodeo Drive to Wal-Mart. This was what her life had come to.

"I don't think so. He made a choice. And I don't care what Yvette says, I'm sure she didn't have to hold a gun to Harrison's head to get him to take her home that night. He walked into that mess with both eyes open. And knowing her, she's going to cuckold another fool soon, if she hasn't already."

"Well, that's for sure," Nicole said with a touch of sarcasm. "She's one rolling stone that won't ever gather any moss. That sister rolls around more than a Chinese marble. Shit, she's already involved with someone else. And it must be serious; she's already moved in with him. Remember that blind rapper?"

Teri gasped and her mouth dropped open so wide her jaws almost locked. "Well, only a blind man could not see what a piece of shit she is."

"Not him," Nicole said, shaking her head. "His brother. Dude just got out of prison so you know he's not too particular. I guess that just goes to show that there is somebody for all of us," Nicole said rising.

Not all *of us,* Teri thought to herself.

CHAPTER 52

Teri still avoided listening to Harrison's show, and she declined invitations to parties or other events that she thought he might attend. She did hear from Nicole and Miguel and even Victor that Harrison still supported a lot of their artists on his show.

Since Teri was never one to discuss her personal life with her coworkers, most of them didn't even know she'd been dating Harrison in the first place, let alone that the relationship had been severed. Victor was too busy trying to hold his marriage together, so he had no more interest in Teri's love life, or anybody else's. And besides, his main interest in Teri was whether she continued to make him look good.

Teri ran into Carla at a boutique the day before the Fourth of July and the first thing Carla asked her about was her relationship with Harrison.

"Oh, that didn't pan out," she confessed, shifting her rapidly increasing weight from one foot to the other. "I've been meaning to make an appointment to see you, but I've been so busy lately . . . working my fingers to the bone trying to keep the company afloat while Victor takes his spur of the moment vacations."

"Things have slowed down quite a bit for me, so when and if

you're ready to talk, let my secretary—no, you call me direct like always and let's schedule an appointment," Carla told her, patting the side of her arm. "You don't have to make an appointment if you just want to talk on a personal level. We're still friends, Teri. And I hope we always will be."

Under normal circumstances, they would have strolled over to the Starbucks at the corner like Carla had suggested. But Teri avoided that when she remembered she'd promised her grandparents she'd stop by on her way home. She'd been avoiding them lately. Since she'd opened her big mouth and told them that she was bringing Harrison to the Fourth of July cookout with her, that seemed to be all they wanted to talk about. She hadn't told them about the breakup and had decided that she wouldn't. When they did ask her how he was doing she always told them the same thing—"He's doing fine as far as I know."

She assumed the questions would stop after the cookout. It would be painful and awkward for her, but she'd help them talk about him like a dog for not showing up. It was the only way she knew how to save face.

About an hour after Teri had run into Carla, she decided to backtrack and go to Starbucks anyway. Not the same one that Carla had suggested, but one in a strip mall near her condo. As luck would have it, five minutes after she'd picked up her latte and plopped down at a table in a corner outside the restroom, Carla exited the restroom.

"Well, now this is a coincidence," she yelled, ignoring the surprised look on Teri's face. "Do you mind if I join you?" Teri let out a heavy sigh and nodded toward the seat across from her that Carla had already claimed. She wondered why people did things first, then asked if it was all right.

Yes, I do mind if you join me, she wanted to say. And had it not been Carla she would have said it aloud. But in the back of her mind, she knew there had to be a reason for this turn of events.

"Carla, please do me a favor and don't mention Harrison Starr," Teri requested.

Carla gave her an amused look. "That's fine with me. I hadn't planned to. I'm more interested in telling you about all the great sales I stumbled across today."

"You see, things ended on a very bad note. After what Harrison did, I don't think I will ever trust another man," Teri announced. "I don't know how much you know about what happened, but this is my side of the story . . ."

Despite the fact that Teri had just said she didn't want to discuss Harrison Starr, for the next ten minutes she shared with Carla every single detail she could remember about the events that had occurred that night. Some parts she repeated several times. "Now, according to Nicole, Yvette broke down and told Eric she'd set Harrison up."

"Why Harrison? If she wanted to set somebody up, wouldn't it have made more sense for her to go after Eric and Nicole?" Carla asked.

Teri nodded. "Yes, but she couldn't get to them. She knew that by wrecking Harrison's relationship with me, it would affect Nicole and Eric on some level."

"Teri, I can understand your feelings. But this was nothing more than a foolish 'prank' played out by a scorned woman so vengeful she didn't care who she hurt," Carla said, gently squeezing Teri's hand.

"It doesn't matter now. I said some pretty nasty things to Harrison and I can't take any of that back." Teri paused and sniffed. The tall latte that she had ordered remained untouched. "Even if he was telling the truth . . ."

"Teri, listen to me." Carla leaned across the table and squeezed Teri's hand even harder. "He was telling the truth." Teri pressed her lips together and gave Carla a skeptical look. "And wipe that look off your face. You've known me long enough to know that I'm rarely wrong when I reveal something."

Teri knew she couldn't argue with that because it was true. "I could apologize to him for what I said, but I don't know where to go from there." She shook her head. "Do you think I should call him up anyway?"

"You have to make that decision." Carla reared back in her seat and pursed her lips.

There was no place else for this conversation to go. "Uh, I'll call you soon," Teri said, rising. She left the latte on the table, still untouched.

* * *

Teri crawled out of bed the next morning with a splitting headache. As much as she loved her grandparents the last thing she wanted to do today was attend their holiday cookout and deal with a dozen or more of their friends and neighbors. She knew that she'd probably be the only person in her age group present. For a painful moment she even considered calling up Dwight and inviting him to join her—with his sleazy self! But he hadn't pestered her in a while. She wasn't even sure he was still interested. The last thing she needed at this low point in her life was for him to reject her. Knowing how crude he was, he would no doubt reject her in a profoundly brutal way to get back at her for giving him the brush-off so many times.

Her thoughts were interrupted by her cell phone ringing on the nightstand next to her bed. She didn't want to answer it, but on the fourth ring she did. The caller ID was mysteriously blank, which usually meant the call was coming from a telemarketer or some other party who had a blocked telephone number. "Hello," she said softly, yawning. She sat up on the side of her bed and looked around her bedroom. The caller didn't respond. "I said hello," she repeated.

"Teri, this is Harrison Starr."

"What?" She stood up, dragging the bedding behind her like a train. "What in the world—"

"Baby, please don't hang up on me! I know I am probably the last person on the planet you want to talk to, but please don't hang up."

"I won't hang up," she assured him. She was glad he had called and she was anxious to hear what he had to say.

"I called because I need the address and directions to your grandparents' house."

Teri covered her mouth so he couldn't hear her gasp. "What? Why?"

"Well, I promised I'd attend their Fourth of July cookout—if it's still on."

"It is. But I didn't think . . ."

"If you think my presence will be too upsetting for you, I won't come," he offered.

Her headache had intensified and now her head felt as if it were going to explode. "I don't know what to say," she admitted. "The invitation is still open." She was confused and elated at the same time. She rubbed the back of her head, then her neck, and then the side of her face. "I didn't think you'd still want to come after . . . after what happened."

"Teri, that's over and done with. We've both moved on and that's all that matters now."

"I . . . *We* at Eclectic appreciate the fact that you still show our artists a lot of love on your program."

"I know. And you can tell Victor he can stop thanking me by sending me all that damn champagne. I'm running out of room." He laughed. She laughed with him. "Are you going to give me that address or not?"

"Uh . . . uh, yeah." She rambled off her grandparents' address. "Don't ask me to give you directions. You can get them from Map-Quest."

"Sure. Oh, before I hang up, I just need a few particulars. I presume I can dress casually, and can bring a guest? Should I bring a bottle or a pie or something? This would be one way for me to get rid of some of those bottles Victor sent." He laughed again, but this time Teri didn't. She was still thinking about the part where he had mentioned bringing a guest.

"Uh-huh. You can bring a bottle, or two and yes, it's okay to bring a guest."

"Good. Trevor's on his own today and I thought it would be nice for him to do a little celebrating. He loves good barbeque as much as I do."

"Trevor? Uh, yeah. He's welcome to come."

A full minute of silence passed before either of them spoke again.

"Do you want to talk?" she asked, holding her breath as she awaited his response. "About us . . ."

"Will it do any good?" he asked her so quickly he almost choked on the words.

"I think it will," she admitted. More silence followed. "I am willing to listen to anything you want to say to me now. Then, we can go from there."

"I've had a lot of things on my mind that I wanted to discuss, Teri. But so much time has passed, and so much damage has been done, I doubt if they will have the same effect now."

"You don't have to keep your promise about attending the cookout. I didn't expect you to, and if you want to back out now, I will certainly understand."

"What do you want me to do, Teri?"

"I want you to come," she said with a sniff. "After my grandparents stop making a fuss over you, we can sneak off to an empty room and talk." She wanted to say the room she had in mind was her old bedroom, but she didn't.

She could hear him breathing. "What time should we get there? I hope it's not too early because Trevor operates on CP time."

"Him and everybody invited to the cookout operates on Colored People's time—including my grandparents—and even our non-black friends." It felt so good to laugh some more. "Anytime after two is fine, if you still decide to come."

"I will see you at two, Teri. And I'm really looking forward to seeing you again."

"I'll see you then for sure?" she said, asking as if she still needed more confirmation.

"You will see me for sure," Harrison assured her.

A few miles away, Carla Andrews stared at the caller ID on her cell phone. She chuckled and decided not to answer Teri's call because she already knew why she was calling. Carla didn't want to tell Teri that this time things would work out between her and Harrison. She wanted her to find out for herself.

♥